W A H I D A C I

This is a work of fiction. ~~Names, ~~~~
incidents either are the product of the author's imagination or
are used fictitiously, and any resemblance to actual persons,
living or dead, business establishments, events, or locales is
entirely coincidental.

Wahida Clark Presents Publishing, LLC
60 Evergreen Place
Suite 904
East Orange, New Jersey 07018
973-678-9982
www.wclarkpublishing.com

ISBN 13-digit 978-19366496-4-8
ISBN 10-digit 1936649640

Library of Congress Catalog Number 2013912647
1.   Urban, New Jersey, New York, Bronx, Brooklyn,
Orange, NJ, African-American, Street Lit – Fiction

Cover design and layout by Nuance Art, LLC
Book interior design by Nuance Art, LLC
Contributing Editors: Linda Wilson and Rosalind Hamilton

Printed in United States
Green & Company Printing, LLC
www.greenandcompany.biz

THE PUSSY TRAP 3: *Death by Temptation*
~ NENE CAPRI ~

WAHIDA CLARK PRESENTS

Dedication

This book is dedicated to my daughter Princess Khairah. Everything I do is for you.
Mommy loves you.

THE PUSSY TRAP 3: *Death by Temptation*
~ N E N E   C A P R I ~

<u>Acknowledgements</u>

All praises due to the most high, I am blessed to have the favor of god shine on everything I do. To my Beloved I am a better me because of you, thank you. To my mom Birdie, all your sacrifice allows me to chase my dreams; I could not do anything without you by my side, thank you. Princess Khairah thank you for sacrificing some of your time to allow me to write and go to school, you are the best daughter in the world, just know I am doing the things I have to do now, so you will have great things later. Wahida Clark we doing it again, twenty years I've been on this journey with you and I don't regret one second, thank you and I love you. Dad thank you for giving me your strength of mind and character, you showed me what a man is supposed to be and for that I am grateful love you.

To my readers, it is your love and support that fuels my pen. I am grateful and honored to have you grace my pages. Thank you so much for reading my work. This book is for you.

To my Aunt Jackie and Uncle Neville, thank you for being the rock of the family, because of you two our family has guidance and direction may the lord bless you with many years to serve him. Princess you never let me down, you have a heart of gold and a mile to match love you. Iman and Boobie I admire you, always listen to each other and thank you for giving us Yuri. To my nephews Jahar I am so proud of you can't wait to watch you graduate from college. Qadir you make my heart smile keep up the good work. Nagee my Capricorn love, you are the best of your mom and dad, make them proud. Rashad always remember you are destined for greatness, you can do it. Khair my heart, you are so smart and special I love you.

IRoka my baby brother you are everything I'm not, the day mommy brought you home wa the best day of my life I love you from a special place in my heart. Angel I was just holding you in my arms now you're in college, love you my precious baby sister.

Tiko and Tiombe I am blessed to have 32 years of friendship with you. Our memories fill my mind with daily joy and happiness I love you. Chucky everyone should have a brother like you, stay up. KeKe (Kisha Steel) every conversation with you makes me smarter I am honored to have you a true friend, p.s. you are very spoiled lol. Uncle James I got you I see you standing over KeKe shoulder saying what about me, Love you bug brah. Budah my precious godson you have a big heart fill it with the best and always reach for your goals. India Brooks you are going to be my Lawyer. I love you Jameer.

A special shout out to all the book clubs. Because of your hard work and dedication new and seasoned authors get their voice to the readers: DJ Gatsby you're the best, Cyrus Web I owe you one. Joey Pinkney you continue to inspire me, thanks for all the support, Mack Mamma you are a beast on the Radio, Diamond Eyes, Slyce Book Club, Sistas on-lit Papaya thank you, Readers R US, Kindle Reading Club, Urban Book Lovers, Ossa book club, Urban Fiction Lovers, Reading Royalty Book Club, Sistah Reading Sistah Book Club, Let's Talk Relationships & Books, AAMBC, Teamambitious, WCP Divas, True Reviews/interviews, All For one authors supporting authors, Readers Club, Nook Readers, Kindle and paperback lovers, and to all the hard working promoters of Urban fiction I salute you.

WAHIDA CLARK PRESENTS

To Our WCP Divas, you are the best you go hard for Wahida and all the Authors at Wahida Clark Publishing. Erica, Char, Jess, Micole, Cass, Leah, Shatisha, Tanny Tee, Sonia, Monica, Young-lit, we love and appreciate you, you are Urban Fiction.

Hey Pashion Allen I see you. Paris Robinson (smile), Lissha you are so sweet, Courtney Lawson, Carlene, Boo Jackson you keep me laughing, Brandon Spivey (BFF) you are one of a kind, Robyn Mitchell much love, Brenda Tashae, Brandie Davis thank you, Wyrter Chene (smile), Tiffany Byers thanks for giving me my first interview.

Let shout out some of my favorite people, Dc Book Diva I love you, K'wan and Charlotte you're the best, Treasure Blue if they want to be successful they better listen to you, Eyone Williams you make this look easy, Al-Sadiq Banks, T. Styles, Ashley and JaQauvis I look up to you, Raheem Brooks,

WCP team thank you for being the back bone of Wahida Clark Presents. Sherry Porter, Nuance Art.*. I am so proud of you! You did ya thing on this cover. Brenda, Jabar, Shahid Pushbuttinz, Hasana, Rosalind, Jennifer, Rahman, Baseem, Omar, Razzqa, Husain, Intelligent Allah thanks for all your help, Cash thank you for always taking the time to read my work and give me an honest review. Anthony Fields, Mike Jefferies I got your back.

THE PUSSY TRAP 3: *Death by Temptation*
~ N E N E C A P R I ~

- 1 -

Fatal Attraction

KoKo stood between two atomic bombs threatening to go off at the slightest movement. Her knees became weaker by the second; her heart beat in her throat. The intensity between the two men had become so thick it felt as if the walls would collapse.

"KoKo, fuck this nigga!" Boa yelled.

"No, nigga. Fuck you!" Kayson stepped forward.

"What the fuck you wanna do?" Boa asked, moving toward Kayson and closing KoKo in tightly between them.

"Pussy nigga, you don't know what you asking for," Kayson said just as smoothly, not even breaking a sweat. He gripped the nine firmly in his hand.

"Boa, *please*. You making shit worse!" She put her hand on his chest.

"Move, KoKo!" he ordered, quickly knocking her hand away.

KoKo turned and put her hands up against Kayson as he leaned forward. With insistent eyes, she looked at Kayson, praying he would accept her plea for mercy.

Turning back to Boa, she calmly stated, "We not doing this shit, Boa. Now back the fuck up! I need you to leave so I can talk to him." KoKo focused on Kayson and his gun.

Boa tilted his head to the side and raised one eyebrow. "You putting me out for this nigga?" he asked, keeping both fists balled tight.

"I need you to back the fuck up and get the fuck out." KoKo asserted herself and turned her attention back to

1

Kayson. "Baby, please. Stay right here."

KoKo grabbed a T-shirt and jeans from a drawer and snatched up Boa's boots. She placed them in his chest as she pushed him out the room. Kayson and Boa kept their eyes locked until Boa was out of his sight.

"So what the fuck? You just gonna take this nigga back?" Boa asked.

"I have to hear what he gotta say. I owe him that," she answered.

"Fuck you mean, you 'owe him'? That nigga left you." His voice echoed throughout the living room.

Hearing Boa's tone, Kayson walked up behind KoKo. "Ask him why he ain't tell you, KoKo?"

The crease in her forehead deepened as she turned in Kayson's direction. "Tell me what?" She slowly turned back, staring at Boa with cold, piercing eyes.

"I ain't got shit to tell her," Boa said in a smug tone.

"Is that right?" Kayson smirked.

"You got something you need to tell me?" KoKo asked Boa.

"This nigga was paid to come for you, KoKo," Kayson announced, releasing the safety on his gun.

"Look. I am who the fuck I am," Boa said as he stepped into his jeans.

"So you're the muthafucka that wants me dead?"

Boa stared at KoKo for a minute. "Yeah, I was sent after you." He chuckled. "But I had to stop and see what that pussy do." He pulled his shirt over his head.

Kayson looked at Boa sideways and then at KoKo.

"See, that's the difference between me and you." Boa locked eyes on Kayson. "You got love for this 'ho. A dangerous emotion for business." He then turned his attention back to KoKo.

"I was going to give you a chance to be on my team. But I think you served your purpose. So fuck you and this nigga. Y'all ain't got shit for me." Boa stepped into his boots, and he walked toward the door. As he reached for the doorknob, he chuckled again. With his back turned, he decided to leave them with some parting words. "One of my nigga's asked me did I love KoKo. Sheeit . . . All niggas love wet pussy, and if it can make you money, even more so. Catch y'all muthafuckas when I catch you."

KoKo looked up at Boa's back through rage-filled eyes. A half smile formed on her face. "Boa, wait!" she commanded. "There is an old saying: Those who laugh last, laugh best." She took the gun from Kayson's hand. "I know who you are. I have known the whole time." She caressed the trigger with her finger. "Sadeek. Your father. He took my father's life."

The hair on Boa's neck stood straight up.

"At seven in the morning you were going to get a call telling you that they found your mother dead. Her body is in the house, and her head is in a small garbage can out back. A suitable place for a bitch that would sleep with trash." KoKo took the opportunity to chuckle, while raising her arm with the nine firmly in hand. "I would have told you sooner, but I wanted to see what that dick do."

Boa's hand slid off the doorknob. His knees weakened, and the blood in his veins surged through his body fast and hot. Breathing rapidly, his shoulders quickly rose and fell.

"You fucking bitch!" he yelled as he charged KoKo, but was stopped short by the heat that exploded from the gun hitting Boa in the shoulder. He fought through the pain to reach her. With the silencer in place she stepped back and continued shooting, hitting him with every shot. When his lifeless body fell at her feet, she looked down. With all the pleasure and pain in her body, she uttered, "Check mate."

KoKo glanced up at Kayson and squeezed the trigger, shooting Boa in the face. Gripping the gun tightly, she stood breathing heavy. A stream of tears rolled down her cheeks. The color had drained from her brown skin as if she were shell-shocked. Kayson reached for the gun, and she turned the gun on him.

"Don't fucking touch me!" she said with the gun extended toward his chest.

Kayson slowly put his hands up to appear as non-threatening as possible.

"Baby, it's me. Lower the gun," he ordered in a calming tone.

"I ain't lowering shit! And you better not move."

"Look at me, ma. It's me." He moved a few steps in her direction.

Shaken and traumatized, KoKo stood firm. "Don't make me do it," she said as tears ran down her face.

Kayson leaned his chest into the barrel of the gun as he locked eyes with KoKo.

"Follow what your heart says," he barely whispered. Time stood still as the faint sound of Eric Benet singing "Sometimes I Cry" played in the background.

Sometimes I cry, babe,
When I'm all alone with this heart of mine
Sometimes I cry, babe,
Although you've been gone for a long, long time.

KoKo's heartbeat echoed through her body. She felt as if it were shutting down. Overwhelmed with emotion, the only thing she could do was cry.

"Let me have it, baby," Kayson spoke softly.

KoKo looked into his eyes. The anxiety of having him

standing in front of her quickened her breathing. Her teeth slightly chattered.

He slowly placed his hand on the gun and gently pulled it away from his chest. "It's just me, baby." He lowered the gun until it was at her side.

Taking her hand in his, he placed it on his chest. "Feel that?"

KoKo continued to stare in his eyes.

"That's our love, baby. Feel it?"

"Why you doing this to me?" she softly mumbled.

"I need you . . . I need you," he repeated as he moved closer.

"Why . . . are you . . . doing . . . this?" She cried harder.

"Living without you is not an option," he said.

KoKo stood in place as her shock turned into anger. "What am I supposed to do? Just act like all this never happened? Do you have any idea what the fuck I have been through?" She moved to the middle of the floor. Boa's dead body lay at her feet.

"Baby, I know, and I'm sorry."

"Well, sorry ain't good enough. You fucked up, Kayson!" she yelled, turning in his direction.

Her words pierced his heart. He knew he had a lot of explaining to do, and he was well-prepared to tell her everything, until he saw the pain in her eyes. Kayson moved toward her in an attempt to cut the distance between them. When he got up on her, she went in on him.

"What the fuck happened to you? Why would you just leave me by myself? Where have—" Kayson's soft lips, which he placed on hers, stopped the million questions, instantly paralyzing her mind. His tongue parted her lips and intertwined with hers.

KoKo tilted her head. Kayson relished the kiss he had been

5

waiting to give her for almost three years.

Placing his hands on her face, he kissed her deep.

She felt like she had been lifted out of her body, and yet she closed her eyes and savored the moment as his tongue danced with hers. His very touch ignited her soul. *Death never tasted so sweet*, she thought.

Her reasoning overpowered her emotion. Breaking their embrace, KoKo pushed him back.

"How could you?" She moved further away from him.

"I'm sorry, baby." He searched her grief-stricken eyes for any sign of welcome.

KoKo looked at him as if she didn't know him. Kayson reached out to her, and she moved away.

"How the fuck you gonna just show up?" she asked with fury filling her gut.

"Let me talk to you, KoKo." He followed her.

KoKo's head was spinning.

KoKo moved close to him with low eyes and gritted teeth. "You gonna play fucking dead, then show up, pull out a gun demanding shit, and turn my shit upside down. So what? We supposed to just pick up where we left off?"

"Baby, I'm sorry. Just let me explain."

"Explain what!" she yelled.

"I never meant to hurt you. This shit we in is serious."

"Well, no shit, Sherlock. I have been catching shit left and right for the last two years. While your ass been doing what, hiding the fuck out?"

"KoKo. Baby, you gotta trust me."

"Trust you? You want me to trust you? You left me here shot and pregnant with your son. Your son!" She got louder. "I've been doing this shit alone! Niggas coming for my neck, shit falling apart. And you show up talking about trust you.

Get the fuck outta here!"

For the first time Kayson couldn't see the love in her eyes. He knew this shit was going to be hard no matter when he told her, but the pain he was feeling right now was worse than anything he ever felt in his life. As he watched her standing there about to explode, tears and sweat running down her face, he knew his next move had to be the right move. In one quick motion, he stepped forward and grabbed her in his arms.

KoKo tussled with him. The more she struggled, the tighter he held her. "Let me go. Get off me!" she yelled as he squeezed tighter.

"No, not until you calm down."

KoKo continued to struggle, tiring herself out. Then he did what he knew was all it took to get her to submit. He bit hard into her neck.

"Kayson, stop!" she pleaded.

Walking her over to the wall, biting harder with every step, he held her tight as she continued to struggle. "You gonna calm down?"

"Stooooop . . . let me go!" she yelled as she tried to free herself.

"Not until you calm the fuck down." His order vibrated from her head to her feet.

"Okay. Stop, you hurting me!"

Slowly releasing her from his grip, he asked, "You gonna allow me to explain?"

She nodded up and down, unable to speak as she wiped her face.

Kayson grabbed her hand and pulled her into the kitchen. He pulled a chair out for her and put his hand out for her to sit down. Then he pulled the other one out and sat right in front of her.

Sniffing and wiping her face, she stared at him. For a

moment they just looked at each other. KoKo broke their silence.

"I needed you," she calmly stated. A knot rose in her throat as tears again flooded her cheeks.

"I know. And I'm sorry. There was no other way around it." He took her hands in his. "When I woke up and you were not there, I almost lost it. Then knowing that you were pregnant and I couldn't come near you . . . that in itself almost killed me." He looked down, feeling ashamed. Kayson brought her hands to his mouth and began planting a few gentle kisses on them.

"He looks just like you," she said through a shaky voice.

"I know. I saw him." Kayson smiled.

"You saw him?"

"I had to see my son."

"He's so smart." She tried to force a smile.

"Just like his mother."

A strong pain formed in her gut.

"I love you," he said, leaning in and kissing her lips again. This time every emotion came rushing back. The intensity of their love caused their hearts to become heavy. KoKo wrapped her arms around his neck and squeezed him tight.

"I missed you."

"I'ma make it up to you. I promise." Kayson held her in his arms for a few more seconds. She pulled back.

"Let me ask you something. Why? And what was so crucial that you couldn't tell me?"

"Contracts."

"Contracts?"

"Yeah. It's two contracts on my head. And until I figure out who has them, I have to move in the background."

"Move in the background?" She chuckled. "So you're the

ghost in the darkness running around hitting niggas behind my back?" KoKo thought back to that night she and the crew got attacked at the club in New York. There was definitely another gun out there and it had saved her life.

"Hell yeah. They was trying to come for my baby. I had to make them feel me. Sheeit . . . you better be glad I was in the shadows. I been putting them niggas on their knees. I was right where I needed to be."

"But wait a minute, you said *contracts*. I handled that shit a year ago. One of those contracts came outta Cali."

"That Cali shit was a smoke screen. And that nigga, Terrance. He was just a pawn. It's somebody with way more power than he had behind this shit. And I think I'm very close to finding out who."

KoKo thought about his mother and started to reveal her hand, but hesitated, not knowing how much he already knew. "So now what? You sure can't just show up talking about 'I'm back in charge. Niggas fall in'."

"Don't worry about now what. First things first, I need you to keep moving like you been doing. Second, secure all assets and make sure the count stays right. When we finish this shit, we gonna have to get the fuck outta New York. Third, call a party a month from now. We need to bring all the troops together. I'm sending in fresh eyes. I have a whole new team. Last, get the immediate team together tomorrow. Tell them what you need to tell them. I got the rest. When we get more time together, I will tell you a little more."

"Okay, I got it." KoKo hesitated. "So, what about us?" She lowered her head, thinking about what she had been doing while he was gone.

"Baby, it's okay." He placed his hand under her chin, bringing her eyes back to his. "I know you have been doing what you need to do, but you're still my wife."

THE PUSSY TRAP 3: *Death by Temptation*
~ N E N E   C A P R I ~

KoKo looked down again. "Ain't no love lost, baby. However, don't give nobody else my pussy," he firmly stated.

"Well, you left it." She quickly regained confidence.

"Oh, don't worry. Daddy know how to make it his again." He leaned in for another kiss, relishing the softness of her lips. Kayson gripped her thighs while placing soft kisses on her chin. He released her from his grip.

"Now back to business." Kayson sat back in his seat in serious mode. "I need all reports. And sit on the boss's lap while you tell me." He pulled her to her feet.

"Oh, so you think you can just show up and get some pussy?" she shot back as she sat seductively on his lap.

"When I want it I'ma take it."

"Oh, is that right?"

"You already know. Now run your mouth."

KoKo began giving him the gist of the business she had going on, and the behind the scenes information that he didn't know.   After about thirty minutes of back and forth conversation, Kayson asked, "So is that all I need to know?"

"Yes. For now."

Kayson knew it was something she wasn't telling him but decided not to press. He knew time would reveal her hand. "Ai'ight, I gotta go."

"What are we about to do with Boa?" she asked, looking over his shoulder.

Kayson sat quietly, searching her eyes for the reason she was showing concern for the next nigga. The silence became eerie.

"What do you want me to do about him? Send his family a fucking fruit basket? Call the crew and have them clean this shit up."

KoKo looked at him sideways. "Don't get cute with me."

"Lift up." He moved KoKo to her feet and stood up behind her.

"Where you going?"

"I gotta handle some shit. You gotta stay on top of niggas. They need to see you and get instructions before niggas start moving on their own. With this nigga dead."

"Where will you be?"

"I'll be in the background. Don't worry. I'ma send for you in a couple days. In the meantime, handle your husband's business."

KoKo folded her arms and nodded in agreement.

"Come here," he said and pulled her close. He held her firmly in his arms, and she held on tighter as if it was her last time. Kayson could see KoKo wasn't ready to let him go yet, so he held her for a few more minutes. Just the idea of being in her presence caused the Enforcer to come to attention. "See what you do to me?"

"I need to get some of that," she said in a sexy tone.

"Don't worry. I got some shit planned for that ass. Just do like I said. I'ma make that pussy talk in tongues."

KoKo laughed. "I love you, Kayson."

"I love you too. Now go ahead. Be careful. I gotta go put some pain on the streets." With that, he kissed her once more, and then she walked him to the door.

"Another thing, I want you back in my bed."

"Kayson, I have my own house now."

"You heard what I said." He left out the door, pulling his hood over his head. Kayson got on the elevator, both worried and relieved. He went against all orders and revealed himself to KoKo, placing her in as much danger as he was in himself. But fuck it. He wasn't going to be led by anybody. He was a Boss, and the streets were about to feel it. He walked out the building, hopped in his truck, pulling off with the mission in full focus.

- 2 -

Business Not Personal

KoKo sat in the chair staring at Boa's body as the thick, crimson liquid seeped into her carpet. Time stood still as the reality of the night's events played in her head. She rose from her seat and went into the bedroom and threw on a pair of leggings, a T-shirt, and some sneakers.

Grabbing her phone from the dresser, she placed the call to the crew.

"Hello?" Mugsy answered in a slurred speech, as if awakened from his sleep.

"I need you to round up the cleanup crew and come to my apartment."

Mugsy sat straight up in his bed. "You alright?"

"Just hurry up!" she stated and hung up the phone.

Within an hour, they were at KoKo's door. When the door opened, Mugsy's heart sank to his feet. "What the fuck!" Mugsy said as he moved toward Boa. His boy and second in charge lay there lifeless.

Night and Savage filed into the living room, leading the three guys on clean-up inside. The last guy shut the door.

"What happened, ma?" Night asked, looking on with a wrinkled brow.

"He said the wrong shit. The rest is self-explanatory."

"Fuck you mean 'self-explanatory'?" Mugsy asked, apparently feeling a little caught off guard.

THE PUSSY TRAP 3: *Death by Temptation*
~ N E N E   C A P R I ~

"Who the fuck is you talking to?" KoKo shot back.

"I'm just saying . . . this nigga laying on your floor dead. What the fuck happened?" Mugsy raised his voice.

KoKo tilted her head, and Savage went for his gun.

"Hold the fuck up!" Night yelled. "Yo ass need to calm the fuck down." He directed his attention at Mugsy. "This shit ain't personal. It's business. Now everybody need to get their head together and treat this nigga like any other muthafucka we done put on their ass." He gave Mugsy a long, hard stare.

Mugsy huffed. "Yeah, ai'ight. But we need a sit down real soon."

Savage eased his hand from his back and rested it at his side. He stood with Mugsy in his scope, and for the first time he held hatred for his boy.

Night briefly turned his attention toward the clean-up crew. "Y'all get this nigga cut up and in those bags. Hurry up! We gotta get this shit done and get the fuck outta here. Savage, call Bas and tell him to meet us at the office. KoKo, come with me for a minute."

Savage turned the music up. He pulled out his phone, then his nine, and posted himself up by the door. As he dialed Baseem, he held a wicked stare in Mugsy's direction. Musgsy had just put himself in a deadly position and didn't even realize it.

Once inside the room, Night closed the door and looked at KoKo while waiting for her to reveal what happened. After about a minute of intense silence, Night began his interrogation.

"Damn, ma. What happened?"

"That nigga got outta line. So I chalk lined his ass." KoKo looked at Night to see where his head was at. "I know we ain't got a problem with how I take care of my business."

14

"Look. I'm on your side. I'm just trying to find out how to handle shit."

"We go on with business as usual."

"You know Boa was supposed to meet with the Colombians in a week for the new deal."

"I will meet with them. You just make sure these niggas stay in line." She moved to the closet, grabbed her gun holster, and placed both nines in it. KoKo put her vest on and a baseball cap.

"You gonna be alright?"

"Why wouldn't I be?"

Night just looked at KoKo as she moved around the room without emotion. He knew she could handle her business. His only worry was how long could she be strong before she finally broke?

- 3 -

Niggas Better Get Right

aseem sat in KoKo's chair waiting for the crew to return from the mission of burying the treachery that had reared its ugly head. Night sat in a chair placed in the far corner. Each one of them carefully plotting and planning the next move. Times like these were the most crucial. On the level they were playing the game, bitching and moaning about the fallen was a bitch move. They had both learned early that if a nigga wanted to burn a bridge, sell that muthafucka some gasoline.

Just when he had decided to place a call to find out what was taking them niggas so long, in walked Savage, Mugsy, and Pete, all in black sweat pants, hoodies, and boots. Mugsy walked over to the bar, poured himself a drink, and then turned toward Baseem with a wicked scowl on his face.

"What the fuck is wrong with you?" Night asked as he picked up on Mugsy's fucked up mood that lingered on from earlier.

"I'm good," he half-heartedly stated.

"I hope so," Night stated. "KoKo will be here in ten minutes." He paused to look down at his watch.

"Y'all niggas get comfortable." Baseem got up and walked to the bar, grabbed a blunt out of the wooden box, and lit up.

Twenty minutes later, KoKo entered her office. She stopped to take a look around. Savage, Mugsy, Pete, and Night were already posted up and in full investigation mode. KoKo took a deep breath, walked to her chair, and took a seat.

Folding her hands, she looked down and then back up to meet eyes with Night.

"All right. Let's begin. Chucky called. He will be here in a minute. I will catch him up later." Baseem said, "We need to regroup. Split Boa's crew up. Put someone in VA and the rest in Atlanta. Leave his top lieutenant here to handle any pending business." Baseem got quiet to make sure everyone was processing the information.

"So what the fuck happened last night?" Mugsy broke the silence.

"He said some shit I didn't appreciate. You know the rest." She looked at him. "I need you to do damage control."

". . . I got you," Mugsy reluctantly answered, putting his head down. "But I need to know something. That shit was business, right? Not personal?"

KoKo frowned. "Fuck you mean was it business or personal?"

"No disrespect. But damn. Shit was kosher when I left y'all. Then, you call me talking about come handle some shit, and I show up and see my nigga stretched the fuck out on your floor."

Night looked back and forth at KoKo and Mugsy. Savage was also on high alert.

Again, Mugsy shifted in his seat and took in a large amount of air.

"Nigga, if there is a problem. Speak on it." Baseem got loud.

"I guess not. Shit. Niggas sitting around making new plans like we didn't just bury our brother."

"That muthafucka don't mean shit to me!" Baseem growled. "Besides KoKo, all y'all niggas are replaceable."

"Just as I thought," he mumbled.

THE PUSSY TRAP 3: *Death by Temptation*
~ N E N E C A P R I ~

"Fuck is that supposed to mean?" Night said, now losing his voice of reason.

"Fuck it, since we all on the table with shit." Mugsy stood up. "It don't bother y'all that at any minute KoKo could wake up and feel we ain't needed. Then it's our ass on the other end of a clean-up."

"Nigga, have you lost focus?" Savage chimed in.

"Focus? It ain't going to be shit to focus on. We killing everybody."

"This muthafucka done lost his mind." Baseem chuckled. "Nigga, we built this shit. When y'all niggas was playing with your baby nuts, we were building the foundation. And not me, or this nigga here"—he pointed at Night—"is going to sit by and let no pussy ass nigga's conscience destroy it."

"Fuck is you talking about? I put in work just like the next nigga. And I'm loyal. But I guess loyalty ain't in your fucked up foundation."

"Loyal? Nigga, I'm the definition of loyal." He pounded his chest and moved deadly close to Mugsy, who also did not back down. "My brother Kayson saved my life. I breathe because of that nigga's sacrifice. My loyalty lies with him. I don't give a fuck about you, or Boa's dead ass," Bassem yelled, taking the atmosphere from heat to lava.

A flurry of comments went back and forth. Baseem and Mugsy were on the brink. Night stood up to come between them, and before he could extend his arm, Baseem grabbed his gun and shot Mugsy in the face. His body fell into Savage and then hit the floor.

"What the fuck!" Pete yelled out.

"This muthafucka was having trouble making up his mind. Nothing a hollow point can't solve." He looked around the room. "Does anyone else have something they would like to get off their mind." Baseem stopped to give each man a cold stare.

"Nah, we good," Pete answered.

"I'ma ride this shit to the muthafucking end," Savage chimed in.

"Good. Because after this moment, I don't want to hear shit else about Mugs, Boa, or any other weak link. And if one of you niggas wake up feeling conflicted. Kill ya self because I will not have a problem helping you with your suicide." Baseem sat in his chair, not budging on his offer. The game had changed, and so had the players. He wasn't giving anybody a break. If anyone showed a minute of weakness, it would be their last.

KoKo stood up and looked around the room. "We good?" she asked. And when nothing but nodding heads held her gaze, she announced, "Meeting adjourned."

- 4 -
The Next Move

Ever since Kayson felt KoKo in his arms, his whole mission had changed. His whole world had just got turned upside down. He was comfortably seated on the plane and looked out the window as he prepared for the landing.

"Can I take your glass, Mr. Wells?" the woman with the bright smile asked.

"Thank you," he responded. Kayson turned his attention back to the view. He prepared his mind to relay the news to his refuge that he went against all orders and revealed himself, literally placing everyone he loved in grave danger.

Once the plane landed in Georgetown, Guyana, Kayson walked out the front of the airport, grabbed a driver, and headed to his house. He had gotten himself a nice compound on Wakenaam Island. Pulling to the edge of the ocean, the driver parked the car and let Kayson out.

Kayson tipped the man and then headed toward the speedboats to catch a thirty-minute ride to the island. He took a seat on the back row and watched as the natives loaded on with fruit and bags from their day's work.

The waves struck the edge of the banks, and the birds flew by, only an arm's length away. A calm came over his soul, a feeling he welcomed as the intensity of the last twenty-four hours began to dissipate.

When the speedboat came to a stop, Kayson waited for

everyone to get out. He made his exit, again hailing a driver.

After the twenty-minute bumpy ride to his estate, he welcomed the feeling of the moist dirt under his feet. When he stepped inside of his plush baby palace, he hit the lights and took in some air. Throwing his keys on the long black granite countertop, he hit the central air and stepped out of his boots. Then he pulled his shirt over his head and walked down the hall to his bedroom. As he unzipped his jeans, his heart got heavy again thinking about leaving KoKo behind. For a brief moment, he even felt guilty, but quickly regained his footing with the thought that his wife was just as much of a beast as he was. Confidence settled in his gut as he headed for the shower.

Resting his arms on the wall, he embraced the water as it covered every inch of him. Kayson put his head all the way down, allowing the water to pound on his neck and shoulders. At that moment, he released all doubt. It was decided. He was moving forward, and he would be doing it his way. And if killing everyone who was against him lay in the balance, come what may. After carefully lathering his skin several times, he rinsed off thoroughly, stepped out, and quickly got dressed.

Kayson grabbed his guns, tucked them tight, and headed to his truck.

After traveling for an hour, he was at the door of his mentor and confidant.

"Mr. Wells, how was your trip?" the butler asked as he held the door open wide for Kayson to enter.

"I made it back safe," Kayson responded.

"Mr. Odoo is awaiting your arrival in his study."

"Thank you," Kayson said as he proceeded to the study. He stopped and took a minute to look at a new painting hanging right outside the door. It was of Mr. Odoo and his wife. It appeared to be their wedding picture, and again, Kayson's mind went back to KoKo.

THE PUSSY TRAP 3: *Death by Temptation*
~ N E N E   C A P R I ~

"Come, my son," Mr. Odoo yelled out as soon as he felt Kayson's presence.

Kayson snapped out of his reverie and entered the room.

"Welcome home. Is everything okay?" the small stature-sized man asked from his huge chair.

"It's all good. Is everything okay here?" Kayson asked as he took a seat on the light gray suede couch across from him.

"Yes, the show went on," he said, giving Kayson's reaction his full attention

"Good." Kayson gave a quick response.

"Did you accomplish what you set out to?"

"Not really. I went to see my wife."

"How did she take death arriving at her door?"

Kayson chuckled. "Besides the fact that she tried to kill me, it went well."

Mr. Odoo returned the chuckle, but then the mood got serious. "Do you think it was worth it? I mean, the reality of putting her and your son in danger?"

"They were in danger anyway."

"But now the shit has risen to a whole other level." Mr. Odoo folded his hands and laid them on his chest.

"That picture outside your door. It's there because it reminds you of something. It sits right at the entrance to a room where you sit and prepare to make the future prosperous for that woman and the children she blessed you with." Kayson paused. "Well, I feel the same way. I gave that woman my word. I made her a promise I got to keep."

"Understood, but I hope you can live with the decision you made."

"I don't have an option. Because what I can't live with is knowing that I have a wife and a son out there alone fighting for their life and spot in the world while I just walked away," he stated as his chest tightened up at the mere thought.

Mr. Odoo nodded in agreement. "Well, I got your back. This is your home and your family."

"Thank you. And thank you for saving my life."

"No thanks needed. You are a son to me, and your loyalty will live on the pages in my mind forever."

Kayson nodded.

"So when do I get to meet the lovely Mrs. Wells?"

"Real soon. I gotta put her with Yuri."

"We must be very careful. My daughter is a very proud and powerful woman."

"That's true. And my wife is a killer." Kayson rose to his feet. "Let me sooth that beast within, and then we will put them together." Kayson walked over to Mr. Odoo, shook his hand, and then prepared to leave.

"I trust you, Kayson."

"I know. And I will never cross you." He turned and walked out, thinking about the reality of putting those two powerful women in the room together. His allegiance to Mr. Odoo was airtight, but KoKo didn't hold that same respect. And until he could get to her and explain why he made the choices he made, everyone who he came in contact with while gone would be marked.

Ground Control
Back in New York . . .

"I thought we agreed that Boa would handle me from here forward." Alejandro sat up in his chair, apparently aggravated with KoKo's news.

"Well, the nigga had to take some time off," she smugly stated while seated at her desk at the Lion's Den.

"Time off?"

"Yeah, he has a headache." KoKo sat across from

THE PUSSY TRAP 3: *Death by Temptation*
~ N E N E C A P R I ~

Alejandro and leaned forward with an intense look.

"Well, I think we need to put everything on hold until he is feeling better." He stood to leave, and his men started to follow.

"Hold the fuck up!" KoKo stood up. "We are in business. I got people depending on me. I am the one who makes the decisions in this organization."

"Yes, that may be true, but I am in charge of this one. Boa gave me a quote, and we have an agreement, and I will not move forward without him."

"Nigga, you a bitch. Fuck outta here . . . And take your bitch ass crew with you."

Alejandro turned and walked back to where KoKo stood.

Night and Baseem got in position to air his ass out.

With gritted teeth and a wrinkled nose, he leaned in and stated, "All the business that we have conducted, and you speak to me this way. You think that you can go around intimidating people with all that mouth you have? Only a weak man folds for pussy." He paused and chuckled. "I love to eat pussy, but I do it standing, so I never have to bow to it."

"That's cool. Because you'll never get close to my pussy, but you can damn sure kiss my ass. And take whatever deal we had and shove it up yours."

"You just made the biggest mistake of your life."

"Muthafucka, you threatening her?" Baseem stepped forward.

KoKo put her hand up.

"I don't make threats," he said as he turned to walk away.

"Me either. Guard ya grill, muthafucka," KoKo spat as she watched them exit.

"You know we gotta come for him first?" Baseem angrily stated.

"They'll never make it home," KoKo said just as smooth.

The rules of the game had changed. In fact, they no longer existed. Everything was subject to change. Now that Kayson was back, KoKo felt like she had grown a new pair of balls, and she damn sure was going to use them.

- 5 -
Mommy Time

With everything going on, and the major turn of events that had taken place, KoKo figured she needed to head to the islands to check on Quran and Keisha. When she stepped off her jet, the sun and serenity were a welcomed change from all the mental and emotional gymnastics her body had endured over the last couple days. She stood for a moment and just took it all in. The sweat now rolling from her skin was quenching her troubled spirit. She wiped her brow and headed to her driver.

"Good afternoon, Mrs. KoKo?" her driver said, opening the door for her. His smiling face and bright eyes were like life support to a dying woman. It was comforting and just what she needed.

"Good afternoon." She smiled back, also something she had not done in days.

As the door closed, KoKo reflected on what Kayson had said about seeing Quran, and wondered if he would show up while she was there. She quickly looked out the window in every direction with hopes of seeing him emerge from the shadows.

With slight disappointment, she settled into her seat, comforted by knowing she would soon have Quran in her arms.

When she arrived at her estate, the guards jumped to post. They welcomed her as she drove up with a slight salute. The gates opened. It was good to see everyone on point. Having the same staff come with her from Dubai was a must. Not only had they been trained personally by Kayson and Night, but they were all that Quran knew. And she wanted to make sure with the major move that he had some sort of consistency.

As the vehicle pulled up to the door, she barely let the car come to a stop before she opened the door and jumped out.

"Wait, Mrs. KoKo! Please, let me," her driver said as he shifted the car in park and attempted to get to the door before her.

"Don't worry. I got it," she said, closing it behind her.

"As you wish." He bowed as she headed inside.

Once within her sanctum, she breathed in heavy, inhaling all the fresh flowers that adorned the rooms. She walked over to the kitchen and looked out the window to see if Quran was playing outside, and yes he was. KoKo watched his nanny toss the ball and Quran attempt to catch it. She had to laugh. Quran was acting like he was really doing something.

Scanning the yard, she spotted Keisha in a hammock lying back wearing a large straw hat and sunglasses. KoKo just shook her head. She could see that her mom had settled into the idea of being the queen of the palace.

KoKo moved to her room to take a quick shower and change her clothes. She figured she would allow Quran to finish his playtime and then be ready for him when he came in for lunch.

Once KoKo was done with her hot shower, she oiled her skin and slipped into a thin bright yellow sundress. Pulling her hair back into a ponytail, her thoughts again drifted to Kayson. All she could do was question his motives and wonder what he would reveal about his whereabouts and if she could fully forgive him. Pushing the thoughts from her mind, she threw on her flip-flops and headed out the room. As she came down the hall, she could hear Quran running into the house and his nanny right on his heels.

"You must wash your hands first," she said in her soft accent, attending to him as if he was her own.

"I'm thirsty," he said, heading to the refrigerator.

"I know, young one, but your little hands are dirty." She took him by the waist and brought him to the sink.

KoKo watched her wash his hands and kiss his cheeks. He squirmed and giggled. Then he reached out, grabbing a handful of grapes from the counter.

"Want some?" he asked as he tried to stuff them in her mouth.

"No, I am going to eat and so are you. Just have a few."

"Mommy wants some," KoKo said with a smile on her face.

Quran's head turned slightly as he slid out of Maryam's arms, dropping his grapes on the counter and taking off. "Mommy!" he squealed as he jumped into KoKo's arms.

Holding her face and kissing all over her, KoKo pretended to be overwhelmed and backed up to the couch and fell backward with him tight in her arms. "Mommy, Mommy, Mommy," Quran sang as he continued to kiss and rub her face.

"You missed your mommy, huh?"

"Yes, yes, yes," he continued to sing.

Maryam looked on as she began to prepare Quran's lunch. "When did you arrive, Mrs. KoKo?" she asked as she moved throughout the kitchen.

"I just got here," KoKo answered as Quran rubbed his nose on hers.

"Are you hungry, madam?"

"I will eat whatever you fix him. I'm just glad to be home." KoKo squeezed him tight and then began to tickle him all over.

Quran laughed out loud as he kicked and wiggled around. His laughter was music to her ears.

When he was tired out, she stood up and threw him on her hip. "Wow! You getting so big," KoKo said to Quran, who had gotten solid and tall, a trait he inherited from his dad.

"So how is my mother doing?" KoKo asked Maryam as she approached the counter.

"She has her days. The medication does good some days, and then some days not so good. But she has been mentioning names and asking about people I don't know. So I humor her and let her speak freely."

"What names? What has she said?" KoKo went into investigation mode. "Quran, go get mommy your school papers, so I can see what you have been up to." She smiled and let him down.

"Okay." Quran took off running to his room.

"Continue," KoKo requested.

"She says things like, 'I told Nine' and Monique is her only friend. Now, I know Mrs. Mo no longer here, but I don't say that. I just nod and smile. But I don't know Nine or Fred."

"Fred?"

"Yes, she say Fred knows. Fred knows everything. I say okay, and then I try to get her mind to something else. You know like you said 'no stress'." Maryam put the sliced turkey sandwiches on the plate, and then cut up fresh pineapple and papaya. "One thing I worry about though." She paused. "Sometimes she seems as if her memories are real. She comes into the room talking like she has just spoken to these people. You know?" she asked, turning to rinse off the carrot sticks. Maryam placed them on the plate with ranch dressing and a few potato chips.

"Are you encouraging her to write things down like I asked you?"

29

THE PUSSY TRAP 3: *Death by Temptation*
~ N E N E C A P R I ~

"Yes. And she holds onto that book for dear life. She say 'this is for my daughter'. She don't even let the nurse see," Maryam stated as she set the plates and fruit on the table.

When KoKo got ready to make her next statement, Quran zoomed back into the kitchen with both hands filled with drawings. "We will talk later," she said as she watched Quran fumble around.

"See, Mommy. Here, here," he said, shoving his papers into KoKo's hands.

"Awww . . . Let's see what you did," KoKo said, trying to organize them.

"See, I did a good job." He beamed with pride.

"Yes, you did." She leaned down and kissed his lips. KoKo shuffled through the pages until she got to a picture he drew of what appeared to be three people.

"Who is this, Quran?" KoKo asked, awaiting his explanation.

"This is Mommy. This is Daddy, and this is me. Right there." He pointed hard at the figure that was supposed to be him.

"And that's your daddy?" KoKo pointed at the taller figure.

"Yup," he said, moving fast to the table, hopping up in the chair, and grabbing his food."

"He talks about his father all the time. Like he has seen him yesterday," Maryam said as she pushed his chair in and placed his juice cup next to him.

"Is that right?" KoKo sat across from him and stared into his face. She wanted to ask him some questions, but she thought it would be better to let things flow naturally.

Maryam's revelations had KoKo's mind all over the place. She was fixated in thought when the sliding doors opened and in walked Keisha.

"My baby," she said as soon as her eyes met with KoKo's. "Where have you been, baby? You said you were going to the store." Keisha walked over to her and pulled her head into her chest and hugged her tight.

"I just got back."

"Did you get my things I asked for?"

"Yes, they are in my room. Let me get them for you." KoKo rose to her feet.

When KoKo returned, she stopped and watched Quran sit on Keisha's lap and play with the charm on the necklace.

"See, Mommy. That's you." He pointed at the baby on the charm.

KoKo smiled and walked over to them. She kneeled in front of them and placed two Nina Simone CDs on Keisha's lap.

Keisha took them into her hands. "Thank you, baby." She held the CDs to her chest. "This is real music." She smiled.

"Anything for you," KoKo responded as she looked at her mother's beautiful smile.

KoKo didn't know what time would reveal, but she knew one thing for certain. She needed to find out who was behind all of these secrets and make them pay without her mother and son becoming casualties in the process.

For the remainder of the day, Quran wore KoKo out. He wanted to play, run, color, and go outside. He tried to cram a week's worth of fun into one day. Quran had learned early that Mommy traveled a lot, and her time with him was short. Every time she came home, he wanted to do everything possible with her before she was gone again. KoKo, too, had been picking up on the fact that he was getting older and needing her more. She had already decided she needed to spend more time with him.

After giving Quran his bath and reading a dozen books to

31

him, KoKo lay next to him in her bed until he was fast asleep. Inching slowly away from his warm body, she got out of bed, put on her robe, and headed to her mother's room. To her surprise, Kiesha was sitting up in the bed and writing in the small leather covered journal that KoKo had given her.

"I see you're still awake," KoKo called out as she walked to the bed and took a seat.

"Yes, I want to sleep, but my mind won't let me."

"What you writing?" KoKo asked, hoping she would reveal some needed information.

"Just a few memories. You know this mind of mine is tricky. I have to get it as it comes." She smiled.

"Can I see?"

"No, not yet. You are not ready yet." She closed it up and tucked it under her pillow.

KoKo just smiled and rubbed her leg. "Okay. Get some rest. I will see you in the morning."

Keisha didn't answer. She smiled and watched her get up and head to the door.

As KoKo began to pull the door shut, Keisha said aloud, "KoKo."

KoKo stuck her head back in the door to see Keisha wearing a serious look. "Always stay one step ahead of them. That way they can never fool you. Sleep well." Keisha eased down into her huge, soft, goose down pillows and closed her eyes.

Although Keisha's awkward comments required an instant question, KoKo hit the light and closed the door instead. On her way back to her room, the strange interaction she just had with her mother made her uncomfortable. She needed to get her hands on that book. Whatever it was that Kiesha knew was haunting her spirit, and the sooner KoKo knew what it was, the closer she would be to solving all the mysteries that haunted her.

- 6 -

New Blood

Within three days mommy time was over and KoKo was back to business. She knew she could not leave the crew for too many days. As soon as her feet touched the New York concrete, she called Night and Baseem for a meeting at one of her favorite spots in West Village.

She sat in the back of the Hudson Clearwater restaurant waiting for Night and Baseem to arrive. She sipped her drink, watching the warm afternoon sun dance on the moving vehicles as different characters passed by in their array of dress and hairstyles. If you wanted to see weird and absurd, just sit and watch the sea of New Yorkers moving about their day. Entertaining is an understatement.

When she saw Night and Baseem pull up and hop out of a cab, she went right into boss mode. She kept her eyes focused on the door until they walked in and toward the table.

"Why you all the way back here? You on punishment?" Night asked as he approached, throwing the *New York Post* on the table.

Baseem sat down next to him with a solemn look on his face.

KoKo quickly read over the caption under the photo of several police cars and fire trucks, which stated that a car blew up near the docks in Manhattan just last night and the four bodies found were burned beyond recognition. KoKo folded the paper up and looked over at Baseem. The deed had been handled. They had to move on the Columbians before they moved on them.

"Why this nigga looking like his cat is stuck in a tree?" KoKo asked as she reached up and grabbed her drink.

Night chuckled, looking back and forth between Baseem and KoKo.

"Go 'head with all that. I had a rough night." He paused and looked around for the waitress. Locating her, he waved her over. "So what is the next step?" he asked as the waitress approached the table.

"Yes, how may I help you?" the waitress asked, smiling big at both men.

"Let me have two Jack Daniels on the rocks," Baseem said, and then looked over at Night. "You want something?"

"Yeah, let me get a glass of Hennessey Black," Night said and then glanced at KoKo.

KoKo waited until the waitress left the area.

"So this is what it is." KoKo sat forward. "Night, I need you to be in Atlanta. I have a special project that I will present to you in a few days. I want you to get with Chico and have him introduce you to everyone, and then have Goldie show you the ropes of the club. She has a three-bedroom house. Stay there until I get you this other spot. But please don't get her all fucked up. I need her for something else."

"Get her all fucked up? What does that mean?" Night asked with a smile on his face.

"You know how you do. I need her focused. I have to send her after someone. I don't need her distracted right now."

"How you gonna tell a grown ass man what to do with his dick?" Baseem asked as the waitress returned to the table with the drinks.

"Tell her, Bas," Night responded.

THE PUSSY TRAP 3: *Death by Temptation*
~ N E N E   C A P R I ~

"Fuck y'all!" KoKo shot back.

"Here you go," the server said as she set the drinks down. "Can I get you anything else?" She gazed in Baseem's face.

"Yeah, you can give us some fucking space," KoKo stated.

The waitress looked at KoKo with wide eyes. In a low voice she said, "Let me know if you need anything." She left the table in a hurry.

"Why you do that? That could have been some potential late night action." Baseem picked up his drink and looked back at her ass. Turning back to the table, he began to sip his drink.

"Late night action. That bitch look like you might fuck around and find some more dicks in there when you get there," KoKo said. They all started laughing.

"Whatever! So what you want me to do?"

"I need you to stick close to me. I will have to leave town in a couple of days. They need to see us together and know that you're on top of everything."

"I got you."

"How is Mugsy's people responding to his death?" she asked.

"They taking it hard as hell. I told them we on it," Night said as he brought his drink to his mouth.

"All right." KoKo paused. "We putting it on them Marcy Boys. I got a connect over there who said they have this nigga they been trying to get rid of. So his ass is getting it. I got Chucky on that. Just make sure they know he was the one after he fall."

"Got it."

"So when you want me to go to the 'A'?" Night asked.

"Tonight. Give your crew instructions to fall in under Baseem. Get down there and get settled. I will be down in a

36

few days."

KoKo got up to leave.

"Where the fuck you going?" Baseem asked.

"To get some KoKo time. After today, shit is about to get very chaotic. I need to see what it feel like when shit is normal. I'll see you in a little while." She walked off.

Once she was out the door and in her car, Baseem spoke freely. "So what you think is up with KoKo?"

"I don't know. But whatever happened the other night must have been real serious for her to kill Boa. She had that nigga on some big shit."

"I think she needs to fall back and let us take some of this shit off her shoulders," Baseem said as he downed the last of his glass and started on the other.

"You know that shit ain't happening. KoKo needs the streets like she needs air. The only one to calm that ass was Kayson. The rest of us better get prayed up." Night laughed.

Baseem sat thinking about what Night said. His thoughts drifted to Kayson and how much he missed his right hand. The feeling of disappointment came over him as he reflected on the danger KoKo was in and how much blame he would place on himself if anything ever happened to her on his watch.

"You all right?" Night asked, realizing that Baseem had zoned out.

"Yeah, I'm good. Pay the bill. I need to go holla at old girl. Because unlike yourself, KoKo ain't in charge of my dick," he said and walked off.

"Fuck you, nigga. You ain't going to have to worry about KoKo if Zori catch that ass slippin'." Night went in his pocket, pulled out a fifty, and tossed it on the table. He stood and stretched.

"Hating ass nigga!" Baseem shot back and kept on going.

Night took the rest of his drink to the head and then moved

to the exit. On his way to the door, he also zoned out, thinking about Kayson and all the shit he left on KoKo's shoulders and how long it would be before the weight of the world brought her to her knees.

- 7 -
Goldie's World

Night touched down at Atlanta's Hartsfield/Jackson airport around two in the afternoon. As he headed towards the shuttle to go get his bags, his steps were light but his thoughts were heavy. He wondered why KoKo would choose to send him out of state and keep Baseem close to her. The implications could be major or they could mean nothing at all.

Placing his hands on his lap, he looked out the window thinking about the task at hand. He also wondered why KoKo would choose to send him out of state and keep Baseem close to her. He quickly forced the thoughts out of his mind, knowing that KoKo always put the best in position to do the best work.

After twenty minutes more, the cab pulled in front of Goldie's house. He paid the driver and jumped out. Walking up her walkway, he wondered if he was going to have any problems out of niggas who were not willing to fall in, and how many he would have to put on their back before he had total cooperation.

Before he could ring the bell, the door came open. All his present thoughts disappeared when he saw Goldie standing there in a pair of orange terry cloth booty shorts and a matching tight tank top. The frigid air displayed her erect nipples, which stood up in his face like a welcome committee.

"Night, right? Goldie said as she extended her hand.

THE PUSSY TRAP 3: *Death by Temptation*
~ N E N E C A P R I ~

"What's up, ma?" he said, taking her hand in his.

"Welcome to the 'A'?" Her beautiful eyes gleamed.

"I'm feeling the love already," he said, taking in all she had to offer.

"Well, come in." She walked toward the kitchen.

"Got dam!" Night mumbled as he watched her ass shift and jiggle.

"I have two extra bedrooms. You can pick whichever one you want," she announced, stopping at the counter.

"I'm a guest. Where ever you want me. That is where I will be." He looked in her eyes.

"Okay, well you can have the one across from mine. It has a nice view of the park and pond."

"That's what's up. I'll get settled later. Right now I need something to eat." Night rubbed his stomach.

"What you want?" Goldie smiled, noticing his flirtatious jester.

Night smiled. "Whatever you want to feed me."

Goldie stood locked in eye contact for a few seconds. "Let me go throw something on. I'll be right back," she said in an attempt to get further away from the sexual tension.

Dammit, KoKo! Why you send this sexy ass chocolate nigga down here? she thought as she walked up the stairs remembering KoKo telling her to 'stay focused and don't get caught up'. "Shit!" she mumbled as she entered her bedroom. Goldie went into her closet and dressed in some tan linen capris, a white button up shirt, and threw on some Gucci open toe clogs. She grabbed a gun and a small black case from the closet. Tucking her .22 in her Celine clutch, she glossed her lips and sprayed her golden dreads that were up in a neat bun.

Coming down the stairs, Goldie looked around to find Night seated on her couch with his head back and eyes closed.

She walked over to him and set the case down on the coffee table causing him to sit up.

"You ready?" he asked, standing up.

"I done wore you out already?" she joked.

"Never that. And even if you did, all I would need is a few minutes, and then you would be in a whole lot of trouble."

"Maybe. Maybe not," Goldie shot back.

Again, the sexual tension was high.

"What's this?" Night reached down and popped open the case.

"KoKo left this for you."

Two guns sat neatly embedded in the velvet interior. He grabbed one, tucked it in his back, and pulled his T-shirt down. Then he placed the small one attached to a strap around his calve.

"That's why I love that woman. She always knows what a man needs," he said, looking at Goldie.

"You ready?"

"Always."

"Okay, I'm driving. I'm going to hook you up with something real tasty, and then I'll take you to see Chico at the club."

"Lead, I know how to follow," Night responded.

Goldie turned toward the side entrance leading to the garage.

Night followed close behind her, needing to dismiss the feelings of attraction. But he had already decided KoKo was going to have to be mad. Because if the opportunity presented itself, he was getting some of that. And from the looks of things, Goldie was not going to mind giving it to him.

- 8 -

Trust No Man

It was Friday night at the bike club and shit was flowing lovely. Niggas were dropping a grip on the tables and the dance floors were popping. Tonight was a slightly different, in that Baseem had opened a room in the club for private parties. He peeked in on the bachelor party that was in full progress.

Stopping at the bouncer, he questioned, "Niggas spending money up in here?"

"Hell yeah. They getting bottle after bottle and fuck making it rain. It's a thunderstorm in this muthafucka."

"All right. Don't let anybody disrespect the girls. Watch their back, and if niggas get outta hand, usher they ass out immediately," he ordered.

"I got you."

Baseem watched the show for a few more minutes, threw a couple hundred at the dancers, and then moved out.

After running a security check, he headed to KoKo's fifth floor office to wait for the crew to arrive.

One by one, they pulled into the bike area.

Chucky stood and waited for each man to pull in, and as they did so, he escorted them all upstairs.

"Damn, it's bitchamania up in here tonight," Savage said as he looked out into the crowd from the glass elevator.

"Man, when this meeting is over I'm getting white boy

42

wasted," Taz said, slapping hands with Savage.

"Them bitches ain't fucking with y'all niggas. They can smell wife pussy on your breath," Chucky joked.

"Fuck you, nigga," Savage said as Taz laughed out loud.

"We know you ain't talking, latch key ass nigga. Yo' wife got a chastity belt on yo dick," Taz blurted.

They all burst out laughing; even the security guard had to laugh at that one.

When the elevator stopped, they got serious as they piled out and went straight to the office.

"What's good, my niggas?" Baseem said, greeting them with a half hug and handshake.

"Man, it is what it is," Chucky said, taking the first seat.

"We just trying to make this happen," Taz said, taking a seat next to Chucky.

"Fuck all that. Where the weed at?" Savage said, going for the wooden box. "Hell yeah. All my troubles are now null and void." He grabbed the lighter and took a seat.

Baseem poured himself a glass of Patron and positond himself on the other side of the desk.

"So how is the street responding to all the changes?"

Chucky went first. "Most of the crew is falling in, but you got the niggas on the skirts who are questioning their status and longevity in our organization."

"Longevity? What the fuck they think we running? Blue Cross? We in the drug game. Ain't no fucking longevity. These niggas better reevaluate the game. We been doing this shit for over fifteen years, and the only thing that comes with longevity is prison and death." He paused, reaching out to take the blunt from Savage's hand.

"So what are we doing now?" Savage asked, blowing the remaining smoke from his lungs.

"KoKo said she working on some shit. We need to let these

young niggas have these streets. We already put our stamp on it." He passed the blunt to Taz.

"Is KoKo all right with all this shit? She taking on everything. I'm ready to step up," Taz said, inhaling the thick smoke.

"Don't worry. When the time is right she will let us know. Until then, hold your crew down. Keep them niggas calm and keep down suspicion and doubt," Baseem affirmed.

"Me and my crew is down for whatever," Taz shot back.

"Make sure you can live by those words because shit is getting ready to get wicked." Baseem sat back, resting his head on the soft cushion.

"We done?" Savage asked, anxious to get to the party.

"Go 'head, nigga. Have fun." Baseem smiled.

"I'm not in no rush, but I saw some tight ass jeans I want to get into." He rose to his feet.

Taz stood up next, taking one last pull from the blunt and then placing it in the ashtray. "Ai'ight, we'll be downstairs if you need us." He slapped hands with Baseem and then Chucky.

Savage and Taz filed out the office like two kids at an amusement park.

Chucky looked back at the door to make sure it was closed. "I don't trust that nigga, Savage," he stated with a mean grimace.

"What you feeling?"

"I don't know yet. But I don't trust his ass."

Baseem nodded up and down. "Watch that nigga. And if you see him step a centimeter off his square I want to know directly. Bring me all reports. KoKo got enough shit to worry about. If he ain't right we know what to do."

"Got you," Chucky responded, standing up and slapping

Baseem's hand. "Let me go make the rounds. I'll see you downstairs."

"Yeah, I'll be right down."

When Chucky left the office, Baseem sat thinking back on the last meetings they had with the crew to see if he remembered any inconsistency in Savage's behavior. He couldn't recall any, but now with Chucky pulling his coattail, he was going to be all over his ass. He checked the monitors, cleaned up, and headed downstairs.

After checking behind Chucky, he went to the main floor where the bike stunts were underway. Savage was posted up with a redbone chick that KoKo used for odd jobs.

Carefully, Baseem posted himself up behind Savage to get a good look at how he was moving.

When Tori caught his eye, he gave her the nod. She knew exactly what he meant and nodded back, confirming her acceptance of the mission. Baseem knew that if Tori was on that ass, within days he would know exactly what Savage was up to.

- 9 -
Anxious

KoKo was wracking her brain and using the wealth of her resources to come up with a new drug supplier. She knew she had to have the money right to flip it with the Japanese connect. Not to mention the laundry list of shit she had going on from state to state. She was so busy focusing on Kayson, that keeping focus on anything else had become challenging. Three weeks had passed since she last seen him; that alone had her thoughts a bit preoccupied and business was pressing.

"So, did we cover everything?" KoKo asked, walking around her desk and taking a seat. She had been on edge. Her conversations were short, and her tongue was sharp.

"Nah. But I need to holla at you," Baseem interjected.

Even though KoKo had wanted him to stay close to her, she had been avoiding him.

She looked over at him and nodded. Her eyes gazed across the room, feeling for each man's soul.

"Anybody else?" She directed her attention to Savage, Taz, Chucky, and their lieutenants.

No one said anything, but she knew that behind their calm was worry. After Boa and Mugsy's sudden departure, the crew had been filled with mixed feelings. There were questions roaming the crevices of every man's brain. However, each opted for silence, patiently waiting for their fate to be revealed. The room was filled with black. Not the décor, but

46

the emotion. A thick cloud of gloom hovered like a weight threatening to choke the very life from them all.

When no one said anything, Chucky stood up and everyone else followed suit.

"That's it for now. We have a big week ahead of us. Everybody needs to stay focused. Keep your eyes and ears open and your mouth shut."

Each man nodded in agreement as they began to move out. "We'll meet you downstairs in five minutes." Chucky directed his voice in Baseem's direction.

"Ai'ight," Baseem responded from his seat in front of KoKo's desk.

Everyone moved out, closing the door behind them.

When Baseem was sure they were gone, he started his conversation with KoKo.

"So, what the fuck has been going on with you?" he asked in reference to her cold attitude and secrecy.

She sat looking over some papers on her desk as she tossed her options around in her mind. Even though Baseem was one of her most loyal and a true brother, she could not reveal her hand. Deep inside she wanted to put him down, but the Boss was back, and he had made himself perfectly clear about her keeping shit to herself.

KoKo didn't even look up. "What are you talking about?" She continued to go through her papers.

"You know what I'm talking about. Your ass has been off balance ever since you took that nigga out. I'm still unclear about what the fuck happened that night. I need you to tell me something."

"Bas, it's so much shit going on. I haven't had time to think."

Baseem got ready to respond, but the intercom went off. "Mrs. KoKo you have an important call on line two." Lori's voice came through the speaker.

KoKo hit the button. "Thank you." She turned her attention to Baseem. "Hold that thought. Let me take this."

Baseem chuckled and stood up. "Yeah, I know. Business first." He walked over to the bar, got a blunt out of the cigar box, and lit it up.

"Hello?"

"Hey Princess." The voice rang through the phone and was music to her ears. KoKo had to fight to hold in her excitement.

"Yes sir," she said, holding a straight face as Baseem looked on.

"Mrs. Kitty called me this morning."

"Is that right? What did she say?"

"She said 'Daddy, make me cum'," he said real sexy into the phone.

KoKo crossed her legs to stop her clit from throbbing.

"So what do you want me to tell her?" she asked while maintaining her calm yet firm demeanor.

"I want your clit on the tip of my tongue, and I don't wanna hear nothing but moaning."

KoKo squeezed her legs tighter at the thought. "Sounds like a plan."

"When I hang up, go board the jet and meet me at our spot in Vegas. Hurry up, and don't keep me waiting."

"I have a few things pending." She looked at her watch.

"Assign that shit to Night. Dismiss that nigga in front of you. Then bring the Boss his pussy. And hurry up. I still don't do late." He disconnected the call.

KoKo played it off for a few seconds. "Okay, I'll get back to you." She hung up, rose to her feet, and placed her papers in the top drawer of her desk. KoKo slid in her chair.

"Is there anything else? I gotta make a run," she told

Baseem.

"Nah, it ain't nothing. I'll catch up with you." Baseem put his blunt out and placed it back in the box. "At some point you're going to have to tell me something. Until then, I'ma hold you down."

"Thank you." KoKo patted him on the back as they exited her office.

KoKo was glad that Night was in town, she called him to notify him that she was leaving and to meet at the airport in an hour for his instructions. As she hung up, a big ass smile came over her face. She was on her way to see the Enforcer.

- 10 -

What Happens in Vegas...

Like a loyal lieutenant Night, flanked by Chucky and Taz, stood awaiting KoKo's arrival. She pulled up looking straight boss rocking a pair of white skinny jeans, a white crop blouse and stilettos. Spoke a few words to Chucky and Taz as she passed the car. Then she walked to the side to give Night his orders. They stood in full conversation for about ten minutes. Night leaned in and hugged her snug in his arm.

"Go give my boy what he needs," he whispered in her ear.

KoKo broke their embrace stood back and gave him the side eyes. "You knew about Kayson all along, didn't you?"

"Maybe. Maybe not." He smiled and then walked to his car.

"Were going to have a long ass talk when I get back," she hurled at his back.

As the plane took off, she sat in her chair trying to relax. Her stomach was doing flips, and her heart was racing. Once she saw the 'fasten seat belt' sign go off, she ordered a drink in an attempt to calm her nerves. Sitting back and stretching her legs out, she began reflecting on all that Kayson had revealed. KoKo sighed loud. The reality that he was actually alive, and she was on her way to see him, crowded her mind, sending hot surges throughout her body.

KoKo pulled her legs into the seat and threw the cashmere wrap around her shoulders. She relaxed, preparing her mind and emotions for the rest of the night.

An hour before landing, she took a hot shower and put on a sexy strapless, short, black dress and a pair of six-inch, hot pink John Galliano animal print shoe. She stood in the mirror looking herself over as she combed her hair down from the wrap and straightened her bangs. She scented her skin with Flowerbomb by Viktor & Rolf and glossed her lips, wanting everything to be just the way he liked it.

Sitting back in her seat and fastening her seat belt, she took a few more breaths and prepared for landing. When she saw Tiffany, her flight hostess, emerge from behind the curtain, she reached over and grabbed her clutch and unfastened her seat belt. The doors opened, and again her stomach sank, each step becoming heavy with uncertainty. The scent of hot tar and palm trees filled the air. She walked down the stairs and hopped in the car headed to her baby. Inside was a bouquet of flowers and a note that read:

Don't get scared now. I'ma be as gentle as I can under the circumstances.

Love you.

KoKo smiled and brought the letter to her nose to inhale his scent. Cartier cradled her nostrils; her mouth watered. Laying her head back, she closed her eyes and summoned all the memories of his touch. She could feel the wetness begin to seep through the silk of her panties and crossed her legs. The closer she got, the more nervous she became. The glass of wine she drank to calm down only intensified the heat burning inside her.

Pulling up to the doors of the Wynn Hotel, her body slightly trembled at the mere thought that he was only minutes away. When her door opened, she almost couldn't move. The chauffeur put out his hand and pulled her from her seat. The bright lights were blinding as she headed to the front door of the hotel. Strutting into the lobby, she walked straight to the front desk, bypassing the wondering eyes and inquisitive stares.

"How may I help you?" the chipper young man said with all smiles as KoKo approached the desk.

"Yes, Wells," KoKo responded.

"Yes, ma'am. You are in the Encore Tower, Salon Suite. Take those elevators over there and enjoy your stay."

"Thank you," she said, walking away from the counter.

Once the elevator doors opened, she stepped inside and rested against the rail and watched the numbers increase. She pulled out a mint from her clutch and slipped it in her mouth.

"Ding."

The doors opened and she exited to the left. Each step felt so surreal.

"Knock. Knock. Knock."

KoKo took another breath, and then ran her hand over her dress to make sure everything was in place.

Kayson opened the door with that serious look. He was all about business. He stepped back a little so she could enter, but she was frozen in place.

"Why you acting like you scared of me?" he asked, looking her up and down.

"I'm not scared of you," she said and walked in the room.

"You about to be." He closed the door behind her.

"We'll see, playboy." She looked back over her shoulder and then proceeded to the counter where he had a few hors d'oeuvres set up.

KoKo eyed the décor of the room. The balance of white and tan calmed her mood. The mirror over the living room area reflected the view of the city down below, creating the perfect ambiance.

She continued to the white and tan marble bar, looking over

the silver trays filled with fresh fruit, shrimp and cocktail sauce, crackers, and several types of cheese.

Coming up behind her, he scrutinized every detail of her frame. His dick tingled as the memories of how good she felt filled his mind.

"I know that we have a lot to talk about, but tonight I just want your whole heart. I want to climb inside your soul and feel the love you have for me."

KoKo turned to look into his eyes, and he kissed her lips. "I never let you go." She looked at him with intense seriousness. "And I will be surrendering myself to you because you owe me." She turned to choose a piece of fruit.

"So what do you have planned for me, Boss?" she asked seductively, as the aroma of sweet strawberries and fresh pineapple rose into her nostrils. Picking up a piece of pineapple, she bit into it. Kayson watched as the juice painted her lips.

"I don't know yet. It all depends on how the pussy responds." His eyes danced along the curve of her neck.

The heat of his breath tickled her skin as he pressed lightly against her body.

KoKo felt like she was seventeen all over again. Even though fear had rose up in her gut, she still had to talk shit. "Well, I just want to warn you. I'm a big girl now."

"Why don't you step outta this dress." He ignored her little statement, placing his hands at the top of her zipper and bringing it to the middle of her back. The lust in his eyes pierced her spine.

Turning her, he gently tugged at the dress, releasing her breasts from their enclosure. His mouth watered at their perkiness; her nipples were just the way he remembered them. Kayson looked on in anticipation as the dress moved along her smooth skin, gliding down her stomach. Once it reached her belly button, he promptly turned her around.

KoKo inhaled and rested her hands on the counter. He tugged lightly. The dress slid down her ass, exposing her black G-sting and soft, round ass cheeks on its way to the floor.

As his hands slid down her back, KoKo put her head down. His fingertips pressed into her skin, sending chills all over her body.

Kayson grabbed a chair and sat down behind her, staring at all her splendor, carefully planning his every move. Placing his hands on her hips, he pulled her closer and slid his hand up her inner thigh. KoKo waited with anticipation as the precision of his touch set her pussy on fire.

"I've been dying to just touch you." He allowed one hand to ease further up her inner thigh as the other found its way to the softest ass a man could ever touch. He rubbed and squeezed her ass firmly, planting kisses on each cheek. A small hiss left her lips as his soft lips moved over her skin.

"Mmmm . . ." he moaned, nibbling gently.

KoKo stood in front of him trying to keep her composure. In the distance Stevie Wonder's lyrics to "All is Fair in Love" played.

All is fair in love.
Love's a crazy game.
Two people vow to stay in love as one they say.

"You know daddy don't like panties on you," he stated, sliding them off so they could join the dress.

"Bend over," he instructed. KoKo didn't speak a word. She just did as told.

Seductively, she bent forward, giving him a good view of his pussy. KoKo grabbed her ankles, giving him all she had.

"That's what the fuck I'm talking about."

KoKo jiggled her ass from side to side and then stood

straight up, and so did the Enforcer. She looked back to watch his expression.

"Did I say I was done?" Kayson gave her that look that let her know he was getting ready to do something wicked.

"If you want it. Take it," she whispered.

Kayson grabbed her by the waist and placed his hand on the small of her back and pushed her slightly forward as he brought her lips to his. Slowly, he ran his tongue up and down her wetness. Wasting no time, he slithered the tip inside her sweet flower, tasting the nectar within.

KoKo shuddered.

When he felt her weaken, he went to work. Her moans filled the room, giving him confirmation that he still knew all her spots.

KoKo grabbed her ankles tighter for more support, feeling as if she would tip over.

As the feelings intensified, she pulled forward, which only made him go hard. Kayson held her tightly in place, reaching around and massaging her clit as he teased and tickled her lips with the tip of his tongue. Sliding two fingers in gently, he caressed her spot until he felt those muscles contract. He circled fast on her clit and worked her G.

"Oh my God!" KoKo moaned as he showed no mercy.

When her knees wobbled, he stood her up and turned her around, throwing her leg over his shoulder. He gave that clit a fit. Flicking his tongue counter-clockwise until she screamed and released all over his mouth.

She rested her hands on his shoulders as she tried to recover.

With a wicked grin, Kayson released her leg. KoKo could barely stand as her legs destabilized.

Kayson pulled her onto his lap and held her firmly in his strong arms, dancing soft kisses up and down her neck.

THE PUSSY TRAP 3: *Death by Temptation*
~ N E N E C A P R I ~

KoKo closed her eyes as she melted in his arms. The sound of Silk singing "There's a Meeting in My Bedroom" resonated. The invitation was definitely on the table.

"You ready to make love to the boss?"

"Yesss . . ." KoKo whispered.

"Let's go," he commanded.

Barely able to move, she rose and took his hand, turning slowly. As he stood, he gently slapped her ass and watched it jiggle. KoKo didn't even respond.

"You scared as hell," he teased, walking close behind her, knowing he was getting ready to put that dick on her.

Entering the room, KoKo inhaled and covered her mouth. The huge king-sized bed displayed nothing but black silk sheets as the flicker of candlelight illuminted the room. It was the moment she had been waiting for. There she stood next to the man that she loved more than life.

Kayson turned her toward him, pulling her body against his. The softness of her breasts rested against his perfect frame.

"I love you," he said, locking her in his gaze.

"I know," she responded softly.

There they stood at the end of the bed, Kayson confident and KoKo overwhelmed. He began to kiss her face from one side to the other. When he stopped at her mouth, he planted gentle kisses, pulling back every time she attempted to taste him, craving him.

When he gave in, KoKo pushed her tongue into his mouth. The softness of her tongue and lips accompanied by the heat that emanated from inside her sent chills up his spine.

"Lay down. I need to look at you."

KoKo bent over to take off her shoes. "Nah ma, keep those on. Those muthafuckas are shoulder worthy."

KoKo smiled and seductively crawled to the middle of the bed. The cool silk sheets were welcoming to her hot skin as she allowed the Boss his pleasure.

Once he took in all her essence, he climbed between her sweet thighs, placing the tip of his dick right at her opening. He wanted to dig deep, but he needed to savor the moment.

She wraped her arms around his neck as Donny Hathaway crooned "A Song for You" in the background.

I love you in a place where there's no space or time.
I love you for my life, you are a friend of mine.
And when my life is over.
Remember when we were together.
We were alone and I was singing this song to you.

"I missed you," were the words that left his lips as he landed forgiving kisses on her neck, entering her inch by inch.

Slow, short strokes were breaking her down. She gripped him fiercly as his pace quickened.

"Ahhh . . ." KoKo moaned, causing him to pick up his stride. She clenched her eyes shut, trying to readjust to his size. Kayson placed his mouth over hers and kissed her passionately. He moved in sync to the moans that passed her lips, as every curve of her pussy caressed his dick. Looking down into her face, he relished every stroke. He wanted to stroke slow, but her body was asking for more, so he had to answer the call.

"Kaaaay . . ." she repeated as he picked up speed. And within seconds he had found that spot and knew just how to work it. KoKo held him tighter as her whole body became overwhelmed with pleasure.

"I love you," she moaned loudly as she began to cum.

"I love you more."

Tears rolled down the side of her eyes as all her many dreams were now a reality. "I missed you so much," she confessed, kissing and sucking his neck, not wanting to let him go.

"You miss me or this dick?" he teased.

"Both."

"Flip over, so I can give you some of these power strokes." He pulled out and rose to his knees.

KoKo eagerly got in position.

"You sure you a big girl?"

"Yes," she said, looking over her shoulder at him, knowing he was getting ready to act up.

Kayson stroked his dick, making it harder.

KoKo watched as each vein bulged. The look in his eyes let her know he was planning to put her out of her misery, and 'to be brutally honest' fright set in.

"Pull your knees in," he ordered, and she complied.

Reaching between her legs, he massaged her clit and then slid two fingers inside, making that kitty drip.

"Damn, that feels good!" she moaned as she rode his fingers to her pleasure.

When he felt her muscles constrict, he pulled them out, gripped her ass, and slipped her a few inches of that dick.

KoKo tensed up as he began going deeper.

"Relax your back," he said in his strong sexy voice as he made her reach for shit that wasn't there.

"Oh shit! Kayson, wait!" she pleaded as he began breaking down the walls.

KoKo was on the brink. She tried to move forward, but he locked his grip, refusing to allow her to slow down his rhythm.

"Kay, you hurting me." She reached around and put her hand on his stomach to slow his push.

Kayson grabbed her wrist, placing it in the middle of her back and pushed her down into the bed and stood up in the pussy.

"Kay, wait," she moaned.

"I thought you were a big girl," he taunted, still stroking fast and intense. "Stop being a punk. Shut up and take this dick." Showing no mercy, he hit it from all directions.

Her loud moans and Kayson's grunts filled the room. It was official. The Boss was home and reclaiming his throne. After a few more minutes of pleasurable pain, he was convinced his goal was reached. He pulled back, giving her short, quick strokes, knowing his baby was ready to come.

Relieved for his show of mercy, her body began rewarding him, pushing back into his push. Her muscles strangled his dick as ecstasy took the place of fear. "Yes . . . Just like that," she moaned.

"You want it like this?"

"Yes, like that."

Kayson released her arm, and she gripped the sheets with both hands. "I'm about to cum, baby."

"Let me have it. Let that shit go."

KoKo began cumming and screaming his name.

"This is Boss pussy. Handle your business." Kayson leaned forward and bit into her back. She threw that ass back at him, triggering her orgasm to come on fast and in multiples.

"Ahhhhh . . . I love. I love. I love," she repeated as she fell forward, unable to handle his pleasure. Her arms were stretched straight out as she struggled to catch her breath. Marsha Ambrosius sang loud in the background "In Your Hands":

Here's my heart, now don't you break it,
I'm leaving it here in your hands.

Kayson looked at her body glistening with his sweat. "You love me?"

"Yes," she murmured.

"Forever?" he asked, stroking his dick, ready for the next round.

"Forever, baby," she confirmed.

"Come ride this dick. Let me know it's real." He smacked her ass and then lay next to her. Dick standing straight up, thick and pretty.

KoKo got up and drunkenly crawled on top of him and straddled him backward.

"You know this is the only time it's okay for you to turn your back on me?"

"Stop talking shit and relax, so I can fuck with your head a little bit," she whined.

KoKo took his dick firmly in her hand. Leaning in, she kissed the head, took him in her mouth, tasting their juices and enjoying every lick.

"Mmmm . . . sssss . . ." he moaned, enjoying her tongue action.

"Get up here and get this dick right. Make daddy cum," he ordered, putting an end to her treat. He wanted to gut something.

KoKo released him from her mouth, got in position, sliding down on him and gripping his thighs as she began bouncing and rocking on that pole. Planting her feet firm into the bed, she worked her show. She closed her eyes and gave the Enforcer just what he needed. "Cater To You" by Destiny's Child played, and she rode to the beat.

"That's right, baby. Work that shit!" he moaned.

KoKo didn't say a word. She effortlessly moved her body and fucked the boss, well. Digging her nails into his thighs, she rocked and rotated her hips until Kayson's moans matched hers. Tangled in a web of passion, both of them on the verge of explosion, oblivious of time and space.

Planting his hands securely on her hips, he guided her movements as she bounced and wiggled. Wet juices slid down his dick making the ride slippery.

"Damn, ma," Kayson moaned.

When KoKo's body began to shake uncontrollably, her nails dug into his flesh.

Reaching forward, he wrapped his arms under her legs, lifting her off his dick and pulling her to his mouth. Kayson sucked her clit fast and hard; her body convulsed.

"Ahhhh . . . Kaaaaay . . ." she moaned as he continued to handle that kitty the way only he could. KoKo lay her head on his leg as he slowly ran his tongue up and down her lips. Her body jerked with every touch.

As he rubbed his lips in her wetness, she took his dick into her hand and stroked and squeezed, running the tip of her tongue around the rim. When she heard a light moan escape his lips, it was on. Squirming away from him, she gripped his legs and took him in her mouth and to the back of her throat.

"Oh shit!" Kayson groaned as her jaws tightened. Moving and bobbing, she began to please the Enforcer.

"Sssss . . . Damn, baby," he whispered, holding the sheets with one hand and massaging her clit with the other.

KoKo brought her mouth to the tip and sucked and rotated her head.

"Mmmm . . . Damn, I missed him," she whined as she freed him from her mouth. Again, she took his dick into her hand, squeezing it tight while slowly stroking. Moving forward, she got back into position—got back on that pulsating pole and rode fast and hard.

"Oh shit! Hold up, baby. I don't want to cum yet."

KoKo looked over her shoulder and said, "This is boss dick. Let that shit go."

Kayson smiled, grabbed her hips, and thrust up hard,

matching her every movement. In seconds, KoKo busted long and hard.

Kayson, not to be outdone, flipped her over, climbed back on top, and threw those legs on his shoulders and treated the pussy like it was bottomless.

"Oh my God!" She was taken over by throbbing desire, needing to escape but couldn't, wanting all the satisfaction of his knowing push, but she couldn't take it.

Making sure he broke that pussy down, Kayson placed his feet on the wall behind them. In a diagonal push up, he went in for the kill and punished the pussy.

KoKo put both hands on his stomach to control his thrusts.

"Move your hands," he growled, plowing into her.

"Kaaaaaay . . ." she yelled as he hit that spot.

"I'm still the boss in this muthafucka."

KoKo squirmed to be free. The intensity of his thrust caused loud moans to drip from her lips as her nails pressed into his chest. She couldn't take any more. Kayson grabbed her hands and pinned them to the bed.

"Kaaaay . . . Nooo . . ."

"Am I still in charge?" He continued to stroke.

"Yessssss . . ."

"Tell me!"

"You're still in charge!" she yelled as her head moved fast from side to side.

"Tell me what I want to hear."

KoKo took as much as she could, and when the stroke became unbearable she surrendered.

"You're still the boss."

"Make me believe it." He released her arms, placing his hands behind her knees. Pinning them all the way back, he plowed her back out.

"You're the Boss! Baby, you're the Boss!" she screamed as a soul-rocking orgasm rose up from her core.

With her admittance of his power, he sealed the deal by writing his name all over her walls. When the last drop was released, he let go of her legs.

Out of breath he warned, "You better not ever forget it."

KoKo looked at him through the slits of her eyes, drunken and unable to move or speak. She just lay there as he placed kisses all over her face, stopping to suck her lips.

"I love you, baby," he again confessed.

"I love you too," she said barely over a whisper.

"You still can't handle this dick," he teased.

KoKo gave him a half smile. "And you still strung out on this pussy."

"Well, you said it best. This is 'made-for-a-boss' pussy."

"Sssss . . ." she hissed as he pulled out, kissing down her stomach. KoKo turned over and watched his sexy, sweaty body.

"Come wash the boss up." He smacked the side of her leg while getting off the bed heading toward the bathroom.

"You ain't going to ever change." She shook her head.

"Bosses don't change. We improve. And right now, I'm at the top of my fucking game."

Barely able to move, KoKo turned onto her stomach and watched him move around the bathroom. She wanted to lie there, but one thing she learned early. Don't play with the boss. KoKo wobbled to her feet and followed his orders, joining him in the shower.

As usual, they showered and laughed and played. When they came out, they oiled each other up and lay down, both worn out.

Kayson held her tight as she dozed off. KoKo fell asleep at ease. Her baby was back and he just gave her everything she needed.

Just when KoKo was settling into her slumber, Kayson woke her up and started everything all over again. The Enforcer was greedy for KoKo, and Kayson, being the pussy tamer he is, put that pussy totally out of commission.

The Next Morning . . .

KoKo woke up and stretched. Then she looked over at Kayson's side to discover it was empty. She stretched once again as her eyes scanned the room. Everything that she saw last night was not there and neither was Kayson. For a quick second she feared she dreamt it all, but when she moved her legs to get off the bed, her body told the whole story. She was sore from head to toe. Her legs felt like rubber bands. The boss had definitely put his work in.

When she reached the bathroom and turned on the light, her reflection in the mirror was also confirmation. KoKo was covered in hickies and faint bite marks, the boss's signature.

"This nigga," KoKo spat as she turned in the mirror and saw two circular hickies on each ass cheek. The boss had marked his territory.

KoKo looked around to retrieve her things. She grabbed a small overnight bag he left her and set it on the sink. When KoKo reached in the bag, she saw a black ring box with a note sticking to it, which read:

Hey Babe,
Sorry Daddy couldn't give you some morning wood,
but we're at war, so I'm back in the trenches.
In that box is my ring. Put it back on and don't take it off.

KoKo opened the box. Inside was her original wedding ring, which confirmed that he had not only been close by, but he had also been in the house. She looked back at the note and continued reading.

Oh yeah, tell Miss Kitty I said thank you.

The Enforcer woke up with a smile on his face.

See you soon.

Love you.

KoKo chuckled, slid her ring on her finger, and got in the shower.

Retrieving the other bags he had set up for her, she began popping tags and getting dressed. Fully clad, she packed up her things and headed to the airport. When the plane landed, Baseem and his two goons were waiting.

KoKo walked off the plane sporting a pair of pink Tod's 'Gommini' moccasins, black thick stretch pants, and a pink tank top.

"What's up, Boss?" Baseem greeted her with a smile, responding to the shine that radiated off her skin.

"I'm good. How you doing?" she asked as he opened the door for her to enter the car.

"Time will tell," he said and closed the door. Immediately, his mood changed as he noticed the many hickies that covered her body.

KoKo's secrecy brought forth visual proof that she had some shit going on, and he was about to get all in her business.

- 11 -

Just Be Patient

Kayson had been following lead after lead and hitting one dead end after another. Frustration was about to set in until he saw Nine walk into Delmonico's restaurant at one o'clock sharp just as his informant had told him. He slouched in his seat and watched as Nine was directed to a seat and given his menu.

With the utmost caution, Kayson eyed his every move. Nine placed a phone call, and then he called the waitress over and placed his order. He motioned her to lean down, putting her ear to his mouth. When he finished, the woman stood up blushing and giggling. She carefully removed his menu and walked off.

Kayson stayed in the cut waiting to make his move, when in walked his twin. His eyebrows wrinkled at the sight of the older gentlemen, who looked exactly like him.

Tyquan walked over to the table in a black two-piece suit with a gray shirt and black and gray striped tie. He pulled the chair out and unfastened his jacket, sitting across from Nine.

Nine waved the waitress over, who poured them both a drink. The two men began their conversation. They went back and forth for a few minutes before Tyquan folded his hands, and with an intense stare he gritted his teeth. He made his final statement, and as he got up he bumped the table. Tyquan stood over Nine, beaming down at him like a disappointed parent.

"Fix this shit!" Tyquan shouted. Several customers looked

in his direction. "Mind your fucking business and eat your food!" he said, fastening his button and walking away.

Nine sat unfazed. He grabbed his glass and brought it to his mouth.

Kayson took this moment of distraction to get up and move to Nine's table. He sat down.

"It's funny what a man can find out when he just sits quietly," Kayson said, picking up the glass Tyquan left behind and taking it to his nose. He set it back down.

"What the fuck are you doing here?" Nine asked, looking around.

"I was going to ask you the same question." Kayson locked eyes with Nine.

"Look, I told you I gotta play this shit out. We can't afford to leave one stone unturned," he said with agitation in his voice.

Sweat appeared on his nose as he feared Tyquan would double back and see him sitting with Kayson.

"You told me that you were done dealing with my father. How is it that I run up on y'all seated and eating from the same plate? Oh, and I see he's mad at you," Kayson said with a smug grin.

"This shit is more dangerous than you know. I have to play my hand my way," Nine stated.

"Yeah, and while you over there playing with your dick, my wife and son are in danger. You need to do what you gotta do to get this the fuck off my back. I paid your ass to handle this shit, and it is still plaguing me."

"I told you, I got you. But I can't do my job if you're going to be popping up intervening." Nine looked around again.

"I'ma give you a week. Then I'm coming for all y'all niggas. And one by one, you will die. And I won't lose one night's sleep behind my choices." Kayson stood up. "Oh, and they are watching you. The man at the table in the back followed you over here. I'ma tell you like my punk ass father told you. Fix this shit!" He spoke his final words and walked off.

Nine put his elbow on the table and rubbed his hand over his face. Taking his phone from his pocket, he placed the call he had been avoiding.

"Hello?" the voice rang through the receiver.

"He's on my ass. We need a meeting."

"Fly out here immediately."

"I'm on my way," Nine responded, hanging up his phone. He looked around the restaurant and then stood to leave.

Tyquan walked into his office with a handful of missed call slips from his secretary. As he thumbed through the pages, his mind reflected on the conversation he had with Nine. His son was alive and stalking everyone down like a skillful hunter after his tender prey.

Unbuttoning his jacket, he hung it over the chair and took a seat. He folded his hands and brought them to his face. Resting his chin on his knuckles, he contemplated his next move.

"Excuse me, you need an appointment to see Mr. Wells," the secretary yelled out as the man stormed into Tyquan's office.

"Should I call security, Mr. Wells?"

"No, I got it. It's okay. Close the door behind you," he instructed.

"Why do I hear that your son is still alive stalking my fucking streets?" The angry man stood in front of Tyquan's desk, damn near foaming at the mouth.

"Don't come in my fucking office being loud and

disruptive," Tyquan calmly ordered.

"Fuck your office! If that hotheaded son of yours comes near me or kills another one of my me—"

"What? What the fuck you gonna do?" Tyquan stood, reached in his desk, and pulled out his golden Star Model .380.

The man's eyes got big as his pale white face turned fire engine red.

"Yeah, that's what the fuck I thought. We down here in the fucking trenches. Don't come down on the front line talking shit. I got this. And in the meantime, don't ever fucking threaten me!" He walked over to the man, only inches away with his gun firm at his side.

"If you're not comfortable with how I'm handling things, bring your fat ass out here, and I'll sit back and watch."

"We got too many people depending on us," he tried to calm the situation.

"I know what the fuck is at stake, and I've been the one taking all the risk. Tell them other muthafuckas to suck my dick. And my fee just went up," he growled. "Get the fuck out my office," Tyquan slowly backed up and went back to his seat. Slamming his gun on the desk, he folded his hands on his chest. "Hurry the fuck up before I change my mind."

Shaken and feeling disrespected to the highest degree, the man backed up toward the door. "I'll be in touch."

"No, muthafucka, I'll get at you." Tyquan's nostrils flared, head to the side.

When the door closed, he picked up a glass figurine off his desk and threw it at the wall. "Fuck!"

Rushing from her desk, his secretary pushed the door open looking around. "Is everything okay, Mr. Wells?" the young naive woman asked.

Tyquan looked in her direction, eyeing her curves in her

tight, red pencil skirt and white blouse that showed off a few inches of cleavage.

"Nah, I need to release some tension. Come in and close the door," he ordered.

"How may I help you?" she shyly asked.

"I need you to help me clean my desk off."

Deborah switched over to him, stepping in between his legs. "Should I stand here?" she flirtatiously asked.

Without saying a word, he stood up, inhaling her scent.

Deborah's breath accelerated as the intensity of his stare caused a flutter in the bottom of her stomach.

"You nervous?" he asked, looking down at her.

Deborah nodded yes. He began to unbutton her blouse.

Running his finger between her breasts, he watched as her nipples stiffened. "Relax, I just want to make you grab tight to the other end of the desk for a little while."

Turning her, he released her breasts from her bra and began to caress them gently.

Deborah pushed her back into his chest as he slipped his other hand down the front of her skirt. Her head slid back and forth against his firm body as he slowly circled his finger on her clit.

"Ain't nothing like wet pussy," he whispered in her ear.

Pushing her forward onto his desk, he spread her legs wide. As he slid his hands up her thighs bringing her skirt over her ass, Deborah looked over her shoulder to see him admiring the view.

Tyquan grabbed a pair of scissors and cut her thong on both sides. Deborah inhaled as he pulled it from between her legs.

Unzipping his pants and releasing his pulsating rod, he positioned her just right and slid all the way in.

"Ahhhh . . . ohhh," she moaned as he stroked with

precision.

Gripping her ass tight, he picked up speed. She did just as he predicted and grabbed tight to the desk as he worked her in every angle. One thing after another fell from his desk as he fucked her long and hard.

Deborah struggled to stifle her moans as the pleasure of his push took over her entire body.

He became more aroused as he watched her breasts slide along his desk. Tyquan hit that pussy like it owed him money. "Make this pussy cum for me," he moaned, hitting her spot just right.

Within seconds, she was cumming and so was he. Pushing all the way in, he rested against her soft ass, breathing heavy.

"You good?" he asked, pulling out.

"No," she responded.

"Is that right?"

"I need to sit on your lap," she purred.

"Well, you know what you need to do." He sat back in his chair.

Turning, she went to her knees and began to make him rise for the occasion.

After his little rendezvous was over, his mind was at ease. His thoughts were now flowing. He knew exactly what he needed to do. While Deborah cleaned up their mess, Tyquan went into his bathroom, freshened up, and changed into another suit. When he emerged from the bathroom she was gone. He grabbed his car keys and briefcase and left his office.

- 12 -

Like Father Like Son

The sound of Tyquan's heels digging into the concrete echoed through the parking garage as he made his way to his car. His mind was racing as he redistributed the thoughts of past and present as he moved swiftly through the cars.

When he approached his Pagani, he hit the alarm and popped the trunk. Tyquan threw in his briefcase and slammed it shut. As he turned to grab the door handle, he was met by a hooded man.

"Make any sudden movements and I'ma make it hard for you to collect your thoughts." Kayson forced his .45 to his father's head.

Tyquan froze in place as the cold steel rested against his temple. His heart pounded in his chest. "If it's the car you want, just let me pass you the keys. I ain't see shit, so you can be on your way."

"Nigga, you ain't got shit I want but information."

"Information?" he repeated the man's words.

"What does the name Monique mean to you?"

"Ummm. That's a name that brings a man many happy thoughts."

Kayson wrinkled his nose and squinted. Then in one move, he hit him in the mouth with the butt of the gun, forcing him up against the car. Placing the gun under his chin, he warned,

"Muthafucka, don't get cute with me."

Breathing heavy and tasting a mouth full of blood, he focused on the man that stood before him. And when those hazel eyes gazed back at him, he spoke. "Kayson?"

"Yeah, nigga. Your worst fucking nightmare."

"What the fuck is wrong with you?"

"Nothing is wrong. I'm here to settle all scores."

"You ain't got shit to settle with me."

"You hurt my mother, and for that you pay with your life." He cocked the hammer.

"Wait!" he yelled out. "Please let me explain."

"Explain what? The only decision left to make is open or closed casket."

"Your mother was a treacherous bitch."

"And you about to be a dead one."

"You sticking up for a woman that caused you to take the lives of innocent men."

Kayson paused to listen. "I took the lives of men who were well deserving of death."

"I'ma tell you like I told your wife. Open your eyes."

"Make the shit plain."

"I didn't leave your mother. She left me. No disrespect, but that was the most expensive pussy I ever had. She cost me everything. Even my best friend."

"And who would that be? Malik?" Kayson chuckled.

"No. Edwin."

"What the fuck is you talking about? That nigga raped my mother, and he paid with his life."

"Did he?"

"What the fuck you mean 'did he'? I was there," he growled.

"But did you really see what you think you saw?"

Kayson went back to that day and began reviewing the

events. "I know what I heard."

"That shit was an illusion. That was her thing. That man didn't rape her, son."

Kayson lowered his gun and allowed Tyquan to explain. "Being the man that I am, I stood by her, gave you my name, and took very good care of you. Until one day she took all of that from me."

Kayson's head was spinning. Here, the woman he loved and cared for and made every possible sacrifice for to give her the world had deceived him, and then made him kill her enemies without good rhyme or reason. How could she?

"Son, listen. All this shit is bigger than you know. Your mother has connections on top of connections. She had been manipulating everything for years."

Breathing heavy and now full of rage, Kayson said, "I need proof. I can't ride with this shit you telling me."

"What the fuck do I have to win by revealing my hand? The only thing I have ever wanted was to tell you this years ago. I stood back and let you grow. But when I found out you were dead, my silence began to kill me. I reached out to Nine and instructed him to tell your wife everything." He paused, grabbing his handkerchief to wipe blood from his mouth. "He is the one who holds all secrets."

"I'ma give you a pass today. But if I find out that you lied to me, the pain that you'll receive will be of epic proportions."

"I see where KoKo gets all that attitude from."

"You met my wife?"

"Yeah, she came and threatened my life." He chuckled. "Yeah. When you get to the bottom of all this shit, find out why your mom stooped to the level of fucking that young boy."

"Excuse me."

"Yeah, the nigga that came after your wife. Boa, that's Mo's little flunky."

Kayson was now livid. He needed to get some answers and quick.

- 13 -
Careful Eye

Before KoKo left for Atlanta, Kayson needed to get into her ear. He left Tyquan ASAP and went straight to the mansion.

As Kayson and KoKo sat in the back of the cab heading to the airport, he grilled her for the missing information.

"Who was it that brought Boa to you?"

"Night, but he was already on my radar."

"Did the nigga take you to meet anybody?"

"No. But I had niggas all in his business. That was how I found out he was foul."

"But did you find out he knew my father?"

"Yes. When I went to see him, he gave Boa up." The cab came to a stop at the airport, and the driver jumped out to open her door. "Why? What's up?" she asked inquisitively.

"We will have to see. Keep your eyes open. I'll see you in a couple days."

KoKo leaned over and kissed his lips. "Baby, be careful."

"Be good," he responded.

"I'm always good. Even when I'm bad."

"That's the problem." Kayson gave her a little smile, smacking her ass on her way out of the cab. He watched her until she was no longer in sight. "Let's go," he instructed the driver and sat back.

KoKo planted her feet on Atlanta soil with mission in hand.

She knew there were too many loose ends dangling in the air, and she needed to begin tying them up. One of the main things she needed to handle was the investigation that she and her organization had hanging over their head. With careful examination, she had found out who was the leading detective, a man named Greg Warren and she was about to unleash Goldie on that ass.

KoKo's first stop was the club. She needed to get with Chico and make sure Night was getting all the assistance he needed to keep everyone in order.

Pulling up to Golden Paradise, she noticed a few females arguing with the bouncer. She looked down at her watch that read 11:30. It was apparent the females were angry they missed 'ladies free before 11 PM' and were acting a damn fool. Patiently, she watched as the man on the door tried to calm the situation. When she saw one female in the crowd of three spit in his face, and he began tossing her around, KoKo sprung from her vehicle and went right into action.

She put two fingers in her mouth and whistled. Everyone within earshot looked in her direction. The bouncer threw up his hands and backed up.

The female who was the most indignant threw her hands on her hips and rolled her neck. "Who the fuck she think she is?" the woman turned and said to her friends.

"Is there a problem?" KoKo calmly asked as she approached the irate woman.

"Yeah, it's a muthafucking problem. This country bama nigga won't let us in," she slurred and stepped back.

Apparently, she had already had a few before she got there, and she was about to get herself in a whole lot of trouble.

"Randy, what's going on?" KoKo turned her attention to the bouncer, who was wiping his face with a napkin.

"We told the young ladies we at capacity right now and that

they missed the free before eleven. But she ain't trying to hear that," he said, glaring at the woman like he wanted to take her head off.

"Miss. Look, we at capacity. You missed the eleven o'clock special. So you can either wait until something opens, or come back another time."

"Nah, fuck that. That nigga Jeezy here tonight, and I got a ticket. Now, y'all need to go in there and snatch some of those other bitches out and let us in," the woman barked and moved a little too close to KoKo.

KoKo pulled in some air and reached around her back. She pulled out Midnight and slapped the shit out of the woman with her gun.

The woman fell up against a car, holding her head.

Gasps filled the air as the nosy onlookers watched in surprise.

KoKo moved close to her and the lesson began. "Bitch, I tried to give you an opportunity to get your shit together. First, you disrespected my people." KoKo slapped her again. "Then you disrespected me." Another forceful blow hit her again, almost knocking her out.

Panic stricken and bloody, the woman pleaded for KoKo to stop. But unfortunately, she had just brought herself an ass whooping, and KoKo was making sure she got her money's worth.

Placing the gun under her chin, KoKo pushed the woman's head back.

"Now, like we both told you, we at capacity. Which means we filled the fuck up. And if you ever try that bullshit again, I'ma fill you the fuck up."

KoKo pulled the woman to her feet. Bloody and shook up, she dragged the woman to the bouncer. "Apologize!" KoKo barked.

With fear and tears in her eyes, the woman mumbled, "I'm sorry."

"He can't hear you. I want you to use the same loud, belligerent tone you used to disrespect that man to now rectify this situation." KoKo held the woman tight by the arm.

"I apologize for disrespecting you," she said, as embarrassment filled her gut while glancing over at her two friends.

KoKo turned her around, lifted her face by her chin, and looked in her eyes. "You could have avoided all this bullshit. But you wanted to act like a gotdamn fool. Let this be a lesson to you. Even when a nigga piss you off, always conduct yourself like a lady." KoKo reached in her pocket and pulled out a knot of hundreds. "Usually, I would kill a bitch like you, but you caught a bitch in a good mood. So today you get a pass." KoKo grabbed her hand and put the money in it and closed it tight. "Randy, let me get some VIP passes for the next big show."

Randy reached in his back pocket and pulled out three passes.

"Give them to her," she ordered.

Once they were securely in her hand, KoKo commanded, "Thank him."

"Thank you," the woman said through her sniffles.

"Go get yourself cleaned up, and the next time I see you, there better be nothing but respect dripping off your tongue."

"Get ya bitch," she said to her friends. They rushed to the woman's side, taking her under the arms, and leading her away.

The crowd looked on in amazement as KoKo took some napkins from Randy and cleaned off her gun. Tucking it back in place, KoKo made a final statement before entering the building. "These bitches gone learn today."

Randy chuckled. "Let me find out you watch Kevin Hart."

"Yeah, every so often I try to be a regular person." KoKo half smiled and walked inside.

Randy put the call in that KoKo was there and for them to also fix the tapes as he started to let a few people in the club.

KoKo stopped at the bar and grabbed a drink. She was pleased with the crowd. Jeezy was set to take the stage in an hour, and shit was jumping. As she moved to the offices, she noticed a dude looking her over.

KoKo took note of his features. He stood about 5-feet 9-inches, and he was pleasantly put together. Short, nice cut, pretty brown skin with a thin outlined beard that led to his goatee. She had to admit the nigga was fine. She caught his gaze and humored him with a quick smile. He returned it, and she kept it moving.

Before she could get a few steps, Chico was on his way to her and moving fast. "Everything all right?" he asked, looking KoKo over.

"Yeah, I'm good."

"Sorry for not meeting you outside. I got caught up with counting money and making sure Jeezy and his crew are straight," he humbly stated.

"It's all good. I'm a big girl. I handles mine."

"All right, come on." He took her by the arm, leading her to his office.

"So what's good?" she asked as he closed the door.

"We doing good with the club. We had His and Her Entertainment down here from Jersey twice. They threw a banging party. They know how to cater to the celebrities, so that is a weight off my mind."

"Okay, see if you can get them on contract for the winter

shows."

"Got it."

Chico walked over to the monitors for a minute, but then turned his attention back to KoKo.

"I do see a problem coming out of Diablo's corner though."

"Speak on it."

"She got new blood, and they don't want to bend to the territory split."

"What's been said?"

"It's not what's said, it's what's not said. Niggas attitudes is shifting. I had to bring in more muscle, and I moved my family out to Marietta."

KoKo sat for a minute, contemplating. "Alright. Change the way we move. Times, places, and people we deal with." She paused. "Light something," she ordered.

Chico pulled out two fat blunts from his drawer. He lit one up and then passed it to KoKo.

Inhaling deep, KoKo carefully plotted her next move. "We need to make a good example out of somebody. They think we out here playing."

"You just say the word."

"Nah, not you. I need to put something in between us and them. We gotta throw down some red herring."

"Red herring?"

KoKo shook her head. "Do me a favor. When you off, read, nigga." KoKo chuckled.

"Ai'ight." Chico laughed.

"I don't know how you niggas expect to get to the next level without intelligence." She got serious. "Red herring is something that you do to throw a hunter off the scent. We need to paint the situation with another nigga's blood, so they get off our asses."

"Ummm . . ." Chico said, nodding his head.

"Don't worry. I got it. Let me get with Night and sit on it for a couple days. Plus, I need to sit down with Diablo and feel her out." KoKo pulled hard on the blunt, savoring the flavor.

"Always remember . . ." She blew out the heavy smoke. "Always find out what they know without letting them know what you know. Then use both to fuck them in the ass, hard," she spat.

"Got you," Chico responded. He looked at KoKo like: pass that shit.

"You might as well light something else. This shit is stuck to my fingers."

They both burst out laughing.

Lighting the other blunt, Chico again turned his attention toward the monitors.

"How is Goldie?"

"She good," he answered, turning back to KoKo. "She been with Night. She comes through to check shit out, but other than that, she is with him."

"Is that right?"

Chico quickly picked up that maybe she hadn't been following KoKo's orders.

KoKo pulled hard, staring at Chico. She knew she had made her orders clear, and it was apparent that Goldie was getting a bit sidetracked. She needed to pull that ass back. KoKo couldn't afford to have her catching feelings for Night. It could compromise her whole plan.

After burning a few more stems, KoKo prepared to leave.

"So you good?"

"Yeah, I'm straight." She walked to his bathroom to freshen up.

"So, you not going to slap nobody around on your way out?" Chico joked.

"Sheeeit . . . I didn't want to slap that bitch around. I've been trying to cut back on my slap-a-ho medication. But every time I do, a bitch jump up volunteering to be a case study."

"Oh shit!" he said.

KoKo walked out the bathroom drying her hands. Her eyes settled on the monitors. "Who is that nigga right there?" she asked, referring to the dude who caught her eyes earlier.

"Who?"

"Him." KoKo pointed to the screen.

"That's some cat that's been coming up in here every weekend for the last month," Chico stated. "I been watching that nigga hard. Why? What you see?"

"Nothing yet. Keep close to that nigga. Put some pussy on him. I need to know where he rest and who he know."

"On it. I got the perfect chick." Chico rubbed his hands together.

- 14 -

Playtime is Over

The next morning KoKo awakened with a tight game plan formulated in her mind. This was gonna be some gangsta ass shit, all she had to do was implement it then sit back and watch muthafuckas unfold. Smiling at her own cleverness, she got up and went to get her nails done and did a little shopping at Phipps Plaza. When she returned to her hotel room, she placed a call to Night, letting him know she was on her way over, and meeting with Diablo was set up. KoKo went into the hotel safe, pulled out the credit cards and IDs that Ralphie made for Goldie.

Moving through the lobby, she devised a plan that would throw everyone off course. Diablo had given her word that she would not go against KoKo. However, time revealed that not only had she gone back on her word, but she also planned on running KoKo's organization out of Atlanta altogether.

KoKo ate a good lunch and then got geared up to make her daily rounds. She jumped in a cab and settled into her seat, knowing from this point on playtime was over. These muthafuckas were about to feel her wrath.

When KoKo pulled up, she heard loud music and laughter. It appeared that Goldie was having a pool party. She looked around and took note of the two trucks in her driveway. Somewhat curious, she moved toward the side of the house heading to the backyard. She scanned the area, taking note of everyone in attendance.

Several girls from the club were splashing around in the pool. A few dudes sat at a table playing cards with Night.

KoKo moved smooth over to the gate and just stood there.

Goldie walked over to Night, handed him a beer, and then sashayed over to the grill. When she looked up and saw KoKo staring in her direction, her heart skipped a beat.

Immediately, she moved to the gate, tapping Night on the shoulder on her way by.

"Hey, KoKo," she said, hitting the switch turning off the electric fence. Goldie opened it wide for KoKo.

"What's this? A day off?" KoKo sarcastically stated with a mean mug.

"Yeah, we do this every Saturday before the club opens. Just a little something I started to give the girls a break," Goldie responded as she reset the gate.

"You thought that was an actual question?" KoKo shot Goldie a dirty look.

Night slammed his final card and then collected his money. "Yeah niggas, keep them pockets on the table. I'll be right back," he stated as he stood up to greet KoKo.

"What's up, ma?" he asked, rising to his feet.

"You tell me," KoKo shot back as she approached the table.

"We just having a little down time. Come meet the crew." Night looked over KoKo's facial expressions.

"This is Brian, Goldie's brother. This is Neeko. He holds down the street crew. And this is Roscoe. He is in charge of the runs."

"Is that right?" KoKo went right into bitch mode. "So let me calculate this shit for a minute. You got security and intel off the streets playing cards while I guess the streets are watching themselves."

"Nah, we got people covering all areas," Neeko responded.

"I'm not fucking talking to you," KoKo calmly stated.

Neeko's eyebrows rose and his nostrils flared.

KoKo stopped and caught eyes with each man. "Here it is I been down here for less than twenty-four hours, and I find out niggas are moving against us. And then I walk up on the very niggas who are responsible for this area and find y'all seated out in the fucking open playing fucking games," she barked with her teeth clenched.

Not wasting any time, Night jumped in. "Let's meet up in a little while. Let me get with the boss."

The three men stood straight up feeling like bitches. They were not used to dealing with KoKo. They only had to answer to Chico, and his style was very different.

"Sorry about this. We on point. Don't worry. It won't happen again," Brian said with his thick Atlanta accent.

"It's all good. I just don't want to have to send wreaths to your families. These muthafuckas ain't playing. You gotta stay one step ahead or lose yours." KoKo headed into Goldie's house. On her way past, she looked at Goldie. "Get these bitches outta here. If they need to relax, let them do it on their own time."

Goldie and Night escorted everyone out, and then joined KoKo in the living room.

KoKo sat with her legs crossed and attitude on hot.

"I guess the South don't make you want to chill the fuck out, huh?" Night asked as he took a seat.

"What the fuck is wrong with you? Did you forget that we got niggas coming for our neck?"

"I know what the fuck is going on." Night sat forward. "You need to remember that I got this. You sent me down here to do a job, and I got it. Just like I have been handling everything else, I am handling this."

"Are you sure?" KoKo asked as the crease formed in her forehead.

"Don't ever question my loyalty. I have been in the shadows helping Kayson before you even knew he existed. I took care of you when shit got rough and kept you and Quran safe. You have a habit of going off when you don't know what the fuck is going on, but that is something that you will have to work on." He paused and made eye contact. "For your jumping-the-gun ass information, that was a meeting I was conducting. They know what's up, and we were regrouping per your orders from Chico."

KoKo just looked at Night, searching his face for any inconsistency.

"Yeah, now you ain't got shit to say. I got this . . . I been doing this shit ever since your ass was in Underoos. You better recognize."

"My bad." KoKo smiled. "Where the weed at? You know a bitch be grouchy when she don't burn something."

"Fuck outta here. Your ass just mean as hell for no fucking reason at all." Night chuckled. "You need therapy."

Goldie walked cautiously toward them, preparing her ears for KoKo's bullshit.

"I brought my PowerPoint presentation to the meeting," Goldie said, holding out an ounce of weed neatly rolled in a Ziploc bag." She threw on a smile to lighten the mood.

"Light that shit up and sit down. We got business to handle."

"That's her way of saying sorry," Night stated as he took a blunt from Goldie.

"Fuck y'all," KoKo responded.

Night and Goldie chuckled and puffed as KoKo pulled the IDs from her pocket and started her spiel.

"Okay, his name is Detective Greg Warren," KoKo informed them while taking the blunt from Goldie's hands.

Night and Goldie listened intensively as KoKo laid out the

plan.

When KoKo was done, Goldie stood up to get dressed and began the first stage of the plan: set the trap.

"So, is everything good between you and Goldie?" KoKo probed.

"Yeah we straight," Night sat back folding his hand over his chest.

KoKo just looked at him. She could see in his demeanor that it was more to the situation, but she decided to let it go.

Later that Night . . .

KoKo and Night pulled up to Diablo's Alpharetta home.

"Why you got all this fucking car? A bitch need a stepping stool or something," she said, exiting Night's big, black, murdered out Hummer.

"It's to go with the other big black shit I got," he spat back, coming around to her side.

"I don't need that information for nothing." She wrinkled her brows.

"You asked," he responded as they headed to the door.

"Well, keep your big black shit to yourself. Don't fuck up my mission."

"Why the fuck you keep saying that? You act like I be fucking everybody."

KoKo looked at him with her lips twisted.

"I ain't thinking about yo' ass. Knock on the door."

"You need to keep a good eye on me, because if this bitch says the wrong thing we might have to come out shooting."

"Don't worry, we walking in and we walking out. It's business. It ain't personal."

Before KoKo could knock on the door, it opened.

Two of Diablo's goons stood looking at them like they

were selling Bibles or some shit.

"We have an appointment," KoKo stated.

"I know that," the big baldheaded, muscle bound dude said, pulling the door open wider.

"Then why the fuck you staring at me like you didn't know I was coming?" KoKo quickly forgot she was going to try and be cool.

The guy didn't even dignify her smart ass remark with a response. "Diablo is downstairs next to the pool," he instructed.

KoKo rolled her eyes and headed to the basement door.

"I thought we were being cool," Night reminded her.

"I can't stand that nigga," she spat, walking down the stairs.

After turning a few corners, they arrived at the glass doors that led to Diablo's indoor pool.

Pulling them open, KoKo scanned the room to do a head count. Then she got disgusted when her eyes rested on some lesbian porn and a group of naked bitches acting the shit out on a stack of pillows right next to the screen.

"This that bullshit," KoKo mumbled as she approached the table where Diablo was sitting smoking a cigar and watching the action.

"KoKo," she sang in her raspy voice as a smile came across her face.

"What's up?" KoKo asked, placing herself with her back to the action.

"Nothing much. Just enjoying a little poolside fun," she responded as her eyes rested back in the direction of the orgy that was well underway.

KoKo's stomach turned as the surround sound belted out moans that filled the whole area.

"What's up, Night? Please have a seat and enjoy the show."

THE PUSSY TRAP 3: *Death by Temptation*
~ N E N E   C A P R I ~

She extended her hospitality.

"Sheeiit . . . I'll fuck around and get fired for eating on the job," he said, looking over at the contorted bodies. Titties, ass, and bald pussies all moving in sync to their pleasure. His mouth watered as his dick slightly nudged his zipper.

"KoKo don't let y'all have any fun. She all work. But a nigga like me like a little 3D in the afternoon." She looked up at Night and then back at the show.

"So what can I do for you, Mrs. KoKo?" she asked, not looking up.

"We need to settle any pending beefs and get back on track."

"Beefs? I haven't heard anything," Diablo said, pulling on her cigar.

"I don't give a fuck about what you haven't heard. I operate on what I know."

Diablo sat silent for a few seconds. "So what you want me to do about your so-called knowledge?"

"I need you to make your bitches act right, because they don't want none of my get right," KoKo spat.

Diablo chuckled. "You should know by now I don't bend to threats."

"And you should know by now I don't make 'em."

Diablo looked into KoKo's eyes. "Well, I tell you what. Pull your bitches back, and I'll instruct mine not to smash them if they don't obey."

KoKo took in some air, swallowed her spit, and said as diplomatically as she could, "Let me explain something to you. Everybody on my team is family. And the only thing worse than fucking with me, is fucking with them. What I am going to do is continue to get money, because we got shit on the table, and I don't fuck with my money. I'll stay out your way. You stay the fuck outta mine. But if you fuck with my family, we all gonna fill some black bags and deep holes." She planted her eyes firmly on Diablo.

"You sexy as hell. You need to switch teams, so I can help you relax. Because obviously, dick ain't doin' it," Diablo shot back.

"Bitch, you don't even know what team you on. Y'all bitches hate men, wanna eat pussy, but got strap ons . . . Fuck outta here!" KoKo said, backing up to leave. "You wish you could taste KoKo. Then I would have some more things I can own." She looked around the room. "Just remember my warning."

"You talk a lot of shit." Diablo watched her ass jiggle as she walked away.

"No, I talk facts, then shit happens," KoKo said without even breaking her stride.

"Thanks for the show," Night said, following KoKo.

"Anytime." Diablo went back to puffing her cigar and watching the ring of pleasure on the other side of the pool, apparently unfazed by KoKo's threats.

When they got to the car, Night looked over at KoKo. "I thought this was supposed to be a peaceful gathering," he teased.

"Yo' ass was supposed to keep me from going off."

"My bad. I had a pussy block."

"Niggas," KoKo shot back.

"So what you think?"

"We gonna have to kill somebody. Simple as that," she said as he drove off.

- 15 -
Nita's

KoKo arrived back from Atlanta a day before the party. She easily flipped modes from beast to beauty and prepared to make a statement at the effect. Picking up the phone, she dialed her stylist, Benita. "What's up, ma?" Benita said into the phone.

"What's good?"

"Nothing. Trying to make this money."

"Can you come out to the house and hook me up today?"

"Damn, I wish I could, but I had two bitches call off, and the shop is flooded. But you can come through here, and I'll hook you right up."

"You know I can't be sitting in no fucking shop all day."

"Oh nah, never that. As soon as you get here it's all about you. You already know. Plus, I want you to see where your investment went." Benita was smiling from ear to ear. She had been trying to get KoKo down there for months.

KoKo paused. "Ai'ight. I'll be there in an hour." She hung up.

Within an hour, KoKo was pulling up to the salon. She parked and jumped out.

When she hit the door wearing a pair of jeans and a T-shirt, a burnt orange bulletproof vest and a pair of boots, all eyes were on her. She removed her shades to take a quick inventory of all the bitches in attendance; the shop was packed wall to wall.

Benita had it all covered. There was an area for every facet of beauty. One area was for nails, feet, eyelashes, brows, and piercing. Across from that was a set of steps that led to a room that overlooked the shop, which was a barbershop. Toward the back were two waiting areas, one was where females could read, watch TV, and have a drink while waiting. The other was for taking out weaves and braids and was closed off by curtains. Past that were twenty sinks full of heads getting washed. The last two areas were all the way in the back. One large area was for styling hair and the other for massage.

A bitch could get a whole day's beauty in one place. And it was the only one like it in the hood. The floor-to-ceiling mirrors opened the shop up and made it appear bigger than it was. The lime green leather chairs and many palm tree plants gave it an island feel. KoKo had to admit Benita did her thing.

"Hey, Mrs. KoKo," a few of the workers began to yell out.

KoKo nodded and kept on walking.

Females were watching all the respect that she was getting. When she got to the steps leading upstairs, three guys came down, who just so happened to be KoKo's Harlem lieutenants.

"Bosssss . . ." D-Low yelled out. He embraced her. The others each took their turn. He pulled her aside and whispered in her ear. Then he went in his pocket, pulled out some money, and handed it to her.

KoKo smiled and pointed at the ladies sitting in the nail area. "Pookie, pay for whatever they getting," she said, tossing the stack to her.

"No problem." Pookie caught it and put it in the drawer.

"Let me find out you getting your Santa on," D-Low commented on her generosity.

"Those who give with an open hand will always have something in it."

THE PUSSY TRAP 3: *Death by Temptation*
~ N E N E   C A P R I ~

"That's why I fucks with you." He leaned in and hugged her.

"Ai'ight, let a bitch get her some reconstruction on her shit," she said, walking away.

"Catch you later." The three men turned to walk out the shop.

KoKo threw up her deuces and kept it moving.

When she got to the back, Benita was ecstatic. KoKo had given her all the money to start her business. Plus, she supplied the security, so she could run it in peace. Therefore, Benita showed nothing but loyalty.

"Let's go. You know a bitch is busy," KoKo yelled as she approached.

"Hey, momma. Come sit right here." Benita pointed at the sink next to her station, which was only for high paying customers.

KoKo sat down and crossed her legs. She reached into a pocket on her vest, pulled out a fat spliff, and lit it up.

Everyone looked on in amazement. Some people even frowned up.

"Yo, little momma, go get me something to drink and don't open it," KoKo yelled to Benita's sidekick.

"What you want?"

"You choose." KoKo sat back and puffed.

Benita hurried the woman out of her chair, sending her to the dryer. As she rushed over to KoKo, a few females sucked their teeth. They had been waiting for a while, and she had just walked in.

KoKo picked up on it immediately and got ready to say something, but Benita beat her to it.

"Look, be patient. She pay for the air y'all breathing up in this muthafucka, so just read your magazine and shut the fuck up. I'll be with y'all bitches in a minute," she said as she put the apron around KoKo's neck and prepared her for her wash.

Bitches rolled their eyes, but did just like they were told.

Once KoKo was done, Benita brought her to the chair, put a dry apron on her, and continued to dry her hair. She pulled the cart over to the chair and began setting KoKo's hair with the big rollers.

KoKo got under the dryer, and when she was done, Benita began styling her hair. She couldn't help but listen to the chicks talking shit about the niggas they were fucking with and the shit they were going through.

When they started talking about sucking all these sorry ass niggas' dicks, she was glad that Benita was done, because the thing she definitely could not stomach was to hear a bitch proud that she broke off a dead beat ass nigga.

"So, Mrs. KoKo, I heard that fine ass nigga Baseem is home. How he doing?" Nikki asked.

"He good."

"Now that nigga right there can get it. I'd suck his dick in the middle of Time's Square in a bikini with a bumper sticker on my ass that reads: So the fuck what!"

They all burst out laughing.

"Damn, it's like that?"

"Just like that. That nigga fine for no reason at all," Nikki said, turning her customer in the seat. "If that nigga get lonely, tell him to holla at me."

KoKo stood up, shaking her head as she paid Benita. The woman looked over at the knot of money that she was paying her. One of Benita's stylists yelled out, "Damn, ma. I need a customer like KoKo."

KoKo smiled and used the opportunity as a teaching session. "Yeah, this is what not sucking dick will get you," she said, straightening her stack, placing it back in her pocket.

THE PUSSY TRAP 3: *Death by Temptation*
~ N E N E   C A P R I ~

"Oh lord, don't talk about sucking dick around KoKo." Benita knew KoKo was going to drop some jewels before she left.

"Why? She don't get it sloppy sometimes?" one of the hating ass females said, accepting the challenge.

"Nah, not the Diva." Nikki smiled.

"You don't have to suck dick when you got good pussy," KoKo said as she got in 'bitch you about to get it' mode.

"Oh shit! I hear that," Maureen, another stylist said, trying to get it going. She couldn't wait to hear what would come out of KoKo's mouth next.

"Fuck that! I'll suck the skin off a dick," the customer said, slapping hands with the chick she was cool with.

KoKo cracked a half smile and then went in. "You'll suck the skin off a dick, huh?"

"Sure do," she said, turning in her seat and rolling her neck, looking in KoKo's direction for a response.

"How much money you got in your pocket?" KoKo asked. The woman got quiet.

Not wanting to seem soft in front of her girls, she responded, "I got a little bank roll." She pulled out a few dollars and then stuffed it back in her pocket.

"Yeah, I thought so. Bullshit ass paper. That's because you got that French fry pussy. Sheeit . . . If a nigga can fuck you and just feed you, then who needs you?"

"Oh shit. Here we go," Benita said, folding her arms and leaning up against the counter.

"French fry pussy? Whatever, KoKo! I gets mine." The woman waved her hand, trying to bow out gracefully.

"Let me school y'all bitches on my way outta here." She adjusted her vest. "See, a common bitch like yourself will suck a dick anytime any place, but a boss bitch like me. I make him beg for it, make him crave for it, and then when he least expect it, I take that shit to the back of my throat and then make him pay for it. Sheeiit . . . if y'all 'hos sucking the skin off dick and ain't got your name on some shit, then bitch, kill yourself."

KoKo chuckled. "Gonna pull out some bullshit ass paper and flash, talking about you get yours. All my cards are black and my money is long, just like the dick I didn't have to suck to get it."

Benita just held her hand over her mouth, floored.

KoKo turned to walk out. "I gave y'all that for free. Remember, all y'all quick-to-suck-a-dick bitches are a duplicate. I'm an original. Pussy so good have a nigga moaning I love you, and he don't even know where I live." KoKo shook her head. "Fuck outta here. Bitches in here celebrating 'cause they suck dick. Keep on being a nigga's expectations, all you gonna get is a dick in your mouth." She turned back to Benita.

"Next time, you come to my house. This shit is depressing," she said, heading to the exit.

The women sat in their seats bewildered. They had just had a cup full of KoKo raw and uncut.

"Why you let KoKo come in here and go off on customers? These sensitive bitches can't handle all that," Nikki joked.

"Bitch, it's your fault. I told y'all bitches not to get her started." Benita laughed. "Come on, girl. Get in this chair," she said to KoKo's victim. "The rest of y'all get to work," she ordered with a smile. KoKo was that bitch and Benita was loyal to her for life.

As KoKo walked through the salon, she hollered at a few cats on the way out. While engrossed in a conversation with one of her workers out of Queens she saw the same dude from the club looking at her through the shop window. She brought her gaze back to Hak and when she looked back up the guy was gone. KoKo ended her converstion and headed outside.

When she walked out the door she threw on her shades and adjusted her eyes from the blinding sun. Looking in both directions she saw no sign of him. It was the second time she saw him on her turf and she needed to find out who he was and why he was on her ass. KoKo rested her gaze on a female that was picking in the trash.

KoKo squinted. "Can't be," she mumbled, and then headed in the woman's direction. KoKo stood by the woman, who was engrossed in her mission. "Excuse me, are you Chocolate?" she asked the woman.

The woman slowly looked up. "I'm not bothering nobody," the woman yelled. Then she realized it was KoKo. Tears welled up in Chocolate's eyes, as shame overcame her. She looked away, wishing to be as invisible to KoKo as she was to herself.

"Damn, Chocolate. Why you ain't reach out to me?"

"The only person who would ever help me no matter what is gone," she said, continuing to look away.

KoKo reached into her pocket and pulled out a couple hundred. She grabbed Chocolate by the arm and placed the money in her hand.

"Get yourself a room for the night and get some rest. Come to the pool hall tomorrow and ask for Savage. He'll get you straight. This is a one-time extension. You fuck up, that's it."

Chocolate looked up as tears flowed down her face. She broke out into a smile, and KoKo could see the spaces that were left after Fred knocked her teeth out. "Thank you, KoKo. I won't let you down."

"We'll see." KoKo walked off and hopped in her car.

Chocolate looked at the money in her hand and had to fight

the internal struggle to either get right or get high.

"KoKo, Fred has been looking for you. You need to go see him. He's been asking for you," she yelled.

"Yeah, I'll get over there."

"Go soon. He's at the end." Chocolate turned to go to her way.

KoKo sat in her car for a minute, reflecting on the fact that Maryam said her mom was talking about Fred. Then she runs into Chocolate, one of Fred's women. What was the connection? She needed to get to Fred, but first she had to handle something a little more urgent.

- 16 -

Dress Rehearsal

L ook. Let's get in here and get our shit and get back," KoKo ordered as she and Baseem emerged from his truck.

"I only got shoes to pick up. You the one got shit to try on." He chuckled.

"Whatever. I just want to get this shit over with, so we can move to the next level." Even though she was against this party, she knew she had to do things just the way Kayson told her. So she could strengthen the organization and smoke out any deceit lurking in the shadows.

KoKo and Baseem moved through the mall parking lot swiftly. She needed to handle this, so she could catch a flight to GA to meet up with Goldie and Night. Also, she needed to get back for the party.

"What store you going in?" Baseem asked her.

"I'm going in Neiman Marcus," she responded, moving quickly to the entrance.

"I'll meet you over there."

"Ai'ight." KoKo kept moving.

She walked in the double doors and headed straight to the dressing room. There, Amy had the three dresses waiting that KoKo ordered and had sent to the store.

"Hey, Amy," KoKo said as she approached.

"Good afternoon, Mrs. KoKo," she responded with a huge smile on her face. "Just come this way." While mentally counting her commission, Amy guided KoKo to a back dressing room, which was larger than the rest. KoKo walked in to see her usual setup, a bottle of wine and a small fruit tray.

"Thanks, Amy."

"No problem. Call me if you need any assistance." She pulled the curtains shut and left KoKo to handle her business.

KoKo poured herself a glass of wine and took a few sips. After having a bite of cantaloupe, she pulled her shirt over her head, took off her shoes, and then pulled her jeans down. Bending over to place her shoes to the side, she felt a breeze.

"Amy, I didn't even get started yet." She turned in the direction of the doorway. When she looked up, Kayson was standing there smiling.

"Oh shit! What are you doing here?" she asked, looking past him. "You gonna get busted. Bas is with me." Kayson pulled his hood back and moved toward KoKo. He walked up on her, pinning her to the wall.

"Kayson," she whined as he grabbed the sides of her panties, slowly twisting his finger in her strap, giving her his intense stare. KoKo's heart raced in anticipation as she looked up, falling into his gaze.

He pulled tighter, popping the strap. She inhaled deeply. Kayson placed his hands on her waist and lifted her in the air, placing her at dick level. She wrapped her legs around him, ready to receive all he had to offer. "Why didn't you wait for me to bring it to you?" KoKo asked while Kayson's soft lips caressed her neck.

"Fuck all that. Daddy need to get wet." He pulled out the Enforcer. Wasting no time, he slid in and went for that spot. KoKo was full of emotion, the fear of being busted, accompanied by the longing to feel him put her body in a trance, which intensified their encounter.

"Mmmm . . ." she moaned as Kayson handled his business.

"I love you, baby," he whispered in her ear as she hugged

him tight.

"I love you more."

KoKo began to cum. Her breathing increased as pleasure dripped from her vocals.

Amy approached the doorway and was stopped in her tracks by the sound of KoKo's moans. She covered her mouth and nervously turned around, moving away from the door as quick as possible.

Once they both released, Kayson held her tight and allowed his tongue to taste the sweetness of hers, stopping to suck on her bottom lip. "You gonna be able to take care of everything tonight?"

"Yes, I got it." She forced the words out, not wanting to speak or stop.

"Handle it then." He released his firm grip, removing the Enforcer from his favorite spot, allowing her to slide down.

KoKo planted her feet on the floor and tried to balance on her wobbly legs while Kayson fixed his clothes.

"I need this to be over, baby. I need you to be able to hold me every day."

"Hang in there, little mama. It's almost over." He kissed her lips again.

KoKo closed her eyes and enjoyed his hypnotic touch. When he pulled back, she had to talk shit. "Yeah, and don't be doing no drivebys on a sistah no more either."

"Sheeeit . . . you know I don't play. I woke up this morning and looked out the window and Mrs. Kitty sent me a bat signal."

"You so stupid." KoKo burst out laughing.

"Let me get up outta here. I'll see you in a couple days." Kayson pulled his hood back over his head and moved out.

KoKo sat down, picked up her panties, and looked at their

condition and chuckled. "That man . . ." She shook her head and set them on the chair next to her. She grabbed her jeans, put them back on, and then just stood there.

Amy stood outside the curtain listening to see if it was cool. "Knock, knock," she attempted to announce herself.

"Come on," KoKo yelled back.

"So, uh, did you decide on anything?" she asked, avoiding eye contact.

"Just wrap all the shit up. I'll meet you at the counter," KoKo said, feeling relaxed and satisfied.

Amy collected the dresses and headed to the counter. As soon as she walked out, Baseem walked over to the door.

"What's taking you so long, and why you look like that?" He looked at KoKo, who appeared a little disheveled.

"Excuse me?" she responded with a serious look, covering her breasts.

"I've been waiting out there for twenty minutes."

"I had to try shit on, Bas. Go ahead. I have to finish getting dressed." KoKo tried to dismiss him. Baseem took a quick survey of the area, and his eyes settled on KoKo's thong sitting on the chair. He didn't say shit. He just took note.

"Yeah, ai'ight. Hurry up. I got shit to do."

"I said I was coming. I got shit to do also." She put her shirt on as the curtain closed. She had to giggle herself. Here it was she had just had a surprise visit from the Enforcer. "Bitch, you bad," she said, looking herself over in the mirror. After KoKo slipped on her shoes, she exited the room.

When she looked over at the counter, Baseem was standing there talking to Amy.

"What's up?" she asked as she approached.

"Nothing. I wanted to treat you," Baseem said, taking out his card and handing it to Amy.

KoKo glimpsed the sneaky look on Baseem's face, and

knew he was up to something, but could not tell exactly what it was. Then a figure caught the corner of her eye. Her brow wrinkled, and she tried to quickly avert her gaze. Baseem turned to see what had gotten her attention. Outside the store he caught a hooded figure as it passed the door.

KoKo realized he had been alerted. "Bas," she called out.

"What the fuck is you hollering for?" he said, turning his attention back to KoKo.

"Grab those for me." She moved over, allowing him to take the dresses from Amy.

Baseem looked at KoKo like she was crazy as he took the bags. "I'ma get you checked the fuck out." He turned back to the door, but the person was gone.

"Thank you, Amy," she said, taking the card and the receipt.

"Anytime." She winked at KoKo.

KoKo acted like she had no idea what she was talking about as she passed Baseem his card. "Here."

KoKo threw her shades on and walked away from the counter.

As KoKo and Baseem walked out the store, KoKo's eyes were all over the place in search of Kayson, but he haddone what he did best, disappear.

- 17 -
The Organization

Time had tested the organization's strength and the loyalty off its members. Some had failed the test and were rocking headstones as a result. Others had proven that they were built for the challenges of the game, and had not wilted under the recent pressure. In acknowledgement of their allegiance, KoKo blessed them with a little something to show her appreciation.

She rented the Living Room Bar at the 'W' New York in Manhattan. The futuristic patterns of silver, crystal, and glass sparkled against the contrast of gold and red, setting the relaxing mode KoKo was pushing for.

Each crew arrived by state wearing an array of dark red. By 11 PM, each crew was checked in and escorted to the party area.

KoKo sat patiently in her suite waiting for the perfect time to make her appearance. When the clock struck twelve, she slipped into her dark red, draped, belted dress by Derek Lam, which accented her shoulders and toned legs. She wore a pair of all black Giuseppe Zanotti for Anja Rubic punk rock classical high heel sandals with piercings and a gold-colored chain. Twirling from side to side, KoKo checked herself over before carefully tucking her gun.

Entering the elevator, she rehearsed the information she wanted to cover with the organization. She needed to be confident and serious. There were plots against them leering around every corner, and she wanted to impress upon them that now was the time to either tighten up or get the fuck out.

KoKo entered the room, and all eyes were on her. She moved gracefully through the crowd, stopping only briefly to smile and say a few words. Night and Baseem watched her move around like a seasoned politician.

She looked over at Baseem, who then moved to the DJ and signaled him to lower the music. Stopping at the bar, he requested the servers deliver the glasses of champagne. When everyone had a glass, KoKo took to the middle of the room to make a toast.

"Good evening, ladies and gentlemen. I would first like to thank you for coming and for your dedicated service to support the organization. I know we have had some trying times these last six months, but I reassure you that smoother days are coming. Please enjoy the weekend I have set up for you with all the amenities the hotel has to offer. Everything is on me. To life, love, and riches. Salute." KoKo held her glass in the air and toasted at the many glasses that were raised.

Once she had made her presence known, she gave Night the nod.

Night walked over to Chucky and gave him the order to gather all the heads of each city and have them meet them in a private boardroom downstairs.

When KoKo entered the room, each person was comfortably seated at the table. She walked past the men and straight to the head of the table.

"Okay, gentlemen, I am going to make this shit short and sweet. Moe, you are still in charge of Miami, and Slim you are still in charge of the NO." She nodded at Baseem who walked over and set a briefcase full of money in front of KoKo. "And here is a bonus." She clicked the locks on the case, and it popped open. Reaching inside, KoKo grabbed a few stacks and set one on her left and one on her right.

Baseem slid the money in front of each man. He positioned himself back at KoKo's side.

"Chico, you are officially in charge of the 'A'. I want you to maintain leadership down there. However, I am going to be sending Taz down to help you go to the next level. Give him your full cooperation. Chico, I will also need your help with my Florida move. Chucky, I want you to switch places with Pete. Pete, you are reassigned to Virginia. Chucky, I need you here in the city all the time."

Chico, Chucky, and Pete nodded in agreement.

"Now, down to the business at hand. It has come to my attention that we have a few unhappy workers." KoKo scanned the table, looking each man in the eyes. "Sabir, you are no longer needed in DC, and Amin, you are no longer needed in Jersey."

KoKo grabbed a few stacks from the briefcase and tossed them down the table.

"What the fuck is this?" Sabir angrily asked, as he looked at the pile of money.

"It's called buyout money. Or as I like to put it, so I won't have to kill yo' ass money." KoKo folded her hands. "See, I can deal with a lot of things, but treachery is not one of them. "You two muthafuckas are out."

"Hold the fuck up. I need you to explain what's going on, because I ain't feeling this shit right here." Sabir pushed the money back to the center of the table.

"What you think? Because I got a skirt on you can fuck me?" she asked with squinted eyes.

"Nah, it's not like that at all," he nervously responded.

"Good. 'Cause you know I will come from up under this muthafucka with something hot," KoKo barked.

THE PUSSY TRAP 3: *Death by Temptation*
~ N E N E   C A P R I ~

Sabir's heart jumped.

"I know y'all had a meeting. You want more area. Amin wants more money." KoKo paused. "Yeah, nigga, don't look all surprised. The next time you decide to talk shit. Don't take your side bitch with you to the meeting, then beat her ass a week later." KoKo gave him the side eye.

Amin grabbed his stack and looked it over. "What am I supposed to do with this?"

"I don't care what you do with it. You can shove it up your ass if you feel like it. However, you will be escorted from this hotel to the tunnel. I don't want to see you or hear from you. And all the protection is off. Get they raggedy ass out of my face."

Chucky and Taz stood behind them, waiting to escort them out.

When they got to the door, Sabir made one last plea. "I was loyal to you, KoKo. I just wanted to upgrade my situation."

"Well, you should have talked to me. I keep telling y'all niggas no secret council. If you're unhappy, talk to me. I can respect a man who comes at my face, but if you come at my back, I usually take your life. I'm in a transition period, so you get a pass."

"We cool, KoKo?" Amin asked.

"Time will tell," she shot back.

Feeling defeated, they both left the room to face their fate.

The doors closed, and every one turned to face KoKo.

"Now, this is where we are going. I got a lot of legitimate business coming down the pipe. I want y'all to start thinking about what you want to do next. This shit right here is a young man's game. We all have families and children. Kayson was always trying to get something going so we could wash this money and then be comfortable."

"Look. I ain't going anywhere. I been hustling since I was twelve years old. All I know is the streets," Moe cut her off.

"We all have been hustling forever. But it comes a time when we have to look at this shit for what it is."

"I live this, and I'ma die this," Moe responded.

"What the fuck is you talking about? Ain't no honor in dying in the fucking street!" KoKo raised her voice. "You sound stupid as hell. Fuck is wrong with you? Yeah, we all live this. I got more on the line than all of you, but I also understand that at some point I'ma have to let the young boys have this shit. I don't want to be looking over my shoulder and killing niggas for the rest of my life." She paused to let her words sink in. KoKo chuckled as a fond memory crossed her mind.

"My grandmother used to always say, 'Don't always think you're bad, KoKo, because somebody else woke up with the same idea, and one day you will meet your match'."

"I understand, KoKo. I'm just not ready to let go."

"I respect that. But know when to fold 'em."

"No doubt."

"Alright. I am working on a new supplier. We have enough in the stash for about two months. Then we are going to be in trouble. I have something big up my sleeve. It will put us on a whole new level. Once I make the initial connect, Baseem and Chucky will take over. I will be falling back, but I'll be available for council. Y'all will go through them. I will only speak up for you once, so don't misuse my kindness. Don't fuck up with them niggas. They aren't as nice as KoKo," she joked. "It's time for me to change direction. Is everyone in this room with me?"

Each man nodded in agreement.

"I will warn you though. If you want out, leave now. Please don't make me come down off my throne for dumb shit. I will not be patient or merciful with deceit." KoKo got up, straightened her dress, and headed to the door. "If you will excuse me, I have to make one last round in this bad ass dress. Go ahead and have fun. Don't waste my money. Get them dicks wet."

KoKo heard a medley of laughter as she exited the room. She quickly made the rounds, passed out a few more instructions, and then she was off to her room. Baseem rode the elevator with her and watched as she got in safely.

When KoKo entered her room, the view took her breath away. There were different sized candles all over the room, creating a dimly lit setting. Soft music played in the background. She turned the corner and entered the bedroom. Kayson was sitting in a chair with all his sexy on display. KoKo looked him over, eyeing his smooth chest. Her eyes roamed his body, and her gaze set on his thick rod that sat up in his satin Polo boxers.

"I wasn't expecting to see you so soon," she announced in a sexy, shy tone.

"I couldn't wait for you to bring it to me. I had to bring it to you," he smoothly stated.

"Is that right?" KoKo stepped out of her shoes. She slid her hand up her thigh, releasing her .22 and placing it on the dresser.

Kayson moved from his seat and met her in the middle of the room.

"I love this dress on you, but I think it goes better with the carpet." Kayson undid her belt and opened her dress, allowing it to fall to her feet. Exposing all her sexy brown skin. Her white lace thong and bra increased his heart rate.

"You know everyone is here," she whispered.

"You look so beautiful standing here." His hands began to

glide over her breasts.

"Keep it up, and I won't be able to hide your little secret," she said as his teeth sank into her neck.

"I got something else I need you to hide." He took her hand and slid it down the front of his boxers.

Grabbing that steel in her hand, she enjoyed the thickness as her hands roamed all over him.

"Did you handle your husband's business?" His tongue caressed her earlobe.

"Yeeesss . . ." she moaned as his finger found her spot of confession.

"Just hang in there a few more days. I'ma make this city bow to you, baby," he confessed as he flicked effortlessly over her clit.

Gripping his shoulders tight, she closed her eyes in anticipation of erupting in his hand.

He removed the boundaries between them, allowing her bra and panties to hit the floor. Wet and ready, KoKo's body begged for him.

Kayson walked her to the bed and laid her down. "Tonight, I want us to forget about all this shit. I just want to make love to my wife." He slid down his boxers, allowing them to drop to the floor.

Crawling between her legs, he rested against her baby soft skin.

"Kay, I want this all to be over. I don't want to hide. I need to have you with me."

"I'm always with you," he moaned, sliding her those inches as gently as he could.

"Baby . . ." she muttered, holding him tight.

Nibbling and kissing all over her heated flesh, he stroked long and angular, making sure to touch bottom with every stroke.

THE PUSSY TRAP 3: *Death by Temptation*
~ N E N E C A P R I ~

KoKo closed her eyes and drank up all his love. With him, there was no fear. With him, there was no grief.

Sensual, wet kisses filled the spaces where words could not. Hot moans caressed their ears as they matched each other's strokes like a nasty tug of war. He needed her unspoken cries for mercy as much as she needed him not to hear them.

Tenderly rolling back and forth, each taking their place on top, they took turns pleasing each other's heart and soul.

Timeless moments of hot dripping passion ended as two bodies quivered and shook. They swallowed each other whole, cumming long and hard.

Kayson lay buried inside her, raining sweet kisses on her face. KoKo put her head to the side and basked in the afterglow of their love.

"You and Quran are my everything. I am nothing without y'all. You have my word. I will protect you with my life," he vowed as he rested his face on hers.

KoKo said nothing in return. Instead, she caressed his back and savored every minute.

When KoKo woke up, she was pleasantly surprised to feel Kayson lying next to her. She pulled his arm around her waist, bringing him closer.

Kayson snuggled against her warm body. "We leaving in a few hours," he announced.

"Leaving? Where we going?"

"I need to see my son. Then we're off to South America. It's time for you to see where I've been and understand where I am taking this family."

Again KoKo said nothing. She just prepared her mind to face the secrets Kayson had been hiding, and what might develop if she ran into anything that would compromise her feelings for him.

KoKo reached over on the nightstand and grabbed her cell. There were several missed calls from Baseem. Apparently, he had been blowing her phone up all night.

Just as she was about to call him back, she heard a rain of knocks on the door.

"Who you expecting?" Kayson asked, holding her tight.

"No one, but I think it's Baseem. I told you he been in my ass." KoKo moved his arm and got up. She grabbed her robe, closed the door to the bedroom, and headed for the entrance door.

She looked through the peephole, and just as she thought, it was Baseem. She tried to prepare herself mentally as she unlocked the door and pulled it open.

"What the fuck? You got drunk and passed out?" he asked, walking into the room and taking a careful eye to the candles and arrangement of KoKo's clothes on the floor.

"What did you want?" she asked, pulling her robe tight.

Baseem was caught in thought as he looked up and saw her neck painted with passion marks.

"Hellooo," KoKo said, bringing him back to the present.

"Ain't nothing. I was just checking on you." He looked at her suspiciously.

"I'm good."

"I bet you are," he responded on his way to the door. "I'll see you later, I guess."

"No. I have to leave town. I'll hit you when I get back." KoKo opened the door for him to leave.

"Yeah, ai'ight." He paused. "You seen Night?" He looked over at the closed bedroom door.

"No, but if I hear from him, I'll tell him that you looking for him." She gazed firmly in his eyes.

After an uncomfortable few seconds of silence, he turned to

walk out.

Closing the door, KoKo ran her hands through her hair.

Kayson emerged from the bedroom. "Baseem?" He smiled.

"Yes. You gotta get him off my ass. Now the nigga think I'm fucking Night." KoKo walked over to the floor and picked up her dress.

"I got it. Baseem is as loyal as they come. He is going to be on top of everything until shit pans out. Come lay with me." He laughed at her little attitude.

"You think this shit is funny?"

"No, I just like to see you with those sexy lips poked out." He pulled her into his arms, placing his soft lips on hers. "Don't worry. I got it."

- 18 -
The Introduction

KoKo rented a bungalow on the other side of the island. Nervously, she taped her nails on the kitchen counter running her list through her mind making sure she had everything. It was time to put Quran and Kayson together, and she wanted to make it as comfortable as possible. KoKo anxiously moved around the house setting things up.

She put the food away and then prepared Quran's room. Quickly, she set up his bed, his video games, and a few new toys so he would feel at home.

After she prepared Kayson's and her room, she lit a few tropical coconut candles and turned on some music. She tried to relax, but her mind kept coming up with questions. How would Quran act with his dad? She was happy to put them together, but at the same time she was nervous. The last thing she wanted to do was have a situation where Quran would be angry or upset.

KoKo sat for a few minutes. Then she blew out the candles and headed to pick up Quran.

When she pulled up to the house, a smile came across her face. Quran was standing in the yard with his backpack on, all ready to go. She could see him fidgeting with his hands and moving around like he was anxious for his outing.

Maryam grabbed his hand as KoKo pulled up in front of them.

THE PUSSY TRAP 3: *Death by Temptation*
~ N E N E   C A P R I ~

One of the bodyguards opened the door, and Maryam placed Quran in his car seat.

"Hey, little face," KoKo said, turning in her seat.

"Hi, Mommy," he said, all excited as Maryam fastened him in.

"You ready, beloved?" She smiled.

"Yup." He shook his head.

"Maryam, I'll be gone for the weekend. If anything goes wrong just call me. I'm not far."

"Yes, Mrs. KoKo. Have fun." She kissed Quran's face and then closed the door.

KoKo drove in silence, occasionally peeking in the rearview mirror at Quran, who was smiling and looking out the window. KoKo knew from this day forward, his whole world would change.

Pulling into the house, her heart jumped when she saw a car in the driveway. Kayson had arrived. It was official; Daddy was home.

KoKo parked next to his rental, and then she walked around to let Quran out.

"Can you pick me up?" he said, jumping on KoKo.

"Boy, you are as big as me," she said, swooping him up off the ground.

"I love you, Mommy." Quran put his head on her shoulder.

"I love you too." She nestled him in her arms.

KoKo walked to the door and fumbled with her keys. A few seconds later, the door came open.

There he stood, peering down at them.

Quran looked up and a smile came over his face.

"Say hello, Quran," KoKo instructed.

"Hello," he said, waving his hand.

KoKo slid him down her hip.

"I have something to tell you." She looked down at her son.

Quran gazed up at her and Kayson.

Kayson moved aside as they walked to the couch. Closing the door, he too became nervous. Kayson joined them on the couch, sitting next to Quran.

"Quran, this is someone very special." She smiled.

He looked up at Kayson, whom he had seen in New York, and in KoKo's photo album.

"I know that, Mommy," he said, all matter-of-factly.

"What do you know?" she asked with a bit of sarcasm.

"Grandma said that's my daddy, and one day he will come home." He shrugged his little shoulders, looking up at KoKo.

She was at a loss for words. Here she was, agonizing over the introduction, and Quran was acting like it was no big thing.

"You know your daddy loves you, right?"

"Yes. I know, Mommy," he said as if KoKo was getting on his nerves. "I love him too." Quran looked up at Kayson.

"Well, excuse me."

Quran took off his backpack and dug inside of it. "I made this for you." He pulled a dry ball of clay out of his bag and passed it to Kayson.

"What's this?" Kayson asked, holding the small orange ball in his hand.

"A ball," Quran said. "Grandma said you like basketball."

Kayson smiled and closed his hand around the ball. "Thank you. Can daddy have a hug?"

Quran turned and crawled up to Kayson's neck and hugged him tight.

KoKo was full of emotion. She had to fight back tears. The moment she had been waiting for was finally here. So many nights she cried and prayed about how she was going to raise her little man all alone, and now they were in the same room hugged up like no time was lost.

"You know you have always been on my mind and in my heart, right?"

Quran shook his head up and down.

"You are my everything." He held him close.

Unable to hold back her tears any longer, she released the water. KoKo smiled as tears ran down her cheeks.

Quran looked over at his mother. "Don't cry, Mommy," he said, reaching out for her.

KoKo leaned over and kissed his face. Quran wiped her tears and kissed her eyes. Kayson pulled her over to them, and they shared their first embrace as a family.

Not long afterward, she prepared dinner while watching Kayson and Quran play in the pool. Kayson was wearing Quran out. She knew after he ate and bathed he would be passed out.

After dinner, KoKo and Kayson put Quran in the tub. They sat next to the tub watching him play with his toys.

KoKo gathered his pajamas as Kayson walked him into the bedroom.

"Can you sleep in here?" Quran asked Kayson.

"I can't fit in your bed."

"Yes, you can." He laughed. "Mommy sleeps with me," he said, jumping up on the bed.

"Your mother is short."

"Whatever," she said, pulling his shirt over his head.

"You too, Mommy."

"How about you sleep with us?"

"Okay!" He grabbed his pillow and took off down the hall.

"I was supposed to sleep alone with Mommy tonight," Kayson said, grabbing her into his arms.

"Mommy will take care of Daddy when he falls asleep."

"Yeah, that Jacuzzi is calling our name." He squeezed her soft body as his lips and tongue moved slowly around her neck.

"Is that right?" KoKo responded, melting in his embrace.

Kayson looked into her eyes and kissed her lips. "I love you," he said in between kisses. "Thank you for my son."

KoKo was overwhelmed. She didn't know what to say. "Don't leave us."

"I promise."

"Come on!" Quran yelled out.

"Here we come," KoKo yelled back.

"Let me find out we have a little blocker on our team." Kayson released KoKo from his grip.

"That's your son." KoKo turned toward the hallway.

Kayson smiled. *His son.* He had never been this happy, and in reality he was scared. There was so much in the balance that could shatter their happiness. Kayson knew he needed to make his moves and quick.

KoKo popped some popcorn and then joined her men in the room. Quran made it through one movie. But when the second one started, his eyes closed, and he was out like a light.

Kayson wasted no time ushering KoKo outside. He needed some daddy time, and she was happy to give it to him.

KoKo was settled nicely on Kayson's lap and rested against his chest.

"I needed that, baby," she cooed as his hands slid over her back.

"I think you just took advantage of me, but I ain't mad at you." Kayson relaxed with KoKo on his lap, and the hot water bubbling all over his body.

"You enjoyed every second." She kissed his lips.

"I damn sure did." He gave in to her tongue play.

A minute later, he broke from her lip lock. "When we drop

Quran off on Monday, we have to head out of the country. You ready?"

"Yes, I'm always ready." She went back to kissing his lips.

"Somebody else is ready," he warned as the Enforcer rose for the occasion.

"Well, let me have it."

"I'ma let you have it, but can you handle it?"

"I'll try," she responded as he switched to a more power position and gave her just what she asked for.

They moved back into the house and showered, and then dressed in their pajamas. Once they climbed in bed next to Quran they both passed out. The family bond was set. KoKo and Kayson just needed to remove anything that would threaten it.

- 19 -
Treacherous

Caught in her feelings, KoKo was unable to fall asleep. Some of it involved them dropping Quran off and taking a fight to South America. But what bothered her most was Kayson taking a phone call from a woman while KoKo was riding his dick. She sat up and looked over at Kayson, who was fast asleep. She stared at him, trying to figure out what he was hiding and why he was hiding it.

KoKo got out of bed, put on her slippers, and headed to the balcony. Opening the glass doors, the breeze blew the curtains as she walked toward one of the chairs and took a seat. KoKo watched the full moon that appeared to sit right outside the house. It was breathtaking. She had been in Guyana for only a few hours and had mixed feelings about what Kayson was doing down here and the fact that he was set up so well. She was also conflicted about them getting to the bottom of why he left in the first place.

"You couldn't sleep?" Kayson asked, walking up behind her.

"Not really," she responded.

"What's on your mind?" He sat in the chair next to her.

"Everything."

"Speak on it."

"I don't know if I'm ready to be out of the country. I have so much pending, and I have to cut some time out to spend with Quran. Maybe you can handle this without me." She looked over at him.

"That's not an option. I need you for this. I want you to work with Yuri. I need someone I can trust to be right in the mix." He looked in her eyes in an attempt to read her emotions.

KoKo looked at him for a few seconds and then looked away.

"Look. Just make this first meeting. Feel her out."

"I hope you weren't feeling her out."

"What is that supposed to mean?"

"I *hope* you weren't feeling her out."

"Don't play with me. You should know me by now. I would never fuck another woman and then put her in your face. I don't roll like that."

"I would hope not."

"Have I ever lied to you?"

"No. But you taught our son to."

"That was different, and we didn't lie to you. I just didn't tell you everything."

"Why did you allow your mother the freedom to move our son around without my permission?"

KoKo frowned. Just the thought that he was sneaking around behind her back with that bitch, upset her whole situation. She sat thinking, *What the fuck was he and his mother hiding?*

"I know what you're thinking. No, my mother didn't know the whole time. I told her a few weeks before her trip to New York. I wanted to see my son, and I didn't want her to travel down here. I knew you would flip if you couldn't find them. I set up a spot in the city and met them there."

"Why would you do that? You put them both in danger,"

KoKo stated, feeling a bit betrayed.

"I did what I needed to do. Plus, I had to get some information from my mother. She needed to be in the city to take care of some things for me."

KoKo's mind was now all over the place. All the pain from his mother's deceit came to the surface, and she had gotten a major attitude. "Look, I have a lot of questions, but I'm going to save them for a time when I'm not pissed, because I don't want to say something I will regret." KoKo got up.

Kayson grabbed her hand. "Don't let nothing come between us."

"You already done enough of that for the both of us." She looked in his eyes. "I'm tired. I need to lie back down." She gently pulled her hand away.

Kayson turned and stared out over the water. He wanted to go after her and tell her everything, but he couldn't. There were still so many pieces he needed to put into place, and her knowing everything would only make her go after the people he needed to complete his mission. It killed him to see her in pain, but it was a sacrifice he had to make to pull shit off without a flaw.

Kayson got in bed behind her and put his arm around her stomach. "Please know everything I do and have done is for us. I promise I will tell you everything when it's time," he whispered in her ear, and then he kissed her shoulder.

KoKo didn't respond. She just closed her eyes and tried to doze off. She had already decided her hunt for answers was going to begin as soon as her feet touched New York soil.

The next morning, Kayson and KoKo moved in silence around the house, preparing for the day. KoKo got her mind right for this so-called meeting with a woman that she didn't know and wasn't trying to know.

When the driver pulled up and rang the bell, Kayson

opened the door.

"Wait by the car. She will be right with you," he instructed. Turning his attention to KoKo, he said, "Look, just hear her out. We need to make this move. I need to know how you feel and what you see."

"I'm always about my business. But when we get back, we need a sit down."

"I got you." He kissed her forehead.

KoKo walked out and got into the car.

Kayson gathered his things and prepared to meet with Mr. Odoo and his son Peppa. Mr. Odoo was old fashioned. He wanted the men to work together and the women to do the same. He had given his daughter a lot of power, but she was still very green when it came to negotiating and thought with KoKo by her side she would get the confidence she needed to make bigger moves.

As KoKo pulled in front of the house, she took a breath and prepared her mind. She was still dealing with the conversation she had with Kayson. She quickly tucked that shit away and went into business mode.

Walking up the driveway, her eyes explored the surroundings. Everything was beautiful. The lawn was perfectly manicured, and every flower looked like it was planted in its rightful place. She approached the door and grabbed the huge metal ring and banged it a few times.

The door came open.

At 6-feet 1-inch tall and approximately 145 pounds, all curves, Yuri smiled, looking like a Brazilian goddess. She wore her hair long, brown, and curly. Her features were exotic. Beautiful long legs, small waist, a fat ass and double D breasts, leading up to a round face with mezmerizing brown doe-shaped eyes, a thin nose, and pretty pink lips glossed over just right.

"Hello. You must be KoKo," Yuri said as she opened the door wider to her mansion, allowing KoKo to enter.

"Yes, I am," KoKo stated as she moved past the entrance.

Yuri closed the door, giving KoKo the once over.

KoKo walked into the foyer and began to take inventory. She marveled at the brown and tan marble staircase that led to a balcony which gave access to two different hallways, one on each side. The tall ceilings were accented by several bamboo ceiling fans, which were all turning in unison.

"Welcome to my home." She smiled. "Please, come this way." Yuri began walking to a large room that housed an all-white pool table that sat up on four small golden lion heads. Across from it was a large glass table with a throne-like chair on each end, and a gold chess set in the middle. "Please be seated."

KoKo sat down in one of the burgundy plush armchairs and crossed her legs.

Yuri walked over to the bar and poured a drink. "Would you like something before we get started?"

"No thanks," KoKo said, remaining quiet and trying to figure out her angle.

Yuri poured a drink from the medium-sized, clear glass bottle. She replaced the lid, and then walked over and sat across from KoKo.

"So, KoKo, did Kay tell you what everything entailed?"

Yuri's use of a nickname for Kayson immediately put KoKo in a bad mood. Everything this bitch had to say from here forward was going to be carefully scrutinized.

"Look, I came a long way, and running small talk is not on my agenda. So, with all due respect, say what you gotta say. I got shit to do." KoKo looked at Yuri with one eyebrow raised.

"Fair enough. I will get to the point. My father loves

Kayson like a son. He has a huge deal coming up, and he wants him by his side. For some reason, he thinks we need to work together." She paused, taking a sip of her drink. "To be honest, I am not looking for a sidekick. However, if I can get you to sit up straight and pay attention, then maybe we will be a good team." She tried to come for KoKo, but was sadly misinformed about how crazy KoKo was.

"Bitch, you must have bumped your muthafucking head. You don't know shit about me!"

Yuri smiled. *So young, so ignorant.* "I'm quite sure Kay has explained to you many times that a lady needs to be patient and allow the strength in her silence to speak louder than her words."

"And I'm quite sure he has explained many times to you, that a bitch with her head in a lion's mouth shouldn't shake her ass."

Yuri chuckled. "Cute." She paused. "With a little more time I'm sure he will be able to dress you up and take you somewhere." She brought her drink to her lips while staring in KoKo's eyes.

KoKo sat back and rested her hands on the armrest, squeezing them tight while struggling to remain calm.

She slowed her breathing, and then went in. "I don't give a fuck how much of my man's dick you sucked. Say some more shit outta the way to me, and I'ma upset your whole dental plan." KoKo rose from her seat.

"What makes you think I sucked his dick?" Yuri smirked.

KoKo gave a half smile. "I've seen your kind before. You're not original. Plus, if he fucked you, your mouth wouldn't be so slippery. See, you're the type of bitch that'll suck a nigga dick and sit around waiting for that comeback."

Yuri twitched in her seat, trying to maintain her calm

demeanor, but on the inside she was heating up. But one thing was for sure. She thought very carefully before parting her lips.

When she didn't respond, KoKo responded for her. "Yeah, I thought so. Fuck outta here." KoKo started toward the door.

Yuri rose from her seat. "Maybe one day you will thank me."

KoKo quickly turned and moved toward her. "We don't have to wait for no one day. Shit, you ain't said nothing. I would like to thank you right now. I know my man was away from me. And I appreciate a bitch keeping his dick right while lining my pockets. Bitch, I'ma Boss, and therefore, I know how to stay in my lane. Your shit is sloppy, and you all over the road. A boss bitch can fuck your man and smile in your face. A thirsty bitch gotta make it known. The only reason you're still alive is because I respect the relationship Kayson has with your father. But don't get it twisted. I am the wrong bitch to fuck with."

The two women stood eye to eye, neither wanting to back down. KoKo smiled. "Just as I thought. A thirsty bitch." KoKo turned this time, exiting the room. She walked out the door, hopped in her car, and headed back to Kayson's house. She packed up her shit and flew straight back to New York.

Later that night . . .
Kayson slid his key into the door, closing it behind himself. "KoKo! Baby," he yelled as he moved from one room to another. He was interested in finding out if she had gotten the details and was moving on the shit he needed done.

When he got to the last room and saw that KoKo's shit was missing, he became agitated. Immediately, his thoughts went to Yuri and what type of shit she must have pulled. He grabbed his phone and called KoKo, but got no answer. He hit her back to back three times. He stood thinking for a minute, and then placed a call to Night.

"Yo. Where your sister at?"

"She about to be in the front seat of my car. I'm picking her up from the airport."

"Ai'ight. When you get her in the car, hit me."

"Everything good, Boss?"

"Nothing I can't handle. Hit me as soon as she get in the car." Kayson disconnected his call, grabbed his shit, and headed to Yuri's house.

Kayson pulled up to the security system and rang the buzzer. After a few seconds, he heard her voice ring through the speaker. "Yes."

"Don't fucking play with me," Kayson said, and the gate opened. He sped to the door, got out, and walked inside. Yuri was standing there waiting for him. "What the fuck you tell my wife?"

"What are you talking about?" She walked into the game room. Kayson was right on her heels.

"I asked you to bring her up to speed, and instead you do the total opposite."

Yuri poured herself a tall glass of white wine. She then walked to the couch and sat down. "I didn't get a chance to tell her anything. She's the type of woman that thinks she knows it all, and I let her go with it."

"Fuck is you talking about you 'let her go with it'?"

"She got the impression that I sucked your dick. And in the moment, I let her believe what she wanted to believe." She seductively crossed her legs and licked her lips.

Kayson was quiet. He watched Yuri bring the glass to her mouth, giving him that sexy, yet sneaky smile.

"What the fuck is wrong with you? Don't play with my

wife."

"She is not on my level. She needs to respect me."

"No, you need to respect what the fuck I told you to do. Because unlike the rest of my team. She don't give a fuck about killing a bitch and then going right on with her day."

"She isn't the only bitch with a gun."

"Tell your father to call me. I can't work with you."

"Why? You scared you might get into something you can't get out of?"

Kayson chuckled. "Bitch, you must be crazy. You got the wrong nigga. Pussy don't excite me. You had your chance, but you can't hang with a real boss. Now your ass is bitter." He paused and laughed. "Crazy, bitch. Let me get the fuck outta here." Kayson looked at her and shook his head. Then he headed for the door.

Yuri was furious. She jumped up, slammed her glass on the table, and swiftly walked behind him. "No. I don't have the wrong muthafucka. You got the wrong bitch. You work for us. We call the shots. You exist because we say so."

Kayson turned quickly, grabbed her by the throat, and pinned her up against the wall.

"Don't *ever* fucking threaten me!"

Yuri grabbed at his hand in an attempt to loosen his grip. Tears rose up in her eyes as she gasped for air.

"Talk shit. Who exist because of who?" he asked as he watched her struggle.

"Let . . . me . . . go," she tried to say, while pulling at his arm.

"Don't play with me! Stay the fuck away from me and my family." He held his hand on her throat a little longer then released. Turning to the door, he said, "And don't fuck with my money, or we will have a real problem."

Yuri fell to the floor, gasping and coughing. She looked up

with tears streaming from her eyes. "Fuck you, Kayson!" she yelled.

"Suck my dick!" he said, not even turning around. "Oh yeah, that's right. I won't let you," he said, and slammed the door.

Yuri pounded her hand on the floor and cried. She was pissed, but not only at him, but also at herself. She had wanted Kayson to be hers, and instead of playing it cool, she allowed her jealousy of KoKo to cloud her vision. She sat back on her feet and cried. The more she cried, the angrier she became, as the realization set in. Now she had to tell her father she may have jeopardized the mission. Pain struck her chest. Her father's orders were clear and rang loud in her mind. *Don't fuck this up.*

Mad as Hell . . .

Kayson jumped in Night's car, closed the door, and rolled down the window. He was beyond pissed, and now he had to face KoKo and clear up the shit Yuri had put out there.

He pulled his hoody back and ran his hand over his face. "So she mad as hell, huh?"

"Hell yeah! She got in the backseat and didn't say shit. I tried to get her to call you, but she pushed that phone right to the side, sat back and looked out the window all the way to the house. Got out my shit and slammed the door so hard I almost shot her in the pinky toe." He cracked a half smile.

Kayson ran his hands over his face again. He knew he hadn't done shit, but with him being gone and all the shit that surrounded that, plus the new business he had set up that he could not tell her about, caused KoKo to be very insecure. "Yeah, I almost had to break that bitch's neck. She got KoKo thinking we fucking."

"Get the fuck outta here!" Night said.

Kayson got quiet.

Night looked over at him. "Did you?"

"Nah. One night I almost slipped, but I don't eat where I shit. Plus, I can't do my baby like that. I put that shit in check real quick."

"Yeah, ai'ight, nigga. Don't make KoKo act like a fool. You know she crazy as hell. Fuck around and wake up with a dog head in your bed."

Kayson pulled his hood down, turned and looked out the window. He needed to get to KoKo and fast.

When Kayson got to the mansion, she was nowhere in sight. There wasn't even a trace that she had been there. He quickly went to the basement and hit the safe behind the bar. He scanned some paperwork, stuck it back inside the safe, and closed it up. Kayson knew that KoKo always did the disappearing act when she was upset. He figured he would just stick to his plan until she cooled off. He just hoped the shit Yuri did wasn't irreversible.

- 20 -

Southern Comfort

KoKo's mind was all over the place. She arrived in Atlanta around two o'clock in the morning and hailed a cab. She needed to go someplace where she could sit and think. And she knew just the place.

As soon as the cab was within a few blocks of her destination, she hopped out and began to walk. She reached the house and rang the bell and waited.

The lights came on, and a calm came over her mind. KoKo knew she had made the right choice, and she would be able to put everything into perspective.

The locks clicked and the door opened. "Why you always at my door in the middle of the night?" Rock asked as he opened his arms to greet her.

"Can I come in?" she asked, moving from their embrace.

"Of course. You alright?" he asked, recognizing her bloodshot eyes.

"Yeah, I'm good. Just need to sit and think."

"Well, you know you can stay here as long as you need to."

"Thank you." KoKo moved to the couch and sat down.

Rock sat next to her, grabbed the remote, and turned on the satellite radio.

KoKo sat for a minute. She reached in her pocket and pulled out a blunt. "Do you mind?"

"Nah, baby, go ahead."

KoKo lit up, took a few hard pulls, and stared off. "You ever did so much shit that you wish you could turn back the hands of time? But realized, if you did, the shit that you love would also be gone?"

"I have made my mistakes. But the good thing about them is they make me who I am."

KoKo chuckled. "Yeah, and mine make me who I am. But the woman I see everyday, I am not proud of." She took a few more pulls.

"You are a brilliant woman. You are only playing the cards you were dealt. If at any time you feel like you keep getting the wrong hand, change the game," Rock said and put his hand on her shoulder.

A tear rolled down her face. She reached up and caught it with her hand.

"It's okay to cry sometimes. Don't worry. I won't tell anyone that the toughest woman I know, cries." He chuckled.

"I am so embarrassed."

"For what? You're human. You have things on your shoulders that most men can't handle. It's okay to be soft sometimes."

"In my world, soft will get you killed."

"Well, tonight you're in Rock's world. Do you." He reached over and kissed her forehead. "I'ma get you some pajamas and get the spare room ready for you." He stood to leave the room.

"Thank you." KoKo grabbed his hand.

"I told you. I got your back." He squeezed her hand, and then he went to prepare the room.

KoKo finished her blunt and plotted her next move. Her first trip would be to her son. Then she was going to shake up Kayson's whole world.

- 21 -

Just What She Needed

Goldie had gotten cozy with the detective after the upside down blow job she did on him. Within a week his gums were bumping so hard it sounded like his teeth were chattering every time he opened his mouth. She was confident that in no time she would have all the information that KoKo needed. Goldie was seated comfortably in her salon chair getting a manicure when she received a call from Night.

"What you doin'?" His voice smoothly caressed her eardrum.

"Hey, you. I'm getting my nails done. What's up with you?"

"I was about to go to lunch. You wanna join me?"

"Hell yeah, my stomach was just starting to talk shit," she said. They both chuckled.

"Where you at?"

"I'm downtown, but I have my car."

"No worries, I got your brother with me. He can hold on to it until we get back."

"Okay. He knows where I am. See you soon." She disconnected the call.

Night picked up Goldie, and they were on their way to one of her favorite spots, The Floataway Cafe. Night sat comfortably in his chair staring into Goldie's eyes. It wasn't only that she was beautiful. She was challenging to his intellect and always about that hustle. No doubt, his woman Rain was a good woman, but she needed to be kept. Goldie had her own shit, and with her, he could share his dark side and then be gentle at the same time.

"What are you thinking about?" Goldie asked. She placed her mouth on the straw and sucked softly, looking up at him.

"Nothing much. Just tossing a few things around," he responded, picking his drink up and taking it to the head.

"Thank you for lunch. I needed that. I have so much going on, and you know KoKo be on my ass. I love her to death, but can't nobody keep up with her. Damn, do the bitch sleep?" she joked.

"No," Night stated without blinking an eye. "KoKo is built different than all of us. She has a different fire under her pot. She has hustle in her blood. She has been doing this shit since her father's nut sac." He paused. "I think if she couldn't rule, it would kill her."

"Let me ask you something. I heard rumors about her husband. Was he really all that they say he was?"

"More. That was the last of a dying breed. Love that nigga till the death of me," Night said, looking her square in the eyes.

"That's what's up."

Just when she was about to ask another question, her cell phone went off. "Pardon me for a minute. I have to take this. Hello," she said just above a whisper.

Night watched her body language as she turned from a woman into a little girl.

"Yes. I know, bu—Okay dad. I'll be right there." She disconnected the call and stared at the table.

"You all right?"

Goldie just nodded, because if she said a word the tears she

135

fought so hard to keep back might fall at a rapid pace and never stop.

"Can you take me down the SWATS?" she asked as she rose to her feet. "Let me go to the bathroom. I'll be right back."

Night frowned. Whoever had just made Goldie feel the way she felt had just made themselves an enemy.

Goldie and Night went straight to an ATM and then jumped on I-20 headed to Southwest Atlanta. They drove in silence to her father's house, and when they pulled up he could see the anguish all over her face. She stared at the raggedy screen door and filthy windows, dreading the interaction that would take place on the other side of the door.

She got out the car and walked down the cracked up walkway. His wretched dog barked from his stationary position tied to a tree with a heavy link chain. The stench of dog shit hit her nose; her stomach felt sick.

Goldie looked up to see her father standing in the doorway with a dirty white T-shirt and a pair of filthy brown cutoff pants. She walked up on the porch and was greeted with a face full of smoke. He held his pipe firm in hand.

"What took you so long?" he asked as Goldie passed him and took a seat right next to the door.

Her father looked out at Night and spat a wad of brown colored phlegm. He let the door close as he stood in front of Goldie and started his shit.

Night watched her lower her head and listened to him degrade her. He went on and on about how she was nothing but a disappointment, and if she ever missed bringing him his money, she could forget she had a father.

Once he was done, Goldie passed him the money and then left.

Her dad stood in the doorway yelling, "Yeah, go ahead and make that money. Make sure you jiggle their balls while you suck that dick." He started to laugh, but coughed that nasty smoker's cough. Hawking up some more phlegm, he spat on the ground, and then turned, letting the screen door slam shut.

Goldie fought to hold back the tears as she reached the passenger side of the car. Night's nostrils flared as heat surged through his body.

When she got in the car, she put on her seat belt and sunk into her seat. "You okay?"

"Yeah, just get me as far away from here as possible." She folded her arms and turned toward the window as he drove off.

As Night turned from one street to the next, he plotted and planned. He had been hanging with Goldie for the last couple weeks and had built a soft spot for her in his heart. The fact that she was hurting was also tearing him up inside.

When they pulled up to Goldie's house, she exited the car, not saying a word. Night followed her into the house. He wanted to make sure she was in safe before he headed to the airport.

"You gonna be alright?"

"Yeah, I'll be fine. I have grown immune to my father."

"Nobody should have to get used to that kind of pain."

"Well, I guess when you're born with the mark of disgrace on your forehead you learn how to live with it." She leaned against the sofa while looking into Night's eyes, searching for his angle. It had been her experience that the only time a man was nice to her was when her legs were open.

"You're a beautiful woman. And you deserve respect."

"You heard my father. The only thing I'm good for is making that money." As she said the words, a tear ran down her face.

THE PUSSY TRAP 3: *Death by Temptation*
~ N E N E C A P R I ~

At that moment, Night felt all her agony, and all he wanted to do was take on all her burdens. He walked up to her and wrapped his arms around her, fitting her firmly in his arms. The more he squeezed, the harder she cried.

"Let that shit out." Night held her as she cried like a baby. It had been years since she was able to release the pain that she had learned to live with. She cried for her mother dying and leaving her with this man, who instead of being a father, was more like her pimp. Sitting and waiting for her to bring in the money.

"Why is this my life?" she asked, barely able to speak.

"It's not your fault. Don't let that muthafucka define you." Night pulled her face up, so he could look into her eyes.

Goldie's face was wet, and her heart was broken.

"You'll get through this," Night assured her. He kissed her tenderly between her eyes. As he pulled back and their eyes met, he felt the heat between them. And it spoke loud and clear. He answered by taking her head into his hands and began kissing her lips. She had lacerations on her soul that needed to be healed, and he wanted to be the medicine she needed.

Overcome by emotion, Goldie pulled back and looked in his eyes. "I need you to be with me tonight." She reached for his zipper.

"Nah, ma. Relax. Tonight. Let me take care of you. Let a real man give you what you been yearning for."

Night picked her up and carried her to her bedroom.

Standing her next to the bed, he pulled her dress over her head, revealing her body. And for the first time, Goldie actually felt naked. She covered her breasts with her hands as she looked away.

Night placed his hand under her chin and brought her face

to meet his. He placed his lips to hers. She released a soft moan as chill bumps covered her body.

"Night. Wait. What about what KoKo said?"

"Let me worry about that. You worry about how good I'm about to feel inside you. Lie down," he ordered.

Goldie positioned herself in the middle of her king-sized bed, watching as Night removed his shirt and then his pants. When she saw all that dick, her heart sank to her toes.

Sensing her hesitation, he quickly tried to calm her nerves. "Don't worry. He lethal, but he ain't deadly. I know how to make this nigga act right," he assured her as he got on the bed. Taking her ankle in his hand, he began planting soft kisses up her calve and her inner thigh.

Goldie melted with his every touch. The closer he got to her kitty, the more nervous she became.

Night positioned himself to have all access. Kissing her sweet flower gently, he savored her flavor.

Goldie arched her back, placing a hand on his head, and guiding him to her pleasure. She escaped with every soft lick and firm suck. Goldie let go of the day's anxiety and pain.

Night rose to his knees and strapped up that steel. "I'ma make you a woman tonight. Fuck the past. Let me step into your future," he calmly stated, climbing in between her thick thighs.

"I'm afraid to let you in."

"With me you safe, ma. I got you." He began to short stroke between her slippery lips.

"Night, don't hurt me."

"You got my word," he groaned as the passion between them pulled him deeper.

Goldie knew exactly how to work that pussy to a nigga's pleasure. It was like she was reading his mind. Each stroke felt different than the last. She rocked those hips to make sure he hit the right spots with every push.

Soft moans left his lips and sank into her eardrums, putting her in a trance that took over her whole body.

"Niiiight . . ." she whined.

"Goldie." He continued to stroke as her wetness covered his waist and stomach. "Fuck me," he repeated. She grabbed his ass, forcing him further inside while her muscles gripped his thick muscle. She bit into his neck, and then she whispered in his ear, "I need it from the back."

Night wasted no time complying. He pulled out and watched her get into position, perching that ass up and spreading those legs wide. He admired her glistening kitty that was screaming for more. He slid back in, grabbed her waist, and fucked her close. The room quickly filled with the sounds of his thighs smacking her fat ass.

Goldie zoned out, rotated her waist and pushed back, forcing him further inside her with every stroke. Night looked down at her smooth body as she worked his pole; she was throwing that ass and squeezing her cheeks at the same time, causing a knee-weakening suction on his dick. All he could think was, *Damn, I see why KoKo put her on niggas.* He fought hard not to cum, but the slippery, wet pleasure he received was fucking his head up.

Intense contractions came on, forcing Goldie to move away from him.

Pulling her back, he began talking shit. "Mmmm… what I'm hitting, baby? What's that?"

"My spot," she moaned.

"Don't run. Go ahead and wet this dick," he taunted, holding her in place and hitting that spot. Her body seized up and then began to shake.

Goldie grabbed the pillow and buried her face as she

screamed out in pleasure.

Night went into beast mode, repeatedly beating that spot. She came over and over again. He fucked that spot until she begged him to stop.

"Uh-huh," he mumbled as he watched her body jerk every time he entered her. "Dick good, ain't it, baby?" his voice belted out as his stroke quickened.

"Hell yeah," she whined. Goldie regained her composure and twerked that ass, working his dick into a frenzy.

When Goldie felt him pick up speed and moan, she rocked into him until she knew he couldn't take anymore. In one swift move, she pulled forward. Goldie turned to him, slid off the condom, and sucked him until he released the pressure.

She stroked his dick and slid the head over her lips as she looked up at him. "Ain't nothing like the taste of sweet dick after a good nut."

Out of breath and mesmerized, Night looked down and said, "You're welcome, but I'm not done with that ass." He grabbed her by the waist and flipped her upside down.

There Goldie rested on her arms in a handstand as Night ate her pussy like he owned it.

For the next few hours, Night removed mountains from her soul. In the morning, Goldie felt like a new person. He had said things to her that she never heard, and he did things to her that she never had done. It was official. Goldie was hooked on Night and not letting go.

- 22 -

Tell Me Everything

Kayson pulled up to his house, full of uncertainty. When he walked in the mansion it was cold and dark. He went straight to their bedroom. KoKo was sitting up in the seating area of their bedroom watching the news. She didn't even look in his direction.

He moved to the closet, took his clothes off, and put on his robe. Kayson walked to KoKo's side of the bed and sat down.

"Why you leave?"

"You need to deal with your bitches, because I don't have time for bullshit. I'm going to take care of my own shit, and you do the same," she said, looking at the television. She grabbed the remote and flipped through channels.

"We ain't got no separate business. All of this is ours."

"Look, I know that you do what you have to do to make shit happen, and I respect that. But I'm way past fighting with bitches over you."

"What the fuck is you talking about? The only woman in my life is you. Ain't shit changed." He placed his hand on her leg.

KoKo looked at him with coldness in her eyes. "So, you can sit here and tell me you ain't fuck that bitch?"

"No, I did not fuck her. I'm not going lie. I had pussy when I was away from you. But you should know me by now. My love is and has always been with you."

"I used to know you."

"Do you know I love you?"

"Yes. Bu—"

"But what?"

KoKo crossed her arms, and for the first time in months, she released all the emotion building up inside her. As tears ran down her face she said, "I live for this life we live. I know what needs to be done and I do it. Do I fuck up sometimes? Hell yeah. But I don't regret the things I have done to feed my son. However, the major thing I question is my relationship with you." KoKo paused. "Who the fuck are you? And why do you keep hurting me?"

Her question stung his heart. He thought long and hard before answering her. "I made the ultimate sacrifice to be with you. They were never coming for me. They were coming for you." He paused and filled his lungs with air and released it. "After you killed Raul, I was supposed to kill you." A brief silence lingered as he gauged her feelings. "I fell in love with you. I then proceeded to go against orders and married you. That night at the party. That was an ordered hit on your life. But I traded places with you. I was willing to give my life for you and my baby."

"You knew I was pregnant?"

"I'm your husband. Of course I know when the pussy changes," he responded, giving her a sexy smile.

"You can't possibly know what I have been through. How were you able to pull it off?"

"That night we got hit, Night was in town trading money with Mr. Lu Chi. When my mother found out, she called him and they came straight to the hospital. I did die on the table twice, but they were able to stabilize me. When Lu Chi found out, he called in some favors to get me moved. They did what they had to do, and the word was sent out that I was dead.

THE PUSSY TRAP 3: *Death by Temptation*
~ N E N E C A P R I ~

Everything was settled except one contract that I am still trying to buy us out of it. I'm close, but hopefully, time won't be against us."

"Why didn't you tell me?"

"The more you know, the more danger you and Quran would have been in."

"So, what now?"

"I need you to work with me on this Guyana move."

"I'm not working with that bitch. They'll fuck around and snatch our freedom papers. I was ready to kill her ass."

"Don't worry. I want you to work with Peppa, her brother. This shit gotta be clean. All this money is legit. I need you to remember that. I don't want no ties to our old world with this new shit we doing. We're going back down in a couple of days."

"Okay, but you have to tell me everything."

"I promise to tell you what I can. The rest you will have to trust me."

"Well, I have some shit pending. And I need to do some things also, and you will have to trust me."

"Don't get fucked up," he warned.

"I'm not going to do anything that will disrespect you or compromise our relationship."

There was an eerie moment of silence. "I know what happened with my mother. We are in a fucked up game. The only thought that comforts me is that you did what you had to do." He looked at her, gauging her mood.

KoKo returned his gaze to feel him out. She had been avoiding this subject ever since he showed up back on the scene.

"I found out a lot of shit while I was gone. I understand. I know that she was involved in a lot of things that created pain in your life. I'm dealing with it, and we will just leave it at that."

"I'm sorry if I hurt you. That was not my intent. Quran loved her, and she took good care of him. I will love her for that, but I could not live with her role in my parent's death."

"I know the code. We all will pay for what we did. It's just a matter of time."

KoKo lowered her head as his words played over in her mind.

"We had to kill to get in, and we gonna have to kill to get out."

"I'm bad with this muthafucka." KoKo grabbed her gun from under her pillow and set it on the nightstand.

"What the fuck are you doing sitting in our bedroom with a gun?" Kayson looked at her sideways.

"You never know."

"You gotta calm down. You can't kill everybody."

"I don't kill everybody. I didn't kill you," she joked.

"You wasn't going to kill me. But you know I owe that ass for pulling that punk ass nine on me."

"I want to pay."

"Come sit on my lap, so we can work some shit out."

"Why you think the answer to all my problems can get solved by sitting on your lap?" She straddled him and rocked gently.

"You know getting that spot stroked makes you nicer."

"Whatever. Just know you need to handle everything on your end, so I can better do my job."

"You need to do what I tell you to do," he shot back.

"I want you to make me," she whispered in his ear.

"You know you ain't 'bout that life." He stood with her legs firmly placed at his waist.

"You better be glad I'm making up with you."

"I got you, baby. Tonight we spend time making up. Then we have to begin putting our family back together."

"What is that supposed to mean?" KoKo asked, looking attentively in his eyes with her back pressed up against the wall.

"Me, you, and Quran. I need to be with my son. I'm about to make my presence known to these niggas. But before I do, I want our family unit tight and safe." He kissd her gently.

KoKo caressed his strong back as she felt his steel.

"Don't worry. Just let me lead," he said as he went to work.

Kayson was doing his thing, but KoKo couldn't help but think about the reunion they would have with their son. She prayed that it would be a blessing and not a curse.

- 23 -
Feather Fred

It had been plaguing KoKo to take the trip to see Fred in worse condition than he was the last time she saw him. She wanted to remember the wise, slick-talking, healthy Fred, but the reality was, death lay at his feet, and he would never be the same again. KoKo swallowed her emotions and drove on.

The weather had become cold. The trees were bare and the sky was gray and dreary. KoKo drove along the streets of Hoboken bumping "If I Should Die Tonight" by Marvin Gaye. Thinking about how far she had come and how far she still had to go. The thing that pulled most at her heart was the lives she lost in the process.

She pulled up to the nursing home and just stared at the doors. The thought of getting out and saying her last goodbyes to Fred caused heaviness in her legs. After a few more seconds, she cut off the engine and prepared to go inside. She stepped out the car wearing black skinny jeans, a black shearling cape, and a pair of black fur Pajar boots. KoKo headed up to the doors.

After signing in, she walked down the long hall. As she passed the rooms, the smell of urine and sickness upset her stomach. She couldn't believe Fred had been reduced to a nursing home. She reached the end of the hall, knocked on the door, and proceeded inside.

"KoKooo," Fred said, his face lighting up when he saw her

pretty face.

He was thinner than before. His hair was gone, and an oxygen mask covered his nose and mouth.

"How's my favorite person?" KoKo responded as she closed the door.

Fred removed the oxygen mask. "Sheeit . . . I think he took a vacation. I called that muthafucka, and he ain't answering."

KoKo chuckled and took a seat. A brief silence passed between the two before KoKo finally spoke. "I'm in deep, Fred."

"Yeah. Well, you can handle it. Just go back to what you know."

"I never wanted all this," she confessed to her mentor.

"Well, it's too late for all that. You're a boss. Regret is for pussies." Fred held her gaze for a while so his statement would resonate and take root. "Put all them muthafuckas in a category. Assets or liabilities. There's no such thing as friendship when you at the top. Be smart. Remember, pussy makes policy," he said, coughing uncontrollably.

KoKo got up and grabbed the cup of water next to his bed and put it to his mouth. He held her wrist and struggled to drink. As he laid his head back on the pillow, his wheezing rattled deep in his chest, laboring for air.

She didn't know what to say. Fred was dying and there wasn't anything she could do about it, and all the money in the world couldn't stop it.

Fred searched for the next gem he wanted to drop on his baby girl before he left her. He had heard about her and Boa, and he wanted to make sure her mind was right. "Remember, KoKo." He turned to face her. "Don't be out here falling in love with these niggas. Ain't no fucking love." He swallowed his spit and coughed violently. Fred closed his eyes and winced once the coughing ceased. "As far as these niggas are concerned, your love is as long as his dick. When he pulls out. You pull out. You gotta flip this shit on these niggas. Make these muthafuckas bow down."

KoKo nodded. "I'ma miss the shit outta you, Fred." She felt a lump in her throat.

"Sheeiit . . . don't be missing me. I had a good life. I lived, loved, fucked some bad bitches, and they paid me to do it." He chuckled.

"Speaking of bad bitches. I saw Chocolate."

Fred turned and looked at her. "How was she?"

"She was all right. She said Kayson left a message with you for me." KoKo got right to the point.

Fred paused for a minute. "Go see the Dutchess. I told her everything that I could remember. She had instructions to give you everything. But only when I'm gone." He looked over at her.

"Thank you."

"When I leave this bitch, don't let them muthafuckas cry over me. Set my ass on fire and scatter me to the wind. A nigga gotta at least be free in death." He smiled at KoKo as a single tear rolled down his face. "Go handle your business. Make them niggas respect your hustle."

"I will."

"KoKo, make sure you burn me with my gun. Me and that nigga Kayson gonna turn it up down there. Maybe they'll reverse our sentence."

"How a nigga gonna get kicked outta hell?" She shook her head.

Fred tried to laugh and again started to cough uncontrollably.

KoKo got up and tried to help him regain his breath. She grabbed the oxygen mask and attempted to put it over his face.

THE PUSSY TRAP 3: *Death by Temptation*
~ N E N E   C A P R I ~

Fred slowly reached up and grabbed her wrist.

She looked down into his eyes and he nodded no. His soul was tired. KoKo put the mask down as she watched Fred labor for air.

"KoKo, I'm tired," he whispered as his chest heaved in and out. "Don't let me die alone," he requested.

She nodded as the tears she fought to hide rolled down her cheeks. Once she wiped her face and took a seat, Fred turned his head and closed his eyes. KoKo sat and watched over Fred until his chest stopped moving.

KoKo stood up and walked over to his bedside and kissed his forehead. As she walked to the door, she said, "Rest easy."

One week later, KoKo granted Fred his wish, and yes she burned him with his gun. While sprinkling his ashes in the Hudson, she said, "Turn it up."

- 24 -
Daddy Time

KoKo and Kayson were in their hideout in the mountains of Pennsylvania. She had prepared a meal for them, and after eating, Kayson and Quran went out to play in the snow.

KoKo looked out the window while drying the dishes. Kayson was chasing him, and they were throwing snowballs at each other. For that brief moment, she felt like she had a normal life. Seeing the smile on both of their faces took away every bit of what was going on around them. Here death was on their asses, and somehow God had enough mercy on their wretched souls to allow them a small amount of peace.

KoKo turned to the door as her two men came in with snow all over them. Smiling, she said firmly, "Keep that snow over there." She pointed at the corner next to the door.

"Go get your mommy," Kayson said. Quran took off running and threw snow at KoKo.

"Nooo . . ." KoKo yelled out, taking off running.

Kayson blocked her, allowing him to hit her with his two small snowballs.

"Stop, Kay. That shit is cold." She tried to push him off her.

"I got you, Mommy." Quran giggled uncontrollably.

"I'ma get you." She took off chasing him with Kayson on her heels. KoKo wrestled him to the floor, tickling him and nibbling on his cheeks.

"Okay, okay." He surrendered.

THE PUSSY TRAP 3: *Death by Temptation*
~ N E N E   C A P R I ~

It was now Kayson's turn to enjoy their connection. He watched as KoKo laughed and played with Quran. It made his heart feel good and ache at the same time. He had missed so much and would be missing so much more if he didn't make everything right.

"Come on, Daddy," Quran said, waving him over.

"No sir. You gotta get into some warm dry clothes before you get sick." KoKo stopped him in his tracks.

"Awww."

"Nah, solider. Do what your mom says." Kayson gave him a stern look.

Quran looked up at his father and immediately changed his mood.

KoKo took off his clothes, gave him a hot bath, and dressed him in warm pajamas.

Kayson walked into the bedroom as she was cleaning up. "You gonna put Daddy in the tub?" He hugged her around her waist.

"Not while your son is awake. Now be good," she warned, attempting to remove his hands.

"He went to watch TV. You need to warm me up for a little while."

"Kay, no," she whispered as she tried to pull back.

"I'll do it real quick. I promise," he whispered back and kissed her lips.

Just when it seemed like he was about to win, in came the blocker, as Kayson called him. "Daddy, come watch TV with me." Quran entered the bathroom to see his mom and dad hugged up. "Ohhhh . . ."

"Ohh . . . what?" Kayson asked, looking down at his son's blushing face.

Unable to say anything, he just laughed and ran back into

the living room.

"I told you," KoKo stated and pushed him back.

"Damn, you can't blame a man for trying," he said, smacking her ass when she turned to pick up Quran's clothes.

"When he go to sleep you in trouble."

"As much as he be on us, he'll probably wake up and his ass will be at the end of the bed watching."

Kayson started laughing. "I'ma fuck around and give little man his first drink."

"See, that's that bullshit. You ain't right," she said, shaking her head on the way out the room.

Kayson headed to the shower as KoKo headed to the living room.

When Kayson emerged from the bathroom, he slipped on his pajama pants and T-shirt and joined his family.

KoKo was knocked out on the couch and Quran was wide awake next to her. He grabbed the cashmere throw from the loveseat and covered her up. KoKo snuggled under the cover and let out a soft snore.

Kayson checked all the locks and made sure the security system was set. He grabbed his gun and checked the rounds before going to sit by Quran.

Quran's eyes settled on the black shiny object. "What's that, Daddy?" he asked.

"This is daddy's peace maker," he looked down at him.

"Why?"

"Sometimes in life you have to make sure that you and your family are safe."

"We're safe."

Kayson heard him, but he knew different. He knew that he needed to give his son his first shot of manhood. He sat down next to him. "Look at me, Quran." He paused, making sure their eyes met. "Everybody will not love you. And sometimes they will hurt the people you love to destroy you. You understand?"

Quran nodded, maintaining eye contact.

"You see that woman?" Kayson pointed at KoKo

Quran turned and looked at his sleeping mother.

"She is our everything. We have to protect her with our life. Don't ever disrespect your mother. Don't ever let anyone disrespect your mother."

Quran stared at KoKo, and his tiny heart became heavy.

"Look at me," he instructed.

Again, Quran looked up.

"You are a Wells. We don't take shit from no man. There is Boss in your blood. You honor what we built for you and don't let anyone stand in your way." He looked firmly in his son's eyes. He knew he was young. But tomorrow was not promised. Kayson had to make sure that every time he came in contact with his son, he gave him the best of him. Sometimes it would be comforting, and sometimes it would be dark. However, it would be truth, and he was determined not to leave his son without love, values, respect, and his killer instinct. Kayson knew one day Quran would be a man, and he couldn't become a man unless he interacted with and was schooled by a man.

Kayson tucked his son under his arm.

Quran laid his head on Kayson's chest, listening to his heartbeat. Content and comfortable, he fell asleep between his mom and dad.

- 25 -
Marked for Death

Tyquan paced back and forth in his office, gathering his thoughts. All the top dogs were awaiting his arrival in the conference room. He had come to the conclusion that he needed to up his game on hunting the hunter. Kayson was back on the scene and stirring shit up, and he knew he needed to get a handle on it before he lost footing and ended up planning his own demise.

"They're ready for you, Mr. Wells." Deborah cracked his door and peeked inside.

"All right, I'll be right there," he stated as he poured himself a shot of bourbon. He threw on his jacket and then headed down the hall.

When he entered the conference room, he looked at the four men who held his life in the balance.

Each man held a cold stare, causing the room to feel frigid. Tyquan walked to his seat at the head of the table and sat down.

"I am very upset with you, Mr. Wells," the first man spoke from his seat on the right side of the table.

"I'ma tell you like I told your partner. I got this shit under control," he answered calmly.

"You ain't gonna tell me shit, but I will tell you this. If Kayson finds out all the players in the game. I promise you one thing. It will be your ass who is folded. Because from where we sit, we're holding a full deck. Don't fuck with us,

Mr. Wells." He looked at Tyquan, who appeared unfazed by the threats being projected in his direction.

"I have stood by my word and product for over twenty years. If you want to disconnect yourself from me and move on, the choice is yours. But when that nigga comes stalking each one of you down. Oh, and he will not stop until each head is a diamond in his crown—don't fucking double back to me." Tyquan rose to his feet.

"You can see yourself out," Tyquan stated, walking past the table.

When he got to the door, the man yelled, "It's a good thing Nine never knows who to cheer for." They all rose to their feet.

Tyquan stood with his back turned as the men approached him. Turning in their direction, he looked each one in the eyes.

"Make sure it's not your head in his crown," the man said, passing Tyquan on his way out. The other gentlemen trailed behind him.

"May the best man win." Tyquan slammed the conference room door. He reached for his phone and promptly called Nine.

"Hello," he answered on the first ring.

"I told you not to let this shit fall in my lap."

"And I told you handle your end."

"If I go down. You go down, muthafucka." Tyquan ended the call as his gut filled with rage.

Exiting the conference room, he went back to his office and straight to his safe. Typing in the combination, he pulled out his secret weapon. Looking over a stack of papers, he began to smile. "These bitches better not come for me," he said aloud.

Deborah came into his office for what she thought would be the usual pick me up, but bad timing would teach her a lesson she would never forget.

"What the fuck you doing in here?" Tyquan was startled out of his mental standstill.

"I just thought you may need something," she said, walking over to where he stood.

Tyquan pushed the papers back into the safe and closed it. "Check this out. Don't help yourself to me. When I need you I will call you."

"I'm sorry. I—"

"Listen, there is nothing between us. You work for me. I pay you for your services. That's all." He gave her a heartless stare.

Deborah lowered her eyes as her spit went hard down her throat. "I don't deserve that," she stated.

Tyquan chuckled. "Oh, what you thought I was going to marry you? Have a family? Live happily ever after? Bitch, please. How can I have respect for a woman that lets me fuck her in the ass then sucks my dick? See yourself out."

Deborah stood trying to choke back her tears. She had been loyal to him for years. She didn't know if he realized it or not, but he had just crossed the wrong bitch.

"You don't have to dismiss me, because I quit," she said as she turned to walk away.

"Good, and leave a list of tricks that you do for me on your desk, so your replacement will know just how I like it."

Deborah gripped the door handle as she exited, and this time she slammed the door as hard as she could. Rushing to her desk, she grabbed her bag and coat. Quickly, she stuffed a few things from her drawer into her bag. When she got to the bottom drawer, she pulled open a flap and grabbed a thumb drive and sim card. She looked down the hall to see if anyone was looking, and then she stored them in her bra. Moving at top speed, she hit the stairs and ran all the way to the lobby.

Once she got downstairs, Deborah ducked into the bathroom and called a cab. She then made a call that would redeem her life.

"Hello, is this Kayson?"

"Who is this?"

"The missing piece. I got your information from Nine," she whispered from the bathroom stall.

"What can I do for you?"

"I think I have something you need. I need to see you."

"I'll have somebody pick you up at the McDonalds in Brooklyn on Fulton."

"I'm on my way."

She emerged from the stall and then ran some water over her face. Deborah fixed her clothes, put on her coat, and headed to the door.

When Deborah emerged from the bathroom, she saw the cab pulling to the front door. She walked past security and straight out the door.

Settling into her seat, she breathed a sigh of relief. Tyquan had just wrote a check his ass couldn't cash.

- 26 -
Happy Birthday

Night and Goldie had become inseparable. Rain had just about given up on him. Whenever he was home, he was distant and cold. Tonight would be no different.

"When am I going to see you again?" Rain asked as she watched him pack his bag.

"You know not to ask me those types of questions," Night shot back, moving around the room double-checking to make sure he was not leaving anything.

"I can't do this shit any more. Don't ask you shit. Don't expect shit. What the fuck are we doin'?"

"Look, I don't have time for this shit. You got everything you need. I'm taking care of business. I will see you soon."

"You think I'm with you because you take care of me? I can get any nigga to take care of me. I need you, Night. The Night I am used to, not this stranger that climbs in and out of my bed every other week."

Night took in heavy air, but did not entertain her tantrum.

"I understand that you have obligations to the organization. And I never stand in the way of that. But you're not honoring the code KoKo set up. She said take care of home. And our shit is falling apart," she yelled.

"Don't yell in my fucking house," he tranquilly ordered.

"I don't even know why I'm talking to you." She folded her arms and shook her head in disgust. "Leave the money on the nightstand. Oh yeah, and I know. Call your pimp KoKo if I need anything," she sarcastically stated as she tried to walk out the room.

Night walked up behind her, and when she turned she was met by a very angry man. Night barked, "Don't you *ever*, in your life disrespect me. You are in my world because I let you in it. Do I care about you? Yes. Are you replaceable? Definitely. You don't want for shit. You drive my cars, you laying in my bed and spending my money. The only responsibility you have is fuck me good and don't stress me the fuck out. Now you always come through on number one, but you are violating number two."

Night looked down at her, seeing in her eyes that the shock of the hour had become grievous. "I need you to act like you got some sense. And don't make me come outta character." He stood there for a few seconds, turned and grabbed his bag and headed to the door.

"Night, I'm sorry. I don't want to fight with you." She came up behind him.

Reluctantly, Night turned and embraced her. He needed to make sure that regardless of the new love he had fallen into with Goldie, that he not fuck up what he had with Rain. KoKo was clear about not creating any new enemies. Plus, Rain had rode for him, and he had love for her, but was no longer in love with her. He just needed some time before he could end it.

"I'm sorry, too. Hang in there. It's almost over."

Rain took his statement literally; she knew she had lost Night. She just needed to ride it out until something else came her way.

Surprise Party . . .

It was a week before Night's birthday, and Goldie wanted to give him something nice. She booked an Ocean Room in the Revel Hotel in Atlantic City and an evening full of surprises.

Goldie had him picked up from New York in a limo and brought straight to the hotel. His evening started with a massage, and dinner that consisted of lobster tails, shrimp scampi, a baked potato with sour cream, and for dessert, chocolate cake with mousse in the middle drizzled with hot fudge.

When he returned to his room, a small bottle of Jack Daniels, a shot glass with his name on it, and three blunts were waiting. Night smiled and poured himself a drink. He took it to the head and then another.

Lighting his blunt, he walked over to the window. He pulled back the curtains and looked out at the black sky touching the ocean. The stars twinkled and shined like they were put in the sky just for him.

Sitting back on the L shaped sofa, he puffed and enjoyed the view. Totally relaxed, he placed the call.

"What's up, ma? Where you at?" he asked.

"I'm downstairs in the lobby. Why don't you come down and get me?" she asked in a sexy voice.

"I'm on my way." Night slipped into the clothes Goldie had set out for him and headed downstairs.

When he got to the lobby, Goldie was posted up at the bar in a yellow knee-length, form-fitting dress that snugged around her curves just right. Night smiled from ear to ear.

"Why a brother got to come all the way to 'AC' to get him some loving?" He pulled Goldie into his arms and kissed her.

"You won't be complaining when you see what I got you for your birthday."

"Mmmm . . . how about you just give it to me? A brother

ain't laid next to nothing soft in a week." He leaned in and kissed her neck.

"Be patient. Trust me, you're going to be loving a sister after tonight," Goldie said with a sneaky grin.

"Keep looking at me like that, and we ain't going to make it to see your little plan through." He held her in his arms while looking in her eyes. Goldie kissed his lips.

"Let's go." They headed to the Ovation Hall for a live comedy show. Kevin Hart was gracing New Jersey with his presence, and it was the perfect gift. Goldie and Night laughed until their stomach hurt.

When the show ended, they headed over to the Revel's HQ Night Club to have a few drinks and dance. Goldie was pulling all her moves out on Night, who just stood there and watched the show.

When they had exhausted all the possibilities, they decided to head upstairs.

As they stood in the elevator, Night couldn't keep his hands off Goldie. Night was running his hands up the sides of her dress and kissing her repeatedly on the lips. "I'm enjoying my birthday," he said in between kisses.

"It's just the beginning," Goldie moaned, enjoying his touch and the taste of his sweet lips.

The doors opened, and Goldie broke from his embrace, grabbing his hand and pulling him toward the room. She could see that Night was definitely in fuck mode, and she didn't want to ruin her surprise.

"Let's hit the shower, so I can give you the last part of your gift."

Night started to undress as he watched Goldie slide out her dress. When she turned, his dick was at full alert. She just needed to keep him distracted long enough to execute her plan.

"You're going to have to give me some before I leave this bathroom. I'm not going to be able to keep him under control much longer." He rubbed his hands between her legs.

"Just relax and let me work my show. You will not be disappointed." Goldie moved his hand, washed him up, and then herself.

Exiting the bathroom, Night was still on swoll and ready to tear something up.

When they got to the room, he couldn't believe his eyes. Three of the baddest bitches he ever saw stood in different places within the room. One was caramel like Goldie, but taller, wearing a white G-string and nothing else. The second female was a Spanish mami with hair to her ass. She was thick in all the right places and also wearing a G-string and nothing else, except hers was neon green. The last one was light-skinned with long pretty legs, a thin waist, and a pretty smile with gray eyes.

The thick Spanish chick took Night by the hand and led him to the bed.

Goldie emerged from the bathroom wrapped in a big white fluffy towel and sat in a chair across from the action. She grabbed the satellite radio remote, turned on something sexy, crossed her legs and prepared to watch the show.

Night sat up between the huge pillows as his eyes roamed over the buffet of titties and asses that stood before him. Each woman crawled onto the bed and began feasting on him, licking and kissing every inch of his body. Spanish Mami took his dick in her hand and then slowly into her mouth. Light-skinned and Carmel created the perfect swirl as they wrapped their bodies around each other and began kissing and caressing each other's breasts.

When Caramel Sister spread her wings, and Redbone went

in for a taste, heat surged through his whole body.

Night allowed his hands to wander over the smooth mounds as the women took turns pleasing him and each other. He was enjoying the show, but he was ready to slide into something hot and wet.

"Goldie, come join me."

"Nah, daddy, it's all about you. Happy birthday. Enjoy." Goldie stayed in her seat.

Night was in heaven. He watched Goldie through the slits of his eyes. She was smiling and enjoying the pleasure on his face.

"Y'all watch out," Night ordered as he motioned Goldie to come over to him.

She stood up, dropped her towel, and sauntered over to him. Crawling between the woman and Night, Goldie straddled his lap sliding all the way down on that pulsating rod, fast and hard. Wasting no time, she effortlessly moved her body to his desire. She sunk her teeth into his neck and bit into his flesh as his thickness tickled her spot.

Night looked over her shoulder as the women devoured each other. Hot tongues traced nipples and legs, hips and thighs. Loud moans and pleas filled the room, as the intensity of passion and pain filled every crack and crease with steamy liquid lust.

Goldie moved in sync with his dick's commands until she began to tremble.

Night held Goldie tight in his arms as she recovered. Sweaty and satisfied, Night spoke into her ear. "I love you."

"I love you too," she moaned.

Night and Goldie got up the next morning and caught a flight to Atlanta. Goldie had gotten a call from the detective KoKo had her on. She needed to get back to lay the groundwork for the last step of KoKo's plan.

Arriving safely at 2 PM, Goldie headed over to the precinct for lunch, and Night headed to make the kill of his lifetime.

Pulling up at Goldie's father's house, Night surveyed the area, reached in the glove compartment, and grabbed his gun. He looked over at the house through the window at the dim light, a sign that someone may be inside.

Emerging from the car, he closed the door gently and moved swiftly to the front porch. Testing the door, he found it to be unlocked just as he expected. Opening it slowly, he made just enough room to fit through and then closed it gently.

Night scanned the living room and saw his helpless victim fast asleep in a dirty, tan recliner. Night moved to the middle of the dirty gray carpet and just stared at him.

Goldie's father began to move in his seat.

When his eyes slowly opened, he saw the Black Night standing there with the look of death on his face. He wanted to yell out, but the hypnotic gaze beaming back at him stole his words.

"You like degrading women?" Night asked in a calm voice.

"Who are you? Why are you in my house?" he asked, squinting to get a better focus.

"You're the type of man that makes it hard for a real man to love his woman."

"Love? I hope the woman you're talking about is not my daughter." He chuckled. "That woman you are talking about is a whore. She fucks for money. Don't you let her fool you. She is the worse type of woman. Sheeeitt . . . I thought you were here to talk about something important." He pushed his chair up and planted his feet in the rug.

"Niggas like you make it easy for me to sleep at night after killing."

"You disrepectfu—" he tried to say, but had to choke back

his words. The bullet from Night's gun lodged in his throat.

The dying man's eyes grew wide as he held his throat in agony, fighting for breath.

"Now you don't have to worry about the woman she is. Die, you dirty muthafucka," Night said as he watched him gasp and wheeze. Thick blood gushed between his fingers, and his soul escaped his body.

Night continued to watch the struggle until his body stopped twitching, and his hands fell to the side. He pulled his sleeve down, opened the door, and walked out.

A surge of emotion flowed through Night's body. For the first time in his life, the kill was personal and not one ounce of regret filled his conscience.

- 27 -
Ready to Get Dirty

Anticipating the meeting, KoKo arrived in Georgetown Guyana a little after five in the evening. Mr. Odoo had her picked up and brought to his estate. She rode in silence and had already made up her mind that if some fishy shit was going on, she was going to commit her first out of the country murder.

When the car pulled up to the mansion, KoKo's stomach filled with butterflies. The car door opened and a hand extended. She placed her hand in the tall, dark gentleman's hand, who gently pulled her from the vehicle and then escorted her inside.

Trailing behind the gentleman, she was taken to a medium-sized room with huge windows, several ceiling fans, and two large navy blue couches, and a hand carved wooden coffee table.

"Mr. Odoo will be with you in a minute." The man bowed and then turned to walk away.

"Thank you," KoKo responded and took a seat.

She looked around the room at the white sheer curtains that blew in and out the window from the nice breeze. The many paintings that adorned the walls seemed to be of family. There were older men and women, and also children. KoKo deduced that this must be an area created to honor the family.

KoKo sat back, crossed her legs, and waited.

THE PUSSY TRAP 3: *Death by Temptation*
~ N E N E   C A P R I ~

Ten minutes later, in walked a short East Indian man with dark skin and straight hair. He was well dressed in a pair of gray slacks and a gray silk dress shirt. There was a calm on his face that most men prayed for. His demeanor immediately put KoKo in a state of tranquility.

"Your husband did not do justice in describing your beauty," he stated, coming over and taking KoKo's hand and planting a tender kiss on it. "Sorry for keeping you waiting. I had to wrap up a little business." He apologetically smiled and took a seat across from her.

"No problem." KoKo smiled.

"Thank you for meeting with me. I must first apologize on behalf of my daughter. Kayson told me of her unkind gestures. I have taken care of it, and you have my word it will not happen again." He put both hands on his heart, and then he dropped them to his lap.

"I appreciate your kindness. Thank you."

"I will get straight to the point. I know you are a busy woman." He grabbed a small bell and rang it.

A woman came into the room. "Yes, Mr. Odoo?" she humbly responded.

"Please bring me something nice to drink. Will you have something?" he asked KoKo.

"No, thank you."

The woman bowed then hurried to fulfill his request.

"Kayson is like a son to me. I need him to help me take this business of mine to another level."

KoKo looked on and listened with a careful ear.

"I started off a lot like him. Ambitious, hungry, and fearless. In a small amount of time I had built an empire. With that came a lot of friends, but even more enemies. The right force of hands later"—he paused and smiled—"I have more

168

friends than I can count, and now my enemies wish they had the same favor."

KoKo nodded her complete understanding. Mr. Odoo was a killer just like her. And what sugar couldn't win, hot pepper would destroy.

"We are planning a huge move to America, exporting and importing. Your husband has invested a great amount into this move, and I need protection and movement of product."

"No disrespect. But what does this have to do with me?"

"Glad you got to the point for me. I am an old man. I tend to ramble." He paused as the maid brought in his drink. He took a few sips and then began to speak KoKo's language, gutter.

"I need you to make sure that if a man's heart holds contempt, you blow his brains out in front of his whole family, so they will never forget that we own the very air they breathe." He dropped the peace from his face, and a dark gaze peered back at KoKo. "I need the work to be clean. My money is legit, and I need to move it and other things across the borders with precision. And I need you to help me make sure that happens."

"What is in this for me?"

"A million on every ten."

"How much are we moving?"

Mr. Odoo smiled. He saw the interest in her go way up when he spit the figure in her direction. "I was going to have you work with my daughter. But I can see that would be like gun powder and fire. So I am asking to have you work with my son. He is a better businessman than me. Plus, he has the same desire you have, kill or be killed. With the two of you together, I know our money will be safe."

As he said that, his son Peppa walked in. Standing about 5-feet 10-inches and 170 pounds and well put together, he appeared to be both Indian and black Guyanese.

"This is my son, Peppa." He will take the meeting from here. Mr. Odoo stood up. "Thank you for gracing me with your presence. I am here if you need me." He kissed her hand and looked at his son.

"Make this young lady feel at home. She is a very smart woman." He patted his son on the back and exited the room.

Peppa was amazed by her beauty, but he was not the type to pick flowers from another man's garden. He had the highest respect for Kayson and would never disrespect his home.

"How are you? I have heard so many great things about you," Peppa said, also taking KoKo's hand and kissing it.

"That's funny. I have never heard of you," she said, feeling a little more on the same playing field as Peppa.

Peppa smiled. "Straight to the point just like Kayson."

"Listen, I have already had a bad taste put in my mouth by a member of your family, so you will have to excuse me if I am skeptical about this whole operation you are running."

"I understand," he calmly stated, enjoying her forwardness.

"I need you to say some shit I can feel good about, or let me go because I have shit to do."

"Fair enough. My father has a vision for this family. But I have another. He is moving products. I need to move something else."

He had KoKo's full attention. "Continue." She encouraged him.

"I have a drug connect that needs to move some heavy weight. I need that done as soon as possible. I have had him on hold for a month waiting to meet you."

She had been looking for a new connect, and with her rations getting low she needed him more than he needed her. "What's in it for me?"

"Whatever you want. I am at your mercy. I will say this. Your money is worth more in my country. I can flip everything you bring in and triple it."

"Why don't you just make the move yourself?"

"I don't have any connection to the streets in America. There, I am green, just like you are green here. But with my connect and your muscle and street savvy, we can blow this shit up." He put a slight smile on his face.

"What did my husband say when you told him?" KoKo probed.

"He turned me down. He is trying to go legit. He wants his hands away from the drug game. He is much like my father. He wants to get out, be safe, and comfortable. Me, I am ready to get dirty."

KoKo sat for a few minutes thinking, and then she went straight into business mode. "You have to get it to a secure place. Florida would be my guess. I will have it picked up and disbursed into several places. The third party will take care of your pockets. I will be responsible for the sales and the transfer of money between me and the connect, who I need to meet before I go forward."

Peppa nodded in agreement.

"Lastly, I will talk to Kayson. I have a different persuasion than you."

"Deal." He reached out to shake her hand. "This needs to stay between me and you," he stated before pulling his hand back.

"The last thing I will ever be labeled is a snitch."

Peppa gave her a bigger smile. "Tomorrow we make you very friendly with a very rich man."

KoKo stood up in an effort to leave.

"Why don't you stay for dinner?" he offered.

"No, thank you. Kayson told me don't eat and shit in the

same place," she said, heading to the door.

Peppa was impressed. He knew he had a real bitch in his presence, and he was going to take full advantage of listening and learning everything she was willing to teach.

KoKo was escorted back to the car by the same gentleman. She couldn't believe what had just fallen into her lap. Here she thought this was all bullshit, when in actuality, it was a blessing in disguise. She had to thank God her husband was so sexy, because if it wasn't for Yuri's attraction to Kayson, she would have never been redirected to Peppa.

- 28 -
Dinner is Served

KoKo made the connect and set up the first shipment, which would come with Mr. Odoo's shipment. She felt a bad for keeping it from Kayson, but she needed to at least do a few drops to get the crew situated before she stepped back. KoKo flew to Atlanta to check on Goldie and Night before she went home. With all the traveling, she was exhausted. She took a long hot bath, and then jumped between her sheets and fell fast asleep.

Kayson had been on the road also for the last couple weeks, and finally he was on his way home. He cruised the streets of the city, fantasizing about Mrs. KoKo and how good it was going to feel being between her chocolate thighs. He grabbed his phone and hit number one on speed dial.

"Hello," KoKo answered the phone with a raspy voice as she rolled over onto her back.

"Baby, what you doin'?"

KoKo tried to adjust her eyes to see the time on her phone. "Kayson, it's five o'clock in the morning. I'm sleep."

"I'm hungry. Can you get up and fix the Boss something to eat?"

"Baby. Where are you? Why don't you grab something on your way in?" she said, rubbing her eyes.

"That's why I have a wife. Get up. I'll be there in an hour." He hung up.

THE PUSSY TRAP 3: *Death by Temptation*
~ N E N E C A P R I ~

Somewhat annoyed, KoKo looked at the phone and then threw it on the nightstand. Pulling the comforter over her head, she contemplated just lying there and continuing her slumber. After about fifteen minutes, she jumped up and hit the shower. She threw on one of Kayson's big 'A' T-shirts and then headed to the kitchen.

For several minutes she stared in the refrigerator. Finally, she grabbed the steak she had marinating and a few potatoes and some fresh carrots. She placed the steak in the broiler, cut up the potatoes, and put them in a pot of water for boiling. After rinsing the string carrots, she oiled a pan, cut up some onions and peppers, fried them, and then added the carrots to the mix.

As KoKo pulled open the broiler, the aroma hit her nostrils and her mouth began to water. "Damn, I'm a bad bitch in every room in this muthafucka." Quickly, she turned the steak and placed it back.

Kayson stood in the doorway watching her ass cheeks jiggle at the bottom of his T-shirt as she stirred the vegetables in the pan. Instantly, his dick rocked up.

Feeling his presence, she turned and looked over her shoulder. "Hey, babe."

"What you got there?" he asked, coming up behind her.

"I'm in here trying to be *a wife* as you so eloquently put it before you hung up on me." She made quotation marks in the air as she said 'a wife'. KoKo went back to stirring the food.

"Is that right?" He began to run his hands up her legs.

"Kay, stop. You're going to get something started."

"I'm trying to get something started." He nibbled on her neck as he pressed against her. KoKo arched her back. She could feel him rising against her. Closing her eyes, she enjoyed the warmth of his lips on the nape of her neck. "Pay attention. You might burn yourself," he said as he moved his hands to her breasts.

"Be good. I thought you wanted to eat." She slid his hands back down.

"I want some backtalk first." He released the Enforcer and spread her legs with his foot.

"Kayson, you gonna make me burn your food."

He placed his hand on her throat and began nibbling on her shoulder.

"Fuck that food," he whispered in her ear, beginning to pull her away from the stove.

KoKo quickly turned the stove and oven off.

Kayson led her to the island and leaned her forward.

Gripping the counter, she braced herself to feel every inch of his power.

Easing in between her sweet walls, he released a breath and a small moan. "I love you, baby."

"I know," she moaned as he began to stroke her just right. Within minutes, he found and pleasured her spot.

KoKo lowered her head as he gripped her hips and devoured her like he hadn't had her in months.

Kayson was in a zone. Her every moan only made him stroke harder and faster. KoKo's grasp tightened with every forceful movement.

"Kaaay . . . be gentle," she pleaded, just as he was on the edge.

Ignoring her call for mercy, he continued to slide in her wetness, not missing a wall on the way in or out. "Shit!" he said as he began to bust long and hard.

As the last drop drained from his body, he pushed all the way in.

KoKo inhaled as he ran his soft tongue along her neck and back. "Damn, ma. The pussy is hot. I'ma need some more of that," he whispered in her ear as he pulled out. Taking his dick in his hand, he began stroking himself back to full potential.

"Baby, wait!" She turned toward him.

Again ignoring her pleas, Kayson kissed her hungrily.

"Baby," she called out. But Kayson was focused as if she hadn't said a word.

Grabbing her waist, he placed her up on the counter and stood, fitting perfectly between her thighs.

"Kayson," she moaned as he began to tear at her T-shirt, releasing her breasts.

Placing his mouth over her nipple, he sucked gently as he slid in fast and hard.

KoKo grabbed at his shirt as he hit the bottom with every forceful blow.

Moving back, KoKo tried to escape all those inches. "Come here," he growled, pulling her back to the edge of the counter. Sensing her struggle, he grabbed her legs and threw them over his shoulders. Holding her in place, he went to work, again finding it hard to hold back. The pussy was wetter and hotter than usual.

After about twenty more minutes, he was again on edge. "Ssss . . . baby, baby, baby," he moaned as he again released his passion all the way inside her.

KoKo arched her back and received all of him.

Out of breath and satisfied, Kayson pulled her to him. Kissing and sucking her lips, he looked in her eyes. "What you do to the Boss's pussy while I was gone?" he asked as he held her tenderly in his hands.

KoKo grabbed him around his neck and whispered in his ear, "I'm pregnant."

- 29 -

I Remember

KoKo awoke from a night of pampering from Kayson. He spent hours holding her and rubbing her belly, ecstatic that she was pregnant. She could not stop him from smiling. When she walked into the kitchen, he was at the stove doing his thing.

"Good morning," she said, walking over to the stove.

"Did you sleep well?" He leaned over and kissed her forehead.

"Mmmm . . . yes I did." She grabbed the back of his head and tasted his lips.

"What you got here?"

"Just a little something. I wanted to return the favor," he stated, taking the last of the food from the pans and placing it on their plates.

"Sit down," he ordered.

KoKo took a seat and watched her husband come toward her with two plates, wearing a pair of boxers and a chef hat that read 'The Boss'. She just shook her head.

"You think you all that."

"You know how I get down," he said, placing the plates on the table.

KoKo's mouth watered when she saw the homemade blueberry Belgium waffles, Italian turkey sausage, and scrambled cheese eggs.

Kayson placed two tall glasses of orange juice down and

then put a napkin on her lap.

She smiled as he sat down, cherishing the feelings of happiness that they shared.

"Eat. I know you been starving my daughter."

"Daughter, how you know it's not a son?" she said, pouring syrup all over her waffles.

"That pussy was so wet I almost drowned. Had a nigga coming all quick. It wasn't like that when you were carrying Quran," he stated.

"You want to put money on it?"

"No, I wanna put my tongue on it."

"You so nasty." She giggled.

"You already know."

They ate and tossed around a few plans before cleaning the kitchen and then showering. And yes, he put his tongue all over her. KoKo climbed every wall in the shower before he finally released her.

After they dressed, they said their goodbyes. Kayson had to get back to Guyana to oversee the shipment to Florida. KoKo had to get to Georgia to make sure Night, Chico, and the crew were on point to make the pick-up.

KoKo sat in Goldie's living room giving Night the full description of how everything was going to go. Night asked as many questions as necessary in order to carry out his mission. When they were done, he reached in his pocket and pulled out an ounce of sour and started rolling it up.

"You smoking?" Night asked as he lit up.

"Nah, I'm good," she responded and then stood up.

"You ain't smoking?" Night gave her the side eye.

"Nah, I think I'm coming down with something. I'll hit something later."

Night smiled.

"Whatever, nigga." KoKo waved her hand at him. "Last thing." She sat back down.

Night gave her his full attention.

"You remember Butchie, right?"

"That cat that you saved at the pool hall?"

"Yeah. He made good on that favor he owed me." KoKo folded her hands. "He has a cousin out Moreland Ave. He informed up that there is a small beef with Diablo's people out Old Bankhead." She paused.

"What you need done?"

"I need you to go down there and put the right amount of deceit and pressure on to get shit going, so we can distract Diablo so we can move this new shipment."

"You checked everything out?"

"Yeah, this is what I wanted you to take care of, but I needed to have all the pieces in place. Everything just lined up," KoKo said, getting up to answer her phone.

"Hello?"

"Mrs. KoKo, you need to come home now," an anxious Maryam said into the phone.

"What's wrong?" KoKo asked with slight panic in her voice.

Night saw the look on her face and jumped up and went to her side.

"Your mother. She is ranting and refusing to eat or bathe until she sees you. She won't take her medication, or leave her room. I am scared for Quran to see this."

"Pack a bag for you and him. Security will take you to the other house. I'm on my way," KoKo instructed.

"Okay. Please hurry. I worry."

"Just relax. I will handle everything."

"Yes." Maryam hung up.

THE PUSSY TRAP 3: *Death by Temptation*
~ N E N E   C A P R I ~

KoKo called the front gate and assigned two bodyguards to immediately take them to the house she and Kayson shared when he was there.

"What's wrong?" Night asked.

"It's okay. I just need to get to the island," she stated.

"I'm going with you," he said.

"No, I need you to handle this business. We can't miss this delivery. I got it. If anything goes wrong I know what to do."

"You sure?"

"Yes, I got it."

KoKo hopped in her car and headed to the airport.

Some twelve hours later, KoKo walked into her island home not knowing what to expect. She moved quietly from room to room looking for Keisha. When she walked into the den, she saw Keisha seated in the corner of the room in a chair staring out the window and holding her journal constricted in her arms.

Approaching slowly, she walked to her side and placed her hand on Keisha's shoulder.

Keisha looked at KoKo with tears streaming down her face and passed her the book. "I remember everything now," she said as a feeling of calm took over her body.

KoKo slid the ottoman next to Keisha, opened the book, and began to read. The first ten pages were bits and pieces of memories, and then she hit a page that was clear and legible. KoKo fixed her eyes as the words jumped off the pages.

I remember it like it was yesterday. That sexy, chocolate man walked into the club with three of the scariest men I had ever seen. I could see he was the type of nigga that was about his money. He walked over to the VIP section and took a seat. All eyes were on him, and I could see he loved every second. Immediately, I went to collect all the information I could find on him.

"Do you know him?" I asked my girl Shay.

"Girl, you don't know who that is?" she asked me with her face all twisted up.

"Bitch, if I knew who it was I wouldn't be asking you," I responded.

"Don't get smart. You asking me questions."

"Whatever! Who is it?"

"That's Malik. You know, from down the hill?"

"Not that nigga that be getting it with them New York niggas."

"Yes, that's the one," she said, slowly nodding.

"Damn, he little as hell."

"Yeah, he is short, but he is a beast, and bitches be all on that dick. So something must be big in his little world," Shay said, turning on her bar stool and ordering a drink.

I sat watching him interact with different people who surrounded his table like he was a superstar. In that crowd I could see the fake and the real. The sad part was, he was a man that had a lot of power, but had surrounded himself with a bunch of yes men. That was always a problem when you're a nigga who might need an honest opinion, because a nigga will be sucking your dick so hard he will let shit slide. That night would prove my every thought to be true.

I went to the bathroom to get my usual, an ecstasy pill and two lines of coke. I stood in a stall in the men's bathroom smoking a joint to top off my high, when I overheard some niggas talking about robbing Malik, and if shit got ugly "kill that nigga". That shit sobered me right up. I waited for them to leave the restroom. I carefully slipped out into the club, grabbed a match book from the bar, wrote my number and name on it and went straight to Malik's table. Cutting through the crowd of chicken heads and hood rats, I walked right up to him. When he saw my openness, he flashed me a pretty white smile that caused my stomach to flutter. Leaning in, I put my mouth to his ear and filled it up with all I heard.

When I stood back, his whole face changed. He went into kill mode. I slid him the match book and walked off.

The next day I got a call from Shay who filled me in about the murder at the club when I left. She rambled on for over five minutes before she said, "Yeah, that nigga you were all eyes on put some niggas on their ass. He ain't no joke," she said, laughing and rattling on like a pebble being tossed around in a big can.

"All right, thanks for the news, As the Hood Turns," I said as I prepared to hang up.

"You going out tonight?"

"Hell no! Shit is going to be rough for a couple days, but I'm sure you will fill me in."

"Whatever, bitch! Bye." Shay hung up.

I put the phone on the receiver and went to the kitchen to fix myself a bowl of cereal. As I poured the cereal and milk, I thought about how I had just helped Malik out, and how the tables would have turned on him had I not pulled his coattail about them fag ass niggas. I grabbed a spoon and my bowl and prepared to sit and eat. Soon as I got comfortable, my phone started ringing again. I almost didn't answer, fearing it was Shay calling back to talk shit, but my instinct said 'get up now'. I ran to the phone, picking it up on the fourth ring.

"Hello?"

"Is this Keisha?" the male voice came through my receiver.

"Why? Who is this?"

"Malik," he answered.

Oh shit, I thought but remained calm. "Oh, whats's good?"

"You," he shot back. "I wanted to come see you. I owe you."

"Oh, it's all good. I only did what your team should have."

"I see." He chuckled. "You live in Orange on Hickory Street, right?"

"Maybe." I tried to feel him out.

"I'll be around there at about four o'clock. Meet me at the Harmony Bar, since you don't want me to know where you live," he said real smooth.

"Okay, see you then." I hung up, ready to scream to the top of my lungs. I sat in my chair, smiling from ear to ear. When I was done eating, I went and took a shower and got dressed.

When the clock read 3:30, my heart began to beat fast. "What is wrong with you, bitch? It's just a man, damn. Calm down," I said aloud to myself as I grabbed my keys and headed out the door.

I sat at the bar until 4:40 before I decided to leave. I paid my tab and got up. When I got close to the door, in walked Malik and this tall, handsome dude who was fly from head to toe.

"All that money you making and you can't afford a watch?" I asked, then walked past him.

"Damn, it's like that?" Malik yelled as I hit the door.

"I don't do late. Maybe next time you will be on time," I said, opening the door. Then I walked out, leaving the two men standing there looking at each other.

When they got outside, I was gone.

A few seconds later, he turned the corner and I was walking fast and picking up speed.

Malik pulled up next to me and rolled down his window. "Yo!" he yelled out.

"Yo?" I stopped and looked at him.

Malik jumped out and walked up to me. "Look, I have an

opportunity for you to make some money. I like the way you carry yourself. But don't get it fucked up, I am not that nigga. I don't chase women, they chase me," he said real serious, then gave me a sexy smile.

"I can get money, but don't ever act like I'm the type of bitch that don't deserve respect, because I will chase that ass all right, and when I catch up to you, regret will be written all over your face," I shot back, staring in his eyes. We shared a few seconds of heat before his boy hit the horn.

"That's my boy, Sadeek. I think he wants to holla at you," he said, filling my heart with disappointment.

"Oh, your boy wanna holla? What about you?"

"I would but my wife might be mad if I brought something this sexy home with me at the end of the night."

Married. The word left a bad taste in my mouth. "The good ones are always taken."

"Be patient," he said, lifting some of the disappointment and replacing it with a little hope.

"Come take a ride with us."

I took a ride with them and that ride changed my life. I went ahead and kicked it with his boy, but he was no Malik. All we did was fight and fuck. That shit got real old real fast. Sadeek was the type of nigga that wanted to be in control, but couldn't maintain self-control. A bad combination for business, Malik used to always tell me when I came running to him about Sadeek. I was on the brink of just killing the nigga and pushing his dead ass in the Hudson, when Malik reminded me that everyone in his organization was important, and I needed to just be patient and things would play into my favor.

One night, me, Malik, Sadeek, and Raheem sat in the club talking shit and relaxing from all the running we had been doing. Malik looked over at a group of girls that were passing bottles and flossing.

"Yo, that's the bitch with all the mouth who tried to get rowdy at The Rink last Saturday," Malik announced.

"Which one?" I asked as I went in 'whoop ass' mode.

"That bitch with the red stretch pants."

Without hesitation, I jumped up, grabbed the champagne bottle by the neck, and headed in their direction.

I gripped the bottle then tapped the girl on the shoulder. When she turned, I smacked her in the mouth, knocking her over the table and causing a stream of teeth and blood to spill from her mouth on her way to the floor.

"Next time, bitch, watch your mouth," I spat.

"What the fuck is wrong with you?" One of her girls jumped up but stopped when I pulled out my gun and stuck it in her face.

"What was that?" I asked, looking at the girl frozen in place. "Yeah, I thought so, punk ass."

I dropped the gun to my side and walked away. When I got to the table, the crew was staring at me with pride in their eyes.

"Damn Key, you fucked her up," Raheem said, looking at the crowd that was forming on the other side of the room.

"Fuck that bitch. She got Medicaid," I said, passing them while heading toward the door.

As I walked off I heard Malik say to Sadeek, "Don't look at me. That's your bitch."

"Yeah, but you got her thinking she Teflon."

Malik laughed as they came up behind me.

From that day on, bitches knew I was that Bitch. I took pride in being the only female in an all-male crew, who could slang and bang.

One night when I came in, Sadeek was fast asleep in the bed, which seemed a little fishy being as though I never beat him home. *I stopped and walked to the closet to take off my clothes. When I opened the closet, this bitch jumped out and tried to run past me. I caught that bitch by the back of her head and pulled my nine.*

"Bitch, make the wrong move and it will be your last move," I warned.

Sadeek jumped up. "Hold up, ma. Let me explain," he pleaded.

I let off a shot in his direction. "Don't make me kill your punk ass."

"Fuck is wrong with you?" he yelled out.

"You got a bitch in my house? In my bed!" I yelled, smacking the woman in the head with the gun. I pulled her to the floor and rested the gun at the top of her head.

"Chill the fuck out, yo!" he yelled again.

"You want me to chill?" I asked as I pulled back the hammer, ready to blast both of they ass.

"Keisha, don't!" he yelled out like a bitch.

The chick was crying and begging for her life, which only fueled my fire.

I smacked her on the side of her face and kicked her in the back. The woman crawled into the corner and cried with her hands over her head.

Sadeek was both relieved and afraid to move.

I looked at him as I struggled to create the words to say to his sorry ass. "The only reason why you're still alive is because I don't want to fuck up my new carpet. Get your shit, get your bitch, and get the fuck out. I'm going to leave this house, and when I get back you better not be nowhere in sight," I warned as I turned to walk away.

"Dirty bitch," I said, passing her and spitting in her face.

As I reached the door, I heard him say, 'Dutchess, are you alright?'

Her name played in my head like a bad record as I drove in pain. I didn't know what to do or think. I drove all the way down Route 1&9 and got a room at the Swann Inn. Once I was settled, I picked up the phone and called Malik.

"Hello?" he answered with a little panic in his voice.

"I am just letting you know I am at the Swann on 1&9, if you were looking for me."

"What happened? That nigga said something about you pulling out on him."

"Yeah, but did he tell you he had a bitch in my bed?"

"That nigga is crazy. You okay?"

"No," I said, then started crying.

"I'm on my way," were the last words he spoke before he hung up.

Within the hour, Malik was at the door.

When I opened it he walked in, grabbed me by the back of my head, and kissed me long and passionately.

"I should have never let him have you," he whispered, pulling back and looking into my eyes.

"Malik, don't . . ." I said as he placed his lips on mine again.

"Don't fight this shit. We been playing with our feelings for months. You're supposed to be mine," he said as he pulled me close to him. His hands were all over me.

I melted with his every touch. The more his hands roamed, the more I erased the worst evening of my life. Within minutes, we were both naked and in a full embrace.

As he laid me down on the bed, I began to replace the love for Sadeek with the pleasure of finally being able to have Malik in my presence and between my thighs. He entered me, filling me up with all he had to offer. The power he had during the day, doubled between the sheets. Finally, I understood why *females were lining up to be chosen.*

Softly he whispered in my ear as he stroked away my pain, "You're mine." He repeated those two words between kisses.

Shit, that nigga had me at hello.

After that night, we were inseparable. The only regret I had was that he begged me to take Sadeek back, and we had to hide what we had. I hated Sadeek. Every time I looked at him, I wanted to choke his ass out.

Two months after Malik and I slept together, I found out I was pregnant. I was ecstatic. But again, I could not celebrate the way I wanted to because I had to pretend the baby was Sadeek's. Thank god I had given him some pussy right before I busted him with that bitch, or it would have been some shit in the wind.

Malik kept telling me I needed to be patient and hang in there. He had some big shit planned that would take us to the next level. He had a new connect, this nigga named Dread out of Chicago. He was moving big weight, and we were going to make a mint. Malik had taken a few trips out to see him and business was picking up. The other thing Malik had cooking was this banker. This dude was supposed to help us start changing our dirty money into clean money. Malik was going to throw an end of the summer party to bring everyone up to speed on what was going on and where we were going.

The night of the party came, and Malik's house was full of all kinds of people I had never seen. This cat named Scarie, who came representing Dread, looked like he had something up his sleeve. A few times I peeped Sadeek trying to get a side conversation going, which he quickly put an end to. The men talked and socialized until the sexy man in the suit came through the door.

The whole room came to attention, and the whole mood

changed. He was dressed in a three-piece chocolate brown linen suit. He looked like he shit dollars, pissed gold, and his dick dripped diamonds. And he had a bad bitch on his arm that looked like she could answer yes to every question.

"Damn, that nigga is a boss," my Aunt Pat came over elbowing me.

"He damn sure is," I said with clenched teeth.

"That bitch look like money too," she whispered.

Just as I was about to respond, Malik called me and he waved me over.

"I'll be right back," I said to Pat, who was all eyes as I walked over to Malik.

"This is Keisha. She is a reliable member of my team. We gonna handle that business we talked about."

"Is that right?" the man said real smooth and looked me up and down. He made my heart drop straight to my coochie. When his sexy hazel eyes met mine, I lost my breath.

I had to pull my shit together real quick. "Hi, how you doin'?" I said.

"I'm good now," he shot back "This is my baby, Mo. She'll be working with you from time to time. I want y'all to exchange information," he instructed. He rubbed her back then pulled her close to him. She looked up at him like he was the only one in the room. He leaned in and kissed her lightly on her lips, squeezing her butt a little before looking back at us.

"Handle ya business," he gently ordered.

That bitch floated over to me like she had helium in her shoes. I stood there thinking that nigga must be eating that pussy for breakfast, lunch, and dinner.

"Where can we talk?" she tranquilly asked.

"Kitchen is good," I said, leading the way.

From that day forward, our shit went straight to the top.

THE PUSSY TRAP 3: *Death by Temptation*
~ N E N E C A P R I ~

The only snag in our perfect life was the day I got busted. There I was facing racks of time. It would be that Mr. Wells, the guy in the fancy suit, had more connections than we knew. He was able to get my baby released to my Aunt Pat and then get me out two months later. When I hit the streets, it was business as usual, except my status was taken up a notch. Something that didn't sit well with the men in the group. And Sadeek was becoming more and more green with envy. I was tight with everyone at the top and making more money than he was. Because he couldn't faze me any other way, he started messing with that bitch Dutchess again, but I didn't give a fuck. I had Malik and my baby.

Everything came to an end when Scarie started making too many trips to Jersey. Dread put him on a short leash, and he was not feeling it. Time passed, and the more I gained respect, the more Sadeek tried to disrespect me.

Sadeek crept in the house at 4 am trying not to wake me up. He lay on the couch and put one of his legs on the arm rest. He had just begun to doze off when he was awakened by an ice cold shower. I doused that nigga with a cup of water, ice and all.

"What the fuck!" Sadeek jumped up and tried to adjust his sight.

"Yeah, muthafucka. You think you can just walk in my fucking house at four in the gotdamn morning and just lay your head down and go to sleep?" I was pissed off. I was starting to hate even the thought of Sadeek.

"I was taking care of some shit. You lucky I ain't jump up and slap the shit out of you!" He walked to the kitchen talking shit and trying to dry off. I wanted to grab a knife and carve his ass up real nice.

"Yeah right, muthafucka! You ain't that crazy. However,

you got to go."

"Go where? Why the fuck is you trippin at four in the fucking morning?" he yelled, bumping me on his way back to the living room. I had to catch myself from going into the wall. I caught my balance and went off.

"I don't give a fuck what time it is or where you go. I can make a suggestion though. Start with the bitch whose pussy you just climbed out of. Go back and knock on her fucking door."

"I wasn't with no bitch. I was taking care of business." Sadeek was lying his ass off. I knew his dirty ass had been fucking with whatever bitch he could get his dick in.

"Look, I can't take this shit no more. You got to get the fuck out. You can leave by will or by force. You draw it up."

Sadeek looked at me like he wanted to knock the shit out of me, but he wasn't crazy. He knew that Malik would take his fucking head.

"Step lively, muthafucka. And give me my keys." I put my hand out with major attitude.

Sadeek reluctantly handed me the keys and headed to the door. He opened the door then turned to me and said, "I guess you can go back to playing house with Malik."

"Don't worry about what the fuck I do with Malik. You just worry about those dirty bitches you stick your dick in."

I guess Sadeek thought about what I said and then responded, "If you wasn't so busy giving my pussy to the next nigga I wouldn't be fucking other bitches." He gave me the dirtiest look then headed out the door.

I slammed the door shut behind him. "Sheeeit . . . you damn right I'm fucking Malik, and his dick is good as hell!" Then I thought about how he was all up in it the other day. I headed back to my room and hopped in the bed. I was free.

The next morning I met with Mr. Wells, and he made me an

THE PUSSY TRAP 3: *Death by Temptation*
~ N E N E   C A P R I ~

offer I could not refuse. And ate my pussy while doing it. I tried to resist, but he had a magnetism about him that rendered a woman incapable of having reasonable thoughts while in his presence. We wrapped up our meeting with him feeling empowered and me feeling ashamed. I defended my behavior with thoughts of, Well, Malik is married. That only worked when we were apart, but when we were together I felt like dirt. I knew Malik loved me, but I knew he would never leave his wife. So to compensate for what I was missing, I met Tyquan for lunch every Wednesday, and he erased all my fear and grief.

Once after our rendezvous in his office, Mo stopped by, and I could tell she smelled sex in the air. He was talking to her but looking at me.

Monique looked in my direction, and I could see disgust in her eyes. She walked out of his office with a plan. It was written all over her face.

The last twenty years of my life have been a blur. The beatings, the pain, the strangers. The only thing that I know to be real is KoKo, my baby. She is the best of me, the only thing I ever got right.

KoKo closed the book and looked over at her mom, who was now fast asleep. She had so many questions, but they would have to wait. Once she covered Keisha up, she sat in the chair by her bed. KoKo wanted her face to be the first one she saw when she woke up.

- 30 -
Tell All or Risk All

Baseem walked into the pool hall with Pete in full 'stay the fuck outta my way' mode. He walked right past everyone in attendance, not even making eye contact. Everybody looked up from the pool table and bar as he went straight to his office.

Pete stopped at the bar to get at Chucky.

"What's up, my nigga?" He shook his hand and gave him a half hug.

"Y'all made some changes up in here. Shit look nice," he said, looking around at the new arrangement. Baseem had the walls painted a glossy black matching a black galaxy granite bar and all black pool tables with glow-in-the-dark balls. With the lighting, that shit was popping. The gray sandstone top tables matched the silver stools and chairs and the smoke gray mirrored walls.

"Yeah, Bas been making a few changes here and there. How was your flight?" Chucky asked Pete, who had just got back from Cali.

"Long as hell. I had a layover, then this lady sat next to me and talked my fucking ear off."

"That's fucked up. What's up with our boy?"

"I can't call it. He was quiet all the way from the airport. KoKo here?"

"Nah, she outta town."

"Ai'ight, let me go have a sit down with Bas. I'll see you

on the way out."

Pete bumped fist with Chucky and headed to the office.

Pete walked in the office and closed the door. Taking a seat on the couch across the room, he kicked his feet up on the coffee table and rested his hands on his chest. "So what's up for the evening?" he asked Baseem as he tried to kick back from his long flight.

"I need you to make some runs before you go to the hotel. I gotta leave town for a few days. Get with Chucky and whatever he got going on, ride with him."

"Got you."

"Everything good on the West?"

"Yeah, we maintaining. That nigga you were locked up with. We finally took care of the last of his crew and expanded on his territory. It was touch and go for a minute, but you know how we get down."

"How is the supply?"

"We copped a few keys from KoKo's boy, Wadoo, but that shit is almost gone. KoKo said a few more days, so we riding on that."

Baseem swiveled in his chair, rubbing his chin.

"Bas, Tori is here to see you." Chucky peeked into the office.

"Let her in. You can go get with Chuck," Baseem told Pete. "I'll see you in a minute."

"Ai'ight." Pete got up and headed to the game room.

Tori walked into the office with her tight black jeans and black shirt, as it was customary to wear black at night to the pool hall.

"Hey Baseem," she said, walking right over to him and kissing him on the cheek.

"What's good, ma?"

"Well"—she perched herself on the desk and crossed her legs—"I have been spending a lot of time with Savage, and I have not seen anything yet. If he's up to something, he is very careful, because I checked that nigga's phone and everything, and I didn't see anything. But you know I will stay on it."

"Nah, fall back a little. I don't want him to know you on him like that. Plus, I need you to do something else for me." He paused, looking into her eyes.

"Anything for you, Baseem," she cooed.

"It's like that?"

"You already know," Tori shot back.

"Meet me at my apartment in an hour. I need a going away present."

"You want it wrapped, or unwrapped?"

"Unwrapped, and you know I like it wet, so feel free to start without me." He stood up and handed her the keys and a knot of hundreds.

"See you in an hour." She turned to walk away.

"Tonight when you're unable to speak or walk, blame it on them jeans," he said real smooth.

Tori looked back and smiled on her way out the door.

Baseem sat back in his seat and thought his plan through thoroughly. He was getting some very mixed feelings about all the stuff that was going on. Although he was holding down New York, he needed to see what Night was doing in Atlanta, and maybe find out what KoKo was doing as well.

Baseem got up and checked the office over. He hit the lights, locked up, and rolled out. Once he hit the bar and left specific orders with the staff, he spoke to security. Lastly, he stopped at Chucky and Pete's table and dropped his flight schedule in their ears.

"Tori was smiling big on her way outta here." Chucky had to fuck with him.

THE PUSSY TRAP 3: *Death by Temptation*
~ N E N E   C A P R I ~

"Oh shit. What happened to wifey?" Pete asked with a smirk on his face.

"She good. But a nigga just did three years. I gotta catch up."

"You know KoKo don't like us fucking with the help," Chucky shot back.

"If it was up to KoKo, none of us would get no pussy. Be walking around this muthafucka with dry dicks and attitudes. Let me get outta here. I'll see y'all in a couple of days," Baseem said, heading to the door.

When Baseem got off the plane, he caught a cab to the hotel. Then he had Chico pick him up and show him around.

"Is this your first time down here?" Chico asked as he pulled off from the front of the Ritz-Carlton.

"Nah, me and Kayson used to come down here for that Freaknik shit back in the day."

"Damn, I haven't talked about that shit in a minute. Freaks use to be acting the fuck up out there." Chico brought up some memories.

"Where we headed first?" Baseem asked, changing the subject. He was not trying to skip down memory lane.

"I'ma take you by a few trap spots. Then I'll take you to the club. Night should be there by then."

"Ai'ight." He sat back and looked out the window. Baseem's eyes bounced all over the sight of women with big colorful weaves and dudes with long shorts and sweat socks pulled up to their knees. It was funny how even though they all had the same kind of hoods, they all were filled with very different people.

After Chico took Baseem on the tour of the trap spots, he headed for Golden Paradise. They pulled into Chico's spot and got out.

When they moved through the back entrance, Chico had to straighten a few workers out. The cook was coming out of the storage room with one of the dancers.

"What the fuck is you doing?" Chico got up on him.

"I was ju—"

"Nigga, don't play with me. I know what the fuck you were doing," Chico barked. "Get yo shit and get the fuck out! I'll let Goldie deal with you." He directed his anger at Pinky, one of Goldie's best girls.

"Where the fuck is the back door security?" Baseem asked.

"Good fucking question," Chico responded.

As soon as the words left his mouth, Big Clay came out of the same direction as the cook and Pinky, zipping up his pants.

"Nigga, what the fuck?" Chico said, but before he could get to the next thought, Baseem went into action.

He grabbed a rolling pin and beat the shit out of Big Clay. Several teeth flew out his mouth and blood splashed all over the walls. His body lie lifeless on the hard cold floor.

Baseem stood up with the bloody wooden object in his hand and began reorganizing the whole situation.

"Chico, call the security team. Put two of your best at the front floor and two at the back door, and tell them niggas they better not fuck up. Get Goldie on the phone and tell her to get over here and get these bitches straight. In the meantime, bitch, go the fuck home. Sucking dick in the closet on company time. Hurry up!" he yelled, causing her to jump. "I'm tempted to slap the shit outta you."

Pinky eased past the angry man, heading to the dressing room.

"No, bitch. This way. You can't get shit." He pointed at the back door. "You need to get your shit and follow that dirty bitch out the same way." Baseem looked at the cook, who was shaking in his shoes.

Nervously, he grabbed his backpack and headed to the door.

"The rest of you muthafuckas get to work!" he yelled at the rest of the kitchen staff.

Several members of security ran into the kitchen and paused when they saw Baseem standing there with the bloody instrument and a team member with his face bashed in.

"Y'all niggas need to step up your fucking game. What the fuck is wrong with y'all? You got the boss in the city, and the place ain't secure. Bitches sucking security dick in the closet, and the cook got cum on his hands serving the fucking guests." He looked in each man's eyes.

"This better be the last time I visit this muthafucka and niggas ain't on point. Tighten the fuck up!" he barked.

Chico was dumbfounded. He began speaking in Spanish to a few men, and they went to the back door and posted up. Then he switched to English.

"Y'all stay in the front and the rest of y'all rover." Every one moved to their post.

Baseem looked at him. "You too comfortable. And they too comfortable with you. Separate business from family."

Baseem handed him the rolling pin. "Clean this shit up. Have one of them bitches take me to Night's office."

Chico sent for one of the girls to escort him and had the dead man cleaned up.

Baseem sat in Night's office watching the monitor and running the events that just took place through his mind. KoKo was nowhere in sight, Night was nowhere in sight, and the place they used as common ground was as secure as a nursing home at Jell-O time.

He sat in the big leather chair behind the desk, lit a blunt, and watched the monitors.

When he saw Night pull up and Chico run over to him, he was ready for a fall out.

Night rushed through the club and right upstairs.

When he busted in the office, Baseem swung around in the chair with the blunt dangling from his lip.

"What the fuck happened?" Night asked.

"I know that fat Spanish fucka already told you, so I won't speak on what happened. But I will speak on what's *about* to happen." He put his hand to his mouth, pulled the blunt out, and dapped the ashes in the ashtray on the desk.

"I'm commandeering this area. Whatever KoKo has you on is you and her business. But these niggas think we running a fucking YMCA. This is a business."

Night just stared at Baseem for a minute to make sure he heard him right.

"Did you run that past KoKo?"

"No. And I don't plan on it. My decision is final. I'ma have Taz come down here and help Chico out, so when you're not around these niggas will be on point."

"You funny as hell. I don't take orders from you," Night said and smiled. "You can tell KoKo whatever you need to. But you better not move Taz, and don't get in my fucking way." He locked eyes with Baseem.

"Let me tell you something. I know you have a brotherhood with Kayson, and I respect it to the highest degree. But me and that man go back like rocking chairs. If no one else does, I'ma make sure the shit we built don't fall down around me while muthafuckas hold they dick," Baseem shot back.

Night wanted to say something to ease Baseem's mind, but Kayson wasn't ready for anyone to know yet. So he had to humor him. "Yeah, ai'ight, do you," he said. Night reached down to answer his vibrating phone.

"Hello."

"Night?" Goldie said, her voice cracking as if she was crying.

"What's wrong?" he said, turning his back on Baseem.

"It's my father . . . Please come get me."

"Where are you?" he asked as he could hear the faint sound of sirens in the background.

"In front of his house," she mumbled through the tears.

"I'm on my way."

"Please hurry," she begged.

Night disconnected the call and turned back to Baseem. "Is there anything else?"

"Yeah, where is KoKo?" he asked.

"Don't you know?" he said and then walked out the office.

Baseem wanted to get up and beat his ass like he did the man in the kitchen. But he needed to remain calm, so he could get the information he needed so he would be justified when he put that nigga on his ass.

He placed a few calls, and then called a taxi to the airport, anxious to get back and make sure everything was in place. He wanted to make sure these niggas weren't slipping.

The taxi pulled in front of the airport, and Baseem dug around in his pocket for the money. He paid the driver as he grabbed his bag in preparation to get out. A dark green, shiny F33 BMW 4 series pulled up a few spots in front of him and out jumped KoKo. He was ready to call out her name when he saw a nigga jump out the driver's seat and come around the car and give her a hug.

"What the fuck!" he said, both shocked and puzzled.

The man released her. They shared a few words and then she was off. Baseem watched until KoKo was inside and the man was back in the car.

"Follow that car," he said to the driver, pushing a few

hundred in the slot.

The driver stayed a safe distance from the car so as not to alert him. Baseem sat back trying to figure out what the fuck KoKo was doing. Whatever it was, he was getting ready to get right in her business. She wasn't going to have any other choice but to tell all or risk all.

Rock pulled up to an apartment building in downtown Atlanta, turned his car over to the valet, and walked inside.

When he got into the lobby, he pulled out his cell phone and placed a call. "Hey. You on the plane?"

"Yes, why?"

"Watch your back. Someone was following me," Rock said as he watched the cab pull off through the tinted lobby windows.

Night picked up Goldie and headed to his hotel room he had gotten to have a little privacy.

They walked into the plush suite and turned on the lights.

Goldie was jumpy and shaken.

"You alright?" Night asked, trying to soften his husky voice.

She didn't speak. Goldie just nodded back and forth.

"Come sit down." He took her by the hand and led her to the couch. "Just try to relax. Do you want me to get you anything?"

Again she nodded no.

Night sat back and pulled her head onto his chest and held her tight.

Goldie settled into his arms as tears rolled down her face. "He was all I had," she mumbled.

THE PUSSY TRAP 3: *Death by Temptation*
~ N E N E   C A P R I ~

Night choked up when he heard the pain in her voice. He didn't know what to say or how to feel. He thought he was helping her by erasing the thing that plagued her the most, but it was the total opposite.

"You'll be okay, ma."

"How am I supposed to live without parents?" she said through sniffles.

"You got me," he said, trying to ease her mind.

"He wasn't always bad. He used to love me more than life itself. Daddy's girl, he used to say." Goldie tried to smile through her tears.

"When did he change?" Night asked.

"When my mother died. He was never the same. He left her for a while when she was sick and had my brother with another woman, which only made her condition worse. When he came back she was near death. He tried to manage at first, but the guilt and grief killed the best part of him."

Night began to feel fucked up about what he had just done.

"Today was supposed to be a happy day. I had a surprise for you."

"I'm sorry this is happening to you," he said, realizing what she'd just said. "You had a surprise for me?"

"Yes. Today I found out I'm pregnant."

"Pregnant?" he shot back. "Sit up."

"Yes, I saw my doctor today. I guess it's an extra birthday present." She tried to force a smile.

"Damn, a baby." Night realized she was telling him she got pregnant the night of his little private surprise party she gave him.

"I'm sorry," Goldie said, trying to get up, sensing he was upset.

"Nah ma, you ain't going nowhere." He pulled her back to

the seat. "I'm not upset. I'm just shocked."

"I didn't tell you to make you stay with me. If you don't want it, I understand. I will do whatever you want me to do."

"What I want you to do? What I don't want you to do is kill my baby." Night was conflicted, but he was damn sure not confused. This would be his first child, and he damn sure wasn't going to let her kill it.

"Are you sure?" she asked, looking in his eyes for any sign of uncertainty.

"Yes, I'm sure." He kissed her lips. "I got you." He pulled her into his arms.

"You're all I have," she whispered, not knowing that the man in her arms took away the only family she had

- 31 -
Dutchess

After leaving the island, KoKo stopped in Atlanta to see Rock for some information. He dropped her off at the airport. She then headed straight to Jersey to follow her leads. Dutchess was a name that had come to her two different ways. In her mother's memories, she wrote that the mysterious Dutchess was a sidepiece of the man who was involved in her father's murder. Dutchess was also the name given to her by Fred on his deathbed. KoKo was embarking on uncovering the mystery and putting the last piece of the puzzle in place.

She pulled up to a large green house on Weequahic Avenue, praying that this would put all the things she had already gathered into perspective.

KoKo paid the cab driver and jumped out. After checking her guns, she walked up on the porch and looked around for a bell, but there was none. She rapped on the big wooden door and waited for a response. Impatient, she knocked again. KoKo stepped back and looked at the windows. She also glanced over the banister and down the alley. When she heard the locks clicking, KoKo positioned herself back in front of the door.

"Hello. How may I help you?" the tall, brown-skinned woman asked.

"Yes, is Dutchess here?" KoKo asked, looking the woman

over from head to toe. She could tell Dutchess was middle aged, but she had a very youthful appearance. Her skin was flawless and her curves were pronounced. She was dripping in labels from head to toe, even her perfume smelled expensive.

"Do I know you?" she asked, giving KoKo the same once over. Dutchess also noticed that she too was well dressed and well put together.

"You don't know me, but we know the same people," KoKo said.

"Okaaay . . . so you would be who?"

"Ce'Asia." KoKo looked directly in her eyes.

One of Dutchess's eyebrows went up. She smiled. "It's a pleasure to see you all grown up. Please come in." She moved to the side, allowing her to pass. Dutchess looked down the street in both directions before closing the door.

KoKo walked into her living room, which was set up like an art museum with paintings of black men and women in all types of positions. African statues were in every corner, but no furniture was apparent.

"Please make yourself at home." The woman walked into the living room, spry and confident.

KoKo looked around like, *Where?*

"Oh, not in here. Follow me." She walked swiftly into the next room.

When KoKo walked in behind her, to her surprise it was set up just like the other one.

"Please forgive me. I do my art thing on Wednesdays." Dutchess walked over to the closet and grabbed two foldout chairs and placed them in the middle of the floor.

KoKo took a seat in one, and Dutchess took a seat in the other.

"So, Miss Ce'Asia. What can I do for you?"

"I'm not sure yet. But I need to ask you a few questions,

and hopefully you will be honest."

"I will be as honest as I can. When Fred came to me and said one day you would come for answers, I almost turned him down. But because your dad was a dear friend, I couldn't."

"Did you know my mother?"

"I can't say I knew her. Let's say we shared a common interest."

"You were fucking her man if I'm not mistaken."

Dutchess cracked a smile. "Well, I see you are your mother's daughter."

KoKo didn't change her mood or her words. She sat staring at the woman waiting for her to spill her guts.

"Well, let me paint you a picture if I may. Yes, I was involved with Sadeek, but whatever it was that he and your mother had was over by the time he met me." She paused.

"Your mother never loved Sadeek. She tolerated him. When Malik stepped up his game and claimed her, nothing was the same."

"What do you mean?"

"Sadeek always knew about her and Malik, but he didn't challenge it, and he knew you were not his daughter. When you were born, Sadeek was so proud. He marched up to the prison with me, his mother, and sister. And when they released you, he took one look at you and the smile drained from his face. He knew immediately you were not his." She sat back, folded her arms, and crossed her legs. "Sadeek loved Keisha, and because of that love he claimed you, but couldn't let go of her deception. He took very good care of you those few months until she came home. Then she flipped the script on him. She and Malik got closer, and Sadeek was pushed out. Not just as his boy, but as his business partner."

"So is that why he had them killed?"

"To be honest, all that did was provide the fire he needed to help with the murder. He did not have the power to pull off anything. One night we were together, and he had gone home really late. Then about an hour later, he was right back at my door. They had a huge fight and that sealed it."

"Sealed what?"

"The deal. There was a guy named Tyquan Wells. He was the corporate type, or so it would seem. This nigga was smooth but devious. Because he was into some type of banking, he was flipping their money. But the shit that got things fucked up was he had their money tied in with some mob type niggas.

"See, Tyquan was a hood nigga, but he was smart. He went to school, came back and showed them niggas how to turn that trap money into clean money. When Malik and Sadeek fell apart, that divided the crew. Malik had all the loyalty and connections, and Sadeek just had greed and envy. Tyquan was smart and greedy also, but the thing that fucked it all up was his taste for beautiful women. He had this high-post bitch named Monique. She was like the empress in the house. But the bitch soon found out that she was not the prettiest flower in his garden, and that's when shit got real."

"What you mean?"

"Keisha became the worm in their big red apple. Sadeek wanted her, but couldn't have her. Malik wanted her, but he was married. But Tyquan wanted her and went for it. Being as though Keisha and Sadeek always fought, Sadeek would send me to get his money and Malik would send Keisha. Well, one of those times I was sent to New York to pick up. I caught a cab as usual. When I got out, Mo was pulling up in her Jag. We both walked inside and got on the elevator. When we got to his floor, Monique walked her high-post ass over to the receptionist and announced herself, and the woman kindly told her 'You have to wait a minute. Mr. Wells is in a meeting.'"

KoKo looked at Dutchess, who was on the edge of her seat like the shit happened yesterday.

"You know how you have the door with glass on both sides? Usually, the curtain would be open, but that day that shit was closed, and I could hear music playing. You know, like soft jazz or some shit. Monique looked at that door. Her eyes closed a little, and she started biting her bottom lip. I was like, Oh shit! I sat my happy ass down and waited." She smacked her mouth and shook her head.

"About fifteen minutes later, the door opened and Keisha and Tyquan came out. And honey, fuck if looks could kill. If reading a bitch's mind could kill, Mo would have leveled a whole city block. Keisha was giggling, and he was smiling and looking all relaxed. When Keisha turned and saw us two bitches over there, she smiled this sinister smile that said, *Fuck y'all looking at?* I could have sworn I heard Monique shit a brick. Tyquan said, 'Lunch again on Wednesday?' Keisha turned to him and said, 'Of course, and until then, don't ruin your appetite on cheap shit.' Then she looked at Mo. Tyquan smiled as Keisha walked away."

KoKo sat listening to her recount the facts. It was like she was listening to some *House Wives of Atlanta* type shit.

"Anyway, after that, Mo went on a mission. She went after every nigga he was connected to. She went after Edwin, who was the connect. He then pulled the dope back from Malik, forcing him to fuck with this Dread from Chicago. Then the thirsty bitch went after Dread, but she couldn't flip him. But that nigga Scarie. He jumped right on the opportunity for a come up, and Sadeek's greedy ass was the scandalous one he needed to help with his takeover. The last one she went for was Malik." Her expression became stoic. "Can't nobody tell me she didn't have something to do with what happened to his family." Tears came to her eyes as she pulled up the memories of that time.

"Malik's wife, Sabrina wasn't in our circle. She didn't deserve that shit. And Keisha, regardless of what she did, she didn't deserve that shit either. They tried everything on that girl, but being the bad bitch she was, she made it." Dutchess caught the tears that fell from her eyes.

"So let me get this straight. My mother was fucking my dad and Sadeek and Tyquan?" KoKo asked, still a bit confused.

"Not really."

"What the fuck is not really? Either you fucking a nigga or you ain't."

"She had stopped giving Sadeek pussy long before she slept with Malik. They were more like roommates, but she would let him eat that shit on a regular. I found out from Mo one night when she came down off her throne and had drinks with us that all Tyquan was doing on those Wednesdays was getting his tongue wet too, or as Mo said it in a drunken slur 'Can you believe that all that nigga do is eat her pussy? Fuck him!'" Dutchess laughed. "Keisha was a bad bitch."

"Let me ask you this. What was your role in all this?"

"I had no role. I was Sadeek's woman. I was around when he needed me and that was that. They paid my rent. I let them cook shit up at my house and occasionally watched a kid or two while they made runs. I even watched you." She smiled. "Keisha and I never had words. I guess she knew she didn't want him and didn't care if I did."

"How did you meet Kayson?"

"A few years ago he found me and asked me some of the questions you are asking, but he was more concerned with his father and Nine."

"What do you know about Nine?"

"Well, Nine was like a mediator. He worked for both sides. He worked for Malik, and he worked for Tyquan. But when shit got rough, I believe he turned on them both. But Nine knows your husband very well."

"What makes you say that?"

"He is the one who brought him to my house."

A puzzled look came over her face. "When Kayson came to see you, Nine brought him. And then what happened?"

"They exchanged some information and then left. Nine got in one car and Kayson got in another. I don't know what happened after that. I never saw either of them after that day. I was contacted by Fred and told that Kayson was killed, and if you ever came to look for me to tell you everything I knew."

"What do you know about Pat?"

"No disrespect. But that bitch is crazy. She is what I call a reacher. She wanted to have Keisha's life, so she stayed close to her and reached out for every crumb that fell off the table."

"I guess when she reached out for my father, he reached back."

"Reached back? He wasn't trying to fuck with her. He would have never done that to Keisha. And all that shit about that being his baby. That's bullshit. She didn't pop up with that one until he was dead and gone. Now granted, people may think she looks like him, but shit I'm old school. I believe when a bitch fuck the same kind of dudes all the time, chances are her kids come out looking a certain way if you know what I mean. If you want the truth, I think she cooked that shit up for some money. But you ain't hear that shit from me." She sat back and took a break, and KoKo welcomed it.

KoKo reached in her pocket and pulled out a knot and passed it to her.

"No. I can't take that." She pushed KoKo's hand back.

"There is a lot I should have said and sooner. I'm sorry for everything that you lost." She looked KoKo in the eyes and again got teary.

"Can you tell me one more thing?"

"I can try."

"Do you know who this is?" KoKo reached in her vest and pulled out the picture of the lady and the little boy.

Dutchess took the picture in her hand and began to smile. "Yes, that's me. I haven't seen this picture in years." She held it in her hands, rubbing her finger over it.

"Can you tell me who the child is?"

"Yes," she responded as tears ran down her face. "He's my son."

KoKo watched as Dutchess began to break down.

"He was all I had. And one day he just didn't come home." She wiped her face and stood to grab a tissue from a small box on a nearby display table. "When he was little, I started calling him Boa. Whenever you wanted to put that boy down, he would cling to you. You know, hold your neck, wrap his legs around you. Anything to keep from walking." She chuckled. "I miss him." She sniffled, looking at the picture tight in one hand and wiping her tears with the other.

"You can hold onto that. I believe it served its purpose." KoKo rose to her feet.

"Thank you."

"I believe it's yours anyway." KoKo turned to leave.

"No. I was thanking you for your kindness."

KoKo turned back and looked the woman in the eyes.

"I know about you and Boa. And I know the game well. You came here to kill me, and to be honest I was ready to go. That is, until I released my demons. Then a bitch had to reconsider." She smiled. "So, thank you."

"I did come to kill you. But I can see that on the inside

211

you're already dead." KoKo turned and headed to the door.

- 32 -

Nine Lives

Kayson waited in the shadows of Nine's driveway, carefully plotting his demise. After his meeting with Deborah, he had everything he needed to get the hits off his back. His hand began to sweat as he gripped his .45.

Nine was playing a dangerous game by toying with both sides of the fence, and it was time to make that nigga choose a side or die trying.

A few minutes passed and Nine pulled into his driveway and looked around. The faint sound of crickets filled the night air as his feet touched the ground. He reached for his keys, realizing he left them in the car. As he turned to go back, a monster stood in his face holding a gun between his eyes.

He paused as a knot formed in his throat.

"You got some shit to tell me. And if it ain't what I need to hear, your third eye is going to be open real wide."

"Kayson, you know I have been nothing but honest with you," he stated nervously.

"Have you? Let's go inside and go over a few things."

"I have to get my keys out the car."

Kayson reached in his pocket and pulled out a set of keys. "Here, use your wife's," he angrily stated.

Nine's eyes grew wide, and his whole body got cold. His mouth filled with saliva as he tried to speak. "Please don't hurt my wife," he pleaded, trying to remain calm.

"She's safe for now. But if you don't say something I want

to hear in the next twenty minutes, the call I place will fill the rest of her life with pain and misery."

"I got you." Nine took the keys and began fumbling with the locks.

"And don't try no slick shit. Because even under pressure I will put holes in you that will make an undertaker wonder," he barked as he held his gun firm to Nine's head.

Once the door was closed, he pushed Nine into the living room and forced him to the couch.

"Look, we don't have to do this like this. Just ask me what you need to know, and I got you."

"It seems like you got everybody."

"You know what I do. I have to play the game hard enough to get what I need and smart enough so that in order for others to get theirs, they need me."

"I have about ten more minutes of patience left, and after that I'ma give you what you need and some shit you don't want," Kayson warned as he carefully placed a silencer on the end of his gun.

"Hold up. We had a deal. You need to honor that." Nine raised his voice.

"A deal?" Kayson chuckled. "Nigga, you helped plan my funeral. Ain't no honor in that, muthafucka." Kayson's livid voice bounced off the walls, causing a vibration in Nine's soul that even fear was afraid of.

"Let me make shit right." Nine tried to calm the situation.

"Who is behind the contract?"

"I don't know. I have access to only the money."

"Who is behind the contract?" Kayson growled as his blood began to simmer.

"I don't know." Nine stood his ground.

Kayson was done with questions. He was ready for

answers, so he took a few steps and stood over Nine with an evil grimace and bad intent.

"Who ordered the hit?"

"I dont kn—"

Before the words could leave his mouth, Kayson grabbed him in the throat and smacked the shit out of him with his gun. Blood flew from his mouth, landing on the light colored sofa and glass end table.

"How is your memory now?"

"I do—"

Kayson smacked him again, this time causing a gash above his right eye.

"Please, wait!" Nine put his hands up in surrender. "Tyquan is behind everything," he confessed.

"Muthafucka, you think I'm pussy. You just tried to fuck me." Kayson smacked his ass again, putting a gaping wound on his forehead.

Nine felt like he was losing consciousness. He tried to focus on Kayson, but the blood that ran from his head blurred his vision.

Holding him down hard to the couch, Kayson peered down at him ready to blow his brains all over the room. But he needed that name, and he knew just how to get it. Kayson hit the button on his Bluetooth and said, "Call Night." A few seconds later, he barked his next order. "How is she holding out?" he asked, watching Nine cringe with anguish.

"I'ma ask this nigga one more time. Then I want you to make that bitch closed casket worthy."

"Wait! Please!" Nine yelled. "Please." Tears ran from his eyes.

"Talk, muthafucka," Kayson yelled.

Nine took a breath. "It was Chi. He is Tyquan's boss," he confessed.

Kayson's rage increased. "And you are his bitch." Kayson put the gun in his mouth and blew his skull and brain all over the wall.

"Night, do that bitch dirty," Kayson ordered and disconnected the call.

- 33 -
Paperwork

Full of vengeful thoughts, Kayson walked into the mansion and went straight to his room. He stripped down, hopped in the shower, and began processing the information he just learned. As the hot water ran over his neck and back, he played Nine's last words in his mind. Chi is Tyquan's boss. Lu Chi had saved his life. He had been loyal to Lu Chi for years and had not once expected that he was secretly trying to destroy him.

Kayson knew he needed to plan wise and accurate. There could be no loose ends and no mistakes. Each person had to be dealt with, and each punishment needed to be tailored to fit their treason.

He wrapped a thick towel around his waist, and then headed to his bedroom. Grabbing the remote, he turned on the radio in an attempt to relax his mind. He walked to the closet and threw on some sweat pants and a T-shirt. Then he moved to the safe, spun the combination, and took out all the paperwork KoKo had shared with him.

Kayson headed to his office and poured himself a drink. He sat on his throne and spread the papers out on his desk, going over each one carefully. When he got to the insurance policies, he scanned them vigilantly. The first problem was the policy numbers. Each one was inconsistent with the dates. Then he looked closely at the signature. It was his mother's name, but her signature was a little off.

Kayson sat back and pondered. "What the fuck is going on? And why would my mother sign her name as Wells?" he spoke aloud. He placed the documents aside and looked at the list of names that his father gave her. At the top of the list was Scarie and several names of his crew members followed. Near the bottom of the list was Brenda Watson. Kayson tried to remember where he had seen that name before, but it wasn't coming to him.

He picked up the insurance papers and compared the handwriting. The 'W' in Wells was written the same as the one in Watson. Kayson searched through all the documents with a careful eye. Every signature had a letter that was inconsistent with the next. He grabbed the folder that he got from Deborah and pulled out a single sheet of paper with account numbers on it. He scanned the list, and his eyes fell on one that matched the numbers on Malik's insurance policies.

"That muthafucka!" Kayson said as he searched for the other policy number among the list. When his eyes rested on it, he knew exactly what his father was doing. "This nigga setting up fake policies to hide money, but for what?" He sat back in his seat, grabbed his drink, and sipped while his wheels turned.

- 34 -
Double Cross

Nervous sweat beaded across Savage's nose as he pulled up to the pool hall to pick up KoKo. He rolled down his window to take in some of the crisp winter air. Chucky came over to the car and stuck his hand inside.

"What's up, my nigga?" Savage asked, giving him some dap.

"Ain't shit. It's slow than a muthafucka out here tonight."

"Word? Where's KoKo?"

"She's coming. She in there talking shit and taking money. Her ass been grouchy all day." Chucky smiled. "Where y'all headed?"

"We just taking a ride. You know how she do. I fuck around and end up across country messing with KoKo's ass."

Chucky chuckled and then looked up to see KoKo coming their way. "Stop all that frowning," he yelled out.

"These niggas get on my nerves." She got in the car and shut the door. "Sometimes I feel like a fucking psychologist. I don't have time to deal with muthafuckas wounded inner child."

"What the fuck?" Savage said, looking at her all strange.

"You know she be reading that shit in Kayson's library," Chucky said.

"No, on the real. A grown ass man should not have to be reminded a million times about his duties. Niggas be wanting pussy and a pacifier. Fuck outta here."

"I told you her ass grouchy today," Chucky stated.

"You need a hug?" Savage asked as he passed her the daily profit in a white envelope.

KoKo took it and placed it on her lap. "Fuck you. Let's go."

Savage smiled and shook his head. "Catch you later, brah." He hit fists with Chucky and pulled off heading for the interstate.

"I wanted to take this drive with you, so I could let some shit off my chest," Savage said, looking over at KoKo, gauging her mood.

"What's up?" she asked, looking forward.

"They flipped Taz," he said as if he was telling her that he wanted ketchup with his fries.

"Fuck is you talking about?"

"A few months ago Taz got picked up, and they been on his ass for information ever since." Savage switched lanes and headed for the exit.

KoKo looked over at him as a frown took over her face.

"Hold the fuck up. You mean to tell me that this nigga is a double?"

"Not really. He ain't telling them nothing they can use against us, only small shit on other niggas. But they really want him to turn me, so I can give you up, but you know that ain't something I would do." He stared forward, now anxious by KoKo's cold stare.

KoKo turned to the side and looked out the window. She could not believe what she just heard. She didn't know who she was more mad at, Savage for withholding the information, or herself for missing it. She gazed out the window a little longer, and then she got started. "So you knew all along?"

Savage looked over at her as he began to filter what it was he would reveal. "No. Not all along."

"So you been all in my face hiding something like this from me?" She looked over at him in disgust.

Savage kept his eyes on the road, daring not to look back in her direction as he could feel the heat coming from her seat. "It's some real complicated shit going on." He paused. "But I knew that this was one thing I could not keep from you."

"One thing?" His words illuminated in her mind. "What else are you hiding?"

His lips wanted to reveal all, but his mind took over, and the only word that would leave his lips was, "Nothing."

"Yeah, ai'ight." KoKo opened the envelope and looked over the neatly stacked bills as she plotted what to do next.

"I do need to tell you something else." He confessed as the weight of deceit felt as if it would crush his chest.

"What?"

"It's more to all this shit than you know," Savage revealed.

KoKo looked over at him as his mouth started to move a mile a minute. He was talking, but her mind and heart had shut down as his words pierced her soul. KoKo stared at him and then back at the road and became enraged.

Savage had released all his demons, and the car fell silent.

Then KoKo said, "You's a dirty muthafucka."

"Look, ma. I could have took all that shit to my grave. But I care about you." Before he could turn to see her response, KoKo said, "Take this to your grave, punk muthafucka. Blow!" She put one in his temple.

Savage's blood and brains hit the window as the car started to swerve on the road. KoKo grabbed the steering wheel, but Savage's foot was heavy on the gas, and off the road they went into a wooded area and careened into a tree. The air bags released on impact, smacking KoKo in the face and knocking her out.

Light was beginning to leave the sky as KoKo opened her eyes to hear a voice saying, "Miss. Can you hear me? Are you all right?" a small voice forced its way through the window, and a rain of knocks followed. KoKo turned her head slightly in the direction of the words. Her head was pounding. She slowly reached over and released the locks. The woman opened the door and freaked out.

"Oh lord. Are you okay, young lady? Just sit tight. I'm going to call 911."

"No! Wait!" KoKo pleaded.

"It's okay. Don't worry. I'll get you the help you need." The woman pulled her phone from her pocket, but was stopped by the hot bullets released from KoKo's gun. The woman fell back against the tree, and slid down as her body convulsed in pain.

KoKo staggered out the car, stood over the woman, and put three more shots in her. "I don't need no help. Nosy ass Good Samaritan." KoKo got her bearings, and then stumbled toward the road. She jumped in the woman's car and pulled off doing ninety all the way home. She pulled up to her boy's chop shop in Brooklyn.

"Ma, you okay?" Big John asked as he approached the car.

"Yeah, I'm good. Get rid of this shit ASAP. Call me a cab. Where is the bathroom?"

"In the back," he shouted as he jumped in the car, parked it in the garage, and closed the big metal doors.

KoKo stood in the mirror dabbing tissue on the small cut above her eyebrow. "Shit!" she yelled as she leaned on the sink. Her body started to ache, and a few sharp pains hit the bottom of her stomach. She rubbed her belly and washed her hands. Replaying Savage's confession, she stood staring at herself in the mirror. Within hours, her whole life had changed. She needed a minute to gather her thoughts, but that would have to wait. Her reverie was interrupted by the words, "KoKo, your cab is here." She snatched the door open and headed outside. Once she got in the cab, she began putting a strategy into action.

The cab pulled up a few blocks away from the mansion and KoKo got out and jogged back. Entering the house, she went straight into business mode. She looked at the clock which read 9:15 PM. KoKo called Night to alert him that a meeting was needed ASAP, and to make sure Taz was with him.

"What's up?" Night responded to the urgency in her voice.

"Just do what I asked you." She hung up.

KoKo quickly showered and changed. She wrapped her clothes in a bag, tucked it in a big Gucci bag, and hit the door. Exiting the garage, she threw the bag in her trunk and headed to the spot.

Busted . . .

"Where we going?" Taz asked, feeling a little uncomfortable about Night's silence.

"We gotta meet KoKo. She wants us to make a pick up. Night looked over at him, and then back at the road.

Taz slid down in his seat, pulled his fitted down, and tried to relax.

Night pulled up to an old building in the Bronx and got out the car. Taz looked around, noticing there were no cars in sight. The block seemed abandoned. He stepped out the car with only the flicker of a streetlight to guide his path.

Night walked up to the gray metal door and knocked three times.

KoKo looked out the small, dirty glass window, and then pulled the latch.

THE PUSSY TRAP 3: *Death by Temptation*
~ N E N E   C A P R I ~

When the door opened, Taz's stomach sank to his feet. Immediately, his mind started to race.

"What's up, ma?" Night asked, passing her.

"What's good, KoKo?" Taz asked, forcing a semi-smile in an effort to appear calm.

"Ain't nothing." KoKo slammed the door and hit the latch hard.

Taz jumped and turned around quick.

"Fuck you jumpin' for?" Night asked.

Taz didn't respond.

"We going in the back room," KoKo instructed.

"Ai'ight," Night said, heading through the maze-like hallway to a back room.

Taz followed closely behind him, occasionally looking back at KoKo. He eyed each room as he passed, afraid that something or someone unexpected might pop out.

When Night got to the last room, he stepped aside allowing Taz to enter first.

Taz looked at the empty room and knew exactly what this was. He stepped inside and stood in the middle of the floor.

"I guess y'all found out," Taz said, giving in to the certainty of death he was now facing.

"Nigga, you know what this is," KoKo barked, pulling out a pink and black Sig Sauer and resting it at her side.

Night pulled out two Cult Double Eagles and held them at his side.

"I promise you. I didn't give you up, KoKo," he confessed.

"Muthafucka, you a snitch. Ain't no integrity in that shit!"

"I'm just saying. They came for me, threatening my family and shit. I had to protect mines." Taz raised his voice.

"Nigga, we're your family," Night growled back.

"I ain't got time for this shit." KoKo shot Taz right between the legs.

Taz staggered back, losing his footing and hitting the floor screaming.

"Did you just shoot this nigga in the dick?" Night asked.

"Yeah, he pussy. He don't need it."

"Wait, please. I don't deserve this shit." Taz screamed.

Night stood over him with an evil grimace. "In your next life, ask to be bulletproof, muthafucka." He filled Taz's body with bullets.

Night stood breathing heavy and peering down at Taz like an angry bull.

KoKo stepped next to Night. "You ready?"

"Yeah, but what the fuck is that?" Night asked, looking at her gun.

"What?"

"Why yo' shit pink?"

"Fuck you. I'm trying to get in touch with my feminine side." She glanced at her gun, turned it back and forth, and then looked up at Night shrugging her shoulders.

Night chuckled. "Good luck with that. Come on. We got to pull shit in and make sure our tracks are covered. They gonna be looking for this greasy muthafucka."

- 35 -

The Cross Over

After finding out about Taz's deception, KoKo closed down all the trap spots and relocated them. She even shut down whole cities and moved everyone around. She could not take any chances. Spring was approaching, and it was a good time to do some cleaning. The drugs KoKo needed were moving well. With every one of Mr. Odoo's shipments was KoKo's product. Chico would meet the shipment in Florida and have it dispersed to Georgia, Virginia, Cali and New York. From those locations, everyone else in the organization would pick up.

Peppa sat back stacking his money and earning his respect. He figured that he would make a trip to New York and feel what the big city had to offer. When he arrived at LAX, KoKo had him picked up and brought to the Lion's Den.

Peppa walked onto the ground floor of the bike club and saw all the bike tricks going on. His eyes roamed the crowd, stopping at the half-dressed females in leather and spandex.

"After KoKo takes care of you, you can come down here and snuggle up with one of these bad bitches," Chucky stated as he escorted him to the elevator.

"Take him to KoKo," Chucky instructed security, who stood firm in his post.

The tall, serious man waved Peppa onto the elevator.

When the doors closed, he was again amazed at the action

going on from floor to floor. He was adding up the figures, and from the looks of it, this place KoKo had set up was a cash cow.

The elevator came to a stop and Peppa was directed to the opened door. Security watched as he approached slowly. When he got to the office door, Baseem walked out to greet him.

"How are you? You must be Peppa," he said, extending his arm.

"Yes, and you must be Baseem. We spoke on the phone." He shook his hand.

"Welcome to the city of nightmares. Please come inside." He extended his arm toward the room.

Peppa walked in, and Baseem closed the door.

KoKo turned in her chair to greet her guest. "Good evening. How was your flight?"

"That plane of yours is fit for a king. Thank you," he said, walking closer to her desk.

"Please take a seat."

Peppa sat in one of the white chairs across from her and put his foot up on his knee. "I love this place you have here. I need one of these in my town."

"Make yourself at home," she said, pulling up to the desk. "Would you like something to drink?"

"Yes, please. Something dark and smooth," he stated.

"Pete, please get Peppa a glass of that black rum we just got from Bermuda," she instructed.

Pete poured as KoKo began the meeting. "So how is business?"

"It's well. Things seem to be moving along at a good pace. I really want to up the volume." He paused as Pete passed him his drink. "How do you feel?"

"I am satisfied with the way things are going and so is

Mocha."

"You spoke to Mocha?" he asked, now feeling a little left out.

"Yes, we spoke and came to the conclusion that we will be going a different route. We both appreciate your initial generosity. However, with the direction that we are taking our business, your services are no longer needed."

"What are you talking about?" he asked as his body began to heat up. Sweat formed on his brow as Peppa tried to wrap his mind around the bullshit coming out of her mouth.

"I know you heard me, so repeating myself is not an option," KoKo spat from her seated position.

"Let me get this straight. I brought Mocha to you. I made it possible for you to have safe delivery, putting my family's business on the line, and you go behind my back and cut a side deal, which now has nothing to do with me," he asked, giving her the side-eye.

"This shit ain't personal. It's business. I am a businesswoman. I can only wish you the best in your affairs. I hope that you wish me the same." KoKo looked him square in his eyes.

"My father has been nothing but loyal to you. How could you cross my family?" Peppa was beyond vexed and ready to go off. However, he was not ready for KoKo.

"Let me tell you something, muthafucka. You are the disloyal one. The day you sat in your father's house and plotted to go behind his back and mix illegal business with his legitimate business, you fucked yourself. I have the utmost respect for him and your family, and that is why I didn't kill your sister, and I decided to not kill you. Please don't make me change my mind," she warned.

"You will not get away with this." Peppa stood.

"Did you just threaten her, muthafucka?" Baseem moved toward him.

"I don't threaten," Peppa responded.

"KoKo, I don't know this nigga's father and don't give a fuck about him."

"Relax, Bas. Trust me. This ain't what he wants. Mocha assured me that if he does not get back there and report that New York is fine, then some very important people will be in danger."

"You will have no luck or good fortune. Please take me to the airport." He turned to the door.

"That can't be true. I'm already about to get your fortune. And luck, I don't need that. I walk with a whistle that will cut a nigga's thought in two. I'm good."

Peppa looked back at her, and then at the men in the room, who looked ready to disobey her order and make his day a short one.

Peppa thought he was getting ready to come up. He just didn't understand that once he introduced her to the connect, his ass would be pushed right out the picture. KoKo was never for a middleman. When doing crooked shit, it was better to have less people on the boat as possible. So when the ship went down, there would be limited people to die or tell.

Pete pulled out his banger and then walked him to the elevator. Baseem stood in the doorway.

"I think that nigga is going to be a problem," Baseem said, watching Pete get on the elevator with Peppa.

"He is way more bark than bite. I'm already shaking his tree, and some big shit is about to fall out," KoKo responded. She knew that Peppa wasn't going to move against her, because his father would be more disappointed that he disobeyed. Plus, she had Mocha on her side. He was going to make sure Peppa stayed in line. However, she knew that he would probably be a bitch and tell Kayson. KoKo did not want to have to deal with that beast when he found out she had risked his plan and went behind his back.

- 36 -
Deceit

Later that evening Night pulled up to the Lion's Den and drove into the bike area and jumped out. KoKo was there to greet him.

"After this meeting, I have to get to Atlanta," she said, walking fast behind him while heading to the elevator.

KoKo looked out over the crowd and smiled. Despite all the shit going wrong, she still had successful businesses and legitimate connections that at the end of the day, made it feel that some of the shit she went through was worth it.

"Let me holla at Chuck right quick," Night said, leaving her standing by the elevator.

KoKo stood with her back against the wall, enjoying the bike tricks when something caught her eye. "What the fuck?" she said out loud.

The guy from Golden Paradise that she saw the night she was in Atlanta stood talking to Tori. She moved toward him. She posted herself to the side and watched him touch Tori's face and whisper in her ear. Heat blazed in KoKo's gut. *Who the fuck is this nigga?* she thought as she eased around the crowd to get a better look.

Tori was all wrapped up in his game, and KoKo was ready to snatch her ass by the top of her Mohawk.

Night saw KoKo and tried to follow her gaze.

When he saw Tori wrapped up with the nigga from Atlanta, he too became alerted. "Hold up, Chuck," he said, heading in

KoKo's direction.

Night slid down into the cut behind KoKo and tapped her leg. "You see that nigga?"

"Yeah, he tried to holla at me in the A," KoKo said. "But you see Tori though."

"You know she sleeping with Bas."

KoKo looked at Night with disgust.

"Get that nigga snatched up. Bring him to my office. Have Tori taken to the pool hall. I want the light on both they faces." She headed to the elevator.

Night rose to his feet and looked around the room to assess the situation. He walked over to security and gave the word.

KoKo sat at her desk carefully maneuvering her thoughts.

Five minutes later, Night walked into the office followed by three security guards and the mystery man of the hour.

"Have a seat," Night instructed.

The man walked over to one of the chairs in front of KoKo's desk and casually sat down.

Two guards held post inside, and the other one posted up outside the door. Night stood right behind him, peering down and daring him to do or say the wrong thing.

"First, I would like to welcome you to New York. Can I get you anything? A drink? Something to smoke?" she asked, extending her arm toward the bar.

"No thanks. I'm good," Damien smoothly stated, his gold tooth with the diamond star in the middle shined bright through his sneaky smile.

"Well, let's get down to business then, shall we? Is there a reason why you all up in my ass?" She looked dead in his eyes.

"It's funny that you should ask that. Because I heard that up in yo ass is the place to be. Deadly but definitely worth it," he said, continuing to lock gazes with her.

"Is that right?" she said, looking at him like he'd lost his mind.

"Yeah, it's right. I have been all over the world and been in the company of the best, but I must say. Nothing has been so intriguing than to follow a beautiful, powerful, yet dangerous woman."

"So let me get this straight. You've been following me even though you know it's both deadly and dangerous?"

"I had to be in the presence of the woman who is responsible for the deaths of—" The man rambled off names, dates, and places.

KoKo's blood pressure shot straight up when he ended his list with Savage.

"Look. I appreciate your extra hospitality, but if you don't mind, there's a woman downstairs that needs a long, deep conversation, and I'm trying to give it to her. Plus, the Atlanta PD is expecting me back to work on Monday." He rose to his feet. "Y'all enjoy your evening." He turned around.

"I hope your wife got life insurance," KoKo said.

"Is that a threat, Mrs. Wells?"

"No, I just heard your line of work is deadly, but I'm sure it's worth it." She gave him an evil smirk. "Travel safe."

"You too," he shot back.

Pausing to look up at KoKo, Night scowled and then headed to the door. The guards were posted up strong, ready to air his ass out.

"Let him go," KoKo ordered.

They stepped aside slowly and escorted the gentleman to the elevator and then out the door.

"How the fuck this nigga get past us?" Night yelled, walking away from the monitors.

KoKo sat in her chair tapping her foot and reviewing in her

mind who knew what and who was talking.

"Did Taz say who he gave up?"

"Nigga, you was in the same room I was in," she said, looking up from her seat.

"What did Savage say?"

KoKo stared at the desk trying to review the conversation. "Well?"

"Hold the fuck up! I'm thinking."

"If yo' ass wouldn't kill niggas so fast, maybe we could get some information out of 'em."

"Fuck you! Don't blame this shit on me. If you weren't down there fucking Goldie into la-la land you could pay more attention. That snake popped up in your city."

"Shit!" Night yelled out.

"This fucking pregnant shit is cramping my style. My shit is all over the place—memory fucked up. I'm missing shit. Can't smoke. You know a bitch need to blow something to have a good thought."

Night paused and looked back at KoKo. "Pregnant?"

"Don't say the word. Just hearing it makes me sick."

"That's why your ass getting thick. I thought it was because my brother been handling his business." He put a little smile on his face.

"Yeah, he handling his business and fucking mine up at the same damn time." She shook her head.

"I slipped up too, KoK," he confessed.

"Oh, shit. Rain gonna kill yo ass."

"It is what it is." He shrugged.

"We both slippin'. This is some bullshit," she said. They both started laughing.

Ai'ight, enough of this mushy shit. We gotta get on point," KoKo said, sliding all the way into her desk.

Night walked over and took a seat. He was about to start talking when he looked up and saw Baseem moving like fifty miles per hour. "Look at ya boy."

KoKo turned to the monitor and could see that Baseem was pissed. His nostrils flared, and his body language said 'I'm about to kill a nigga'.

"Here we go," KoKo said.

"You know he about to come in here with some bullshit, right?" Night sat back.

"Yes, and I am not in the mood. You think Kayson gonna be mad if I kill 'im?" she joked.

"Maybe a little bit," Night held his hand out to measure about an inch with his fingers.

"What the fuck is going on?" Baseem burst in the office.

KoKo and Night were sitting back trying to remain calm.

"What are you talking about?" KoKo asked calmly from her desk.

"Tori hit me up and said they snatched her up and are holding her at the pool hall until they hear from you."

"And?"

"What the fuck you mean 'and'? I had her on some shit. You just fucked that up."

"You had her on some shit, or you had her on your dick?" KoKo spat.

"Don't fucking play with me. I ain't these muthafuckas. You know how I get down."

"Yeah, I heard."

"Look, stay the fuck outta my business! You need to worry about who you fucking."

"What the fuck is you talking about?" KoKo chuckled.

"Yeah, I saw yo ass with that Atlanta nigga. Rock, is it?" he asked, looking at her with the side-eye. "Yeah, talk some shit now. While you was all up in that nigga's face, that

235

detective was all in yo' ass."

"You don't know shit about me." KoKo didn't even bother to clarify her actions.

"I know one thing. Yo' ass is slippin'. Out here chasing niggas and doing sloppy ass murders." He paused and looked at Night.

"This muthafucka," he stated and then continued his rant. "From this moment on, I'm taking over this shit. You're relieved," he said to Night.

Then he turned his attention to KoKo. "I don't know what the fuck you been doing, but go ahead and do you. But New York is mine now. I'm calling a meeting to sit everybody down. This shit has gotten way outta control."

"Relieved? Muthafucka, you can't relieve me." Night stood up in Baseem's face.

"It's already done." He glared back at Night.

Night turned to KoKo. "I'ma let you handle this, because this nigga done lost his muthafucking mind." Night turned and walked to the bar to keep from laying hands on Baseem.

"No, I'm good. It's y'all niggas who got the game fucked up," he yelled.

KoKo was trying her hardest to remain civil, but Baseem was one wrong word away from getting it.

"We built this shit!" he shouted. "My brother put his blood, sweat, and tears into this organization. He sacrificed his fucking life! And you gonna sit here and fuck it up."

That was the last straw.

"Well, Kayson ain't here, and all of this"—she held her arms out—"is my shit, muthafucka." There was no turning back now. "He left all this shit to me. *I* make the fucking decisions around here. Who the fuck you think you are? Come up in my shit and order me around. No, fuck that! *You're relieved.*"

"You always talking about what you owe him. Well, here!" She went in the drawer, pulled out a wad of money, and threw it at his feet. "You paid your dues, and here is the fucking change." She stood breathing heavy as sweat formed on her nose. "But I will tell you this. If you owe somebody, it's me. You owe me some fucking respect!" She looked him square in the eyes.

Baseem was both shocked and pissed. If it were anybody else, he would have blown her fucking head off. Staring intently into her eyes he said, "I gotta take a piss," in an effort to get out of her presence as quickly as possible.

"Well, be careful. Don't let your big balls weigh you down on the way out," KoKo said as he reached the door.

When he left the room, KoKo sat in her chair. Her hands shook and her heart raced.

"KoKo, you had to go there."

"Not now, Night," she said as she tried to calm down. "I almost killed him," KoKo confessed. "But I know Kayson would never forgive me if I killed this nigga for trying to protect his legacy and be loyal to the code they set up."

"Just give him a minute. He'll calm down."

"No he won't. Baseem is not built like that. Kay is going to have to get at him, or I'm gonna get at 'im." KoKo put her hand up to her head.

I'm Taking Over . . .

Right after the big blow up between KoKo and Baseem, things were very cold between them. She had made her position clear. And he made his even clearer by going forward with his plan to fade her ass to the back. He immediately called a small meeting with the heads of each city to regroup everyone. He didn't give a fuck what KoKo said, and as far as he was concerned, she had lost her ability to rule and he was taking over.

He carefully directed each man into their new position. There was a little confusion at first, but when he laid out his plan, each man saw a very profitable role and quickly got on board.

"Listen, this shit may get real dirty for a minute. But I promise you after the fall out, everyone will be in charge of their own city. And the only thing you will need me for is supply. We in the 21st Century. You niggas should be able to stand on your own. If it's heat, then the heat is on you. If it's beef in your camp, then you handle it. We not coming to another man's city and trying to rule. We will still have these meetings to make sure nobody is toe steppin'. But at the end of the day, you are the captain of your own ship."

There was strong agreement in the room.

"That's all for now. Let's enjoy the night," he announced as he passed the long table, patting a few of the men on the shoulder on his way by.

"Yo, Bas," Moe yelled out, stopping him from exiting the room.

Baseem turned as the other men passed him talking and laughing.

"What's up?"

"Is KoKo good with all this?"

"She don't have no other choice."

"I'm just saying. She been running ship well without Kay, and I'm just trying to feel which direction we moving in, that's all," he humbly stated.

"I feel you. And you got my word, we good. She got a lot of shit on her shoulders. I'm just stepping in to make sure we don't collapse under the pressure."

"That's what's up. Well, if you need me, you know me and my team stay at go."

"Good to know." Baseem stepped forward and shook his hand.

"Ai'ight, well let me go have some of this fun you got set up," Moe said as he headed to the main room of the club.

"I'll catch you out there." Baseem left the meeting room and walked down the hall to the bathroom. While walking, he ran the conversation he had with KoKo through his mind. It was the first time he had ever had a blow up with her, and to be honest, he was feeling fucked up about it. The fact that she had not spoken to him since that night put a rip in his armor.

Entering the bathroom, he began putting together the words he needed to say to make things right between them. He knew better than anyone that Kayson would have a serious problem with any man disrespecting his wife, friend or not.

Baseem positioned himself at the stall. When he was done, he quickly zipped up and headed to the sink.

As he grabbed a paper towel, a dark figure caught the corner of his eyes. Carefully, he rubbed his hands, calculating how fast he could get to his gun. Glancing up at the mirror, he watched the figure move slowly in the shadows.

Being the man he is, and not about to surrender to any man, he quickly reached around his back and pulled out. With gun extended firmly in hand, he said what might have been his last words.

"Only a bitch comes at a nigga's back." His heart beat rapidly.

The figure moved from the stall, just enough to make his presence known.

Baseem looked him over for a weapon, but saw there was no threat of life or limb. When his hands moved up and his hood came back, Baseem almost shit his pants.

THE PUSSY TRAP 3: *Death by Temptation*
~ N E N E C A P R I ~

"Damn, nigga. If this is how you treat an enemy, I would hate to see how you treat a friend," Kayson smoothly stated, looking Baseem square in the eyes.

"Muuuthafucka . . ." Baseem slurred, squinting his eyes to make sure they were not deceiving him. "Can't be," he mumbled. "Kay?"

"In the flesh," he responded.

Baseem dropped his gun to his side. His heart raced and he breathed heavy.

"How the fuck?" he asked, still confused.

"It's a long story. I'll fill you in on the way to the house. I'll meet you out back. Do what you gotta do out there. I'll be in my truck." Kayson pulled his hood back over his head.

"Stop shaking, nigga. I almost threw your ass some twenties. I trained you better than that," Kayson joked.

"Nigga, dead muhfuckas don't be in bathrooms and shit," he shot back.

"Hurry up, I'll see you outside." He smirked, and then headed out the bathroom.

Baseem leaned against the sink and shook his head. He was fucked up and didn't know what to think or how to feel. Then it hit him. All of KoKo's sneaking around, the hickies, the panties in the dressing room. "That's why she been acting like that." A surge of relief came over him. For a minute he thought he may have to do something drastic. He tucked his gun away, and ran some water over his face.

Quickly, he rushed out the bathroom, gave out a few orders, and headed to the back. His energy increased as he got closer to the door. It was on now. Kayson was back, and their enemies better get ready for the body count.

- 37 -

Brothers

When Baseem reached the truck, he and Kayson drove around for hours bringing each other up to speed on the shit going on inside and outside of the organization. When they were done, they picked up Night and headed to Atlantic City, where it all began.

Kayson, Bassem, and Night hit the 40/40 and enjoyed the club scene before going to their hotel suite. After a few drinks, they rolled some blunts, sat back on the plush couches with the lights dim, getting fucked up and talking shit.

"When the crew saw Kay walk into that room, I could hear their hearts drop to their toes," Baseem stated.

"Hell yeah. They did not see that shit coming," Night responded.

"I started to bring some chains and rattle them muthafuckas for effect," Kayson said, reaching in his pocket and shaking his change.

"Oh shit! You crazy as hell," Baseem said as they burst into laughter.

"Let me ask y'all something. How the fuck both of y'all niggas got babies on the way?" Baseem slurred out.

"Maaan . . . that shit was a set up," Night confessed.

"Fuck you mean 'a set up'?" Baseem shot back, taking a long pull on the blunt and then passing it to Night.

"Y'all know KoKo did that shit on purpose. Gonna put me in a house with not regular pussy, not okay pussy, but highly trained and skilled pussy. Made a nigga throw all the rules out the window and run them shits over with my truck."

"Oh shit!" Baseem laughed as he reached for his drink and then sat back.

"Y'all niggas already know I got boss pussy. She got all my shit. Be talking shit and pulled a gun on me. Where the fuck they do that at?" Kayson chuckled.

"Y'all know KoKo ass is crazy," Night said.

"When yo' punk ass gonna settle down?" Kayson asked Baseem.

"Who me?"

"No, muhfucka, the nigga behind you," he shot back.

"Fuck that. I'm not 'bout that life. I don't fuck with these bitches like that. Get all caught up in your feelings then a bitch get new on you."

"You gonna die a lonely man," Night joked.

"I won't die a broke one. This nigga just said KoKo got all his shit. How we both gonna be broke?" he slurred.

They all looked at each other and then burst out laughing.

"You stupid as hell," Kayson said as they continued to laugh.

" . . . Shittin' me. These bitches already know. I live by one philosophy. Get on this dick, cook me something to eat, and try not to talk me to fucking death while it's happening. And I might let you ride in the front seat."

"Nigga, you retarded," Night said, still laughing.

Baseem shrugged his shoulders and sipped his drink. "Damn, I miss us together like this," he stated.

"You was about to kill me a week ago, nigga," Night reminded him of his arrogance.

"My bad. You know a nigga need counseling," he said, shaking his head.

"I got yo' counseling, nigga," Night said, and then pulled on the blunt.

"On the real. Out of all the shit we been through. I would have never thought that Al would have been a snitch and Wise a fucking crack head."

"No excuses, but shit got rough when you faded to the back. Al let that shit happen. But KoKo put that heat on 'em."

"She is as loyal as they come," Kayson stated.

"Yeah, KoKo held us down. She kept me and my family straight and made sure everybody ate while I was on lock. Niggas were coming for her, but she did what she had to do," Baseem stated.

As the words left his mouth, Baseem thought about that nigga in Atlanta that he saw KoKo with. He started to say something, but figured now was not the time.

Night nodded in agreement. "So where we taking this shit from here?" he asked.

"We about to bring some pain," Kayson said, sitting up and rubbing his hands together.

For almost three years he had plotted and planned, and with the enemy accurately identified, all he needed now was to make them bow to him.

- 38 -
Defiant

Yuri stood at her father's side with a sly smile on her face. Mr. Odoo had sent Yuri to oversee the shipment, and to her fortune, she found the Miami police snooping around and questioning the workers. She knew instantly Peppa had been dealing drugs out of the warehouse. The other thing she was certain about was that Mrs. KoKo was behind it. Being the daddy's girl she was, her report was swift and accurate.

"Are you trying to ruin us?" Mr. Odoo stared at his son with disgust.

"I was just trying to make some moves. We've been in the same financial situation for the last ten years. It's time to step it up," he said to his father with confidence.

"Step it up? You think that peddling dope means we are *stepping it up*? I thought that I was making a good choice selecting you to take charge. And in return you make me look foolish," he yelled, slamming his hand on the desk.

A smile formed on Yuri's face as she stood next to her dad filled with joy. Their sibling rivalry was intense, and she knew that this would not only put a wedge between her dad and Peppa, but also between him and Kayson.

"You are a huge disappointment. I am sickened by your presence. Leave me!" he yelled.

Peppa stood up and looked at his father. "Your ignorance

of the time is going to destroy you."

"And being plain ignorant is going to destroy you," his father warned.

Mr. Odoo put his hand on his forehead. "Yuri, please have Kayson summoned. I need to see him at once."

"Yes, Dad." She patted her father on the shoulder and sashayed out of his office.

When she got to the hallway, she pulled her phone out to make the call.

"You're an evil bitch, and I promise you are going to pay dearly. I promise you that." Peppa vehemently hurled those words at Yuri as he exited his father's office.

"You laid down with the bitch. Don't blame me for your fleas." She turned and placed the call.

Peppa turned the other way and went out the door.

"Hello," Yuri seductively said into the phone.

"Why you on my phone?" Kayson responded coldly.

"My father wants to see you. I guess your disobedient wife has been doing some shit behind your back."

"Tell him I'll be there in a couple days." He hung up and threw his phone up on his desk. "Shit!" he said aloud and picked up his phone.

"Hello," KoKo said into the receiver.

"Where you at?" Kayson asked.

"I'm at the house. Why?"

"Meet me at our spot." Kayson hung up.

"What the fuck?" KoKo looked at the phone with a wrinkled brow.

She dressed quickly and headed to the spot. When she walked in the door, Kayson stood with his back turned looking out the window in intense thought.

"What's up?" she asked, laying her keys on the table.

"Tell me what I told you to do?"

"What?"

"Repeat to me what I told you to do with Peppa?"

"Oh shit!" KoKo said and sat down.

"Why would you think it was okay to have dope delivered through that warehouse?"

"Kay, on the real, I needed that connect. I was wrong for not saying shit. But I had to make a move."

"Fuck is you talking about?" he growled, turning in her direction.

"We got people depending on us. Yeah, we going legit, but we got shit pending that we have to resolve."

"You talking to me like I just signed up for boot camp. I built this shit! I know what the fuck has to be done!" His voice carried through the living room.

KoKo sat looking at him like he was crazy. "Like I said, I had some shit pending, and I handled it. As soon as I could cut Peppa out, I did. Niggas gotta eat, Kayson."

"Those is grown fucking men. If they hungry then them niggas need to hunt just like we did," he growled.

"Baby."

"You coddle these muthafuckas. But it's all good. I got it from here. You're gonna sit yo' pregnant ass down."

"I can't do that right now."

"None of what I just said is up for discussion. That shit is final. I'm about to meet with Baseem and Night and reel this shit back in. I respect what you did while I was gone, but I'm back, and you're done. If you see something that needs to be handled, run that shit by me first."

KoKo looked at him. She heard him, but she had so much pending, and she needed to make a few more runs.

"Are we clear?" He looked at her with raised brows.

KoKo didn't answer.

"I said. Are. We. Clear?"

"We clear. Anything else, Boss?" she asked sarcastically.

"Don't make me act the fuck up. I need you to take care of our son and make sure my baby arrives healthy. And you can't do that out running into shit."

"Night gotta big ass mouth," she mumbled.

"Yeah, and yo' ass is spoiled and hardheaded."

"It's your fault," she murmured.

"What?"

"Nothing." She headed to the bathroom.

Kayson walked into the other room, sat in the chair, and called Night.

"What's good?" Night said into the phone, sounding as if he just woke up.

"Call a meeting. I'm about to shake shit up."

"You ready for that?"

"I don't have no other choice. Your sister is about to make me fuck her up."

Night laughed. "You know how she get down."

"Another thing, I need you to take a long trip with me. I have to take care of some shit."

"Got you."

He hung up and placed a few more calls. Kayson sat back in his large black chair and continued his plot. When he looked up, KoKo was coming toward him wearing only a tight T-shirt with a sneaky smirk on her face.

"I ain't fucking with you right now."

"You ain't fucking with me?" she asked, squatting between his legs.

Kayson looked down at her as she reached in his sweats and pulled out the Enforcer.

"I'ma do what you tell me, baby," she cooed as she ran the tip of her tongue around the rim of his dick.

247

Kayson held eye contact with her as she began to suck gently on the head, bringing him to attention. When he looked down to see her pretty pussy staring back at him, his shit went from rock to brick.

KoKo squeezed tightly at the base, moving her wrist enough to bring him in and out of her mouth, getting it sloppy with every motion. Tightening her grip and her jaws while rolling her tongue back and forth over that main vein got the reaction she was looking for.

"Sssss . . ." he hissed as his hands gripped the arm of the chair.

"Mmmmm . . ." she moaned, taking in all of him.

Releasing him from her jaws, she stroked him quick and firm while sensually rolling her tongue up and down his length making full eye contact.

When she heard another hiss leave his lips, she took him in her mouth and all the way to the back of her throat. Gripping each hand on his knees, she tilted his dick forward and gave him that no hands action.

The faster and harder she sucked, the heavier he breathed.

"Damn, ma," he mumbled as the intensity of her wet treat brought him to the edge of no return.

"Mmmmm . . ." she moaned, causing the right amount of vibration.

Removing her hands from his knees, she grabbed him with one hand and gently caressed his balls with the other. Rotating her wrist, sucking and caressing him with her mouth brought it on.

Kayson dug his fingertips into the chair as he released.

KoKo allowed a little to enter her mouth and then run down the length of his dick. She then ran the tip of her tongue down the back and up and down the line between his sac, playing in his essence.

"I love you," she whispered, rising from between his legs.

Slightly dazed and satisfied, he moaned, "I love you too. Sorry for yelling at you, baby. But I still need you to do what I say."

"I'ma let you lead, baby. I just wanted to polish the seat of your throne." She bit down on her lip, giving him her 'fuck me' gaze.

"Is that right?" He stood up.

Towering over her, he sized up the situation, realizing he needed to return the favor.

"If I'm sitting on the throne, where do you think you need to sit?" he asked, pulling his shirt over his head and throwing it to the floor.

"Where you want me?" she cooed.

"Right at the top," he said, scooping her up and placing her pussy at mouth level.

KoKo draped her legs over his shoulders and rubbed his head as he walked to the wall, placing her back firmly against it.

When his tongue made the first contact with her clit, she put her head back on the wall and allowed him to worship her, thinking, *If a bitch gotta be at the top, might as well be on the shoulders of the man she loves while she paints his lips with her honey.*

- 39 -

Disappointed

Just follow my lead," said Kayson, as calmly as the quiet comes before a storm. "I know this nigga gonna be mad as hell, and he's justified in that. I'ma let him vent. Then I'll deliver my verdict." Him and Night had just pulled up to Mr. Odoo's estate.

"You know me. I'ma be cool until you say get hot. Then that muthafucka is in trouble," Night seriously stated.

"Let's go."

They exited the vehicle and headed to the door.

Once inside, Night looked around at the décor. "This shit is nice," he said, admiring the artwork and earthy color scheme.

"It's all right," Kayson shot back, leading the way to Mr. Odoo's study.

"Thank you for coming right away. Please have a seat," Mr. Odoo stated from his recliner.

"No problem. This is my brother Night." Kayson made the introduction.

"Welcome to my home," he greeted Night with a smile.

Night walked over and shook his hand.

The two men took a seat on the couch, mentally preparing for this emergency meeting.

"It always surprises me how you can provide a man with what he needs to eat a good meal, and he will still reach over and take food off your plate," Mr. Odoo said, looking down as he moved the golden pieces around on a glass chessboard.

"When a man is full, the only thing he can get off another man's plate is scraps. And I'm very full," Kayson said.

Mr. Odoo nodded and moved another piece. "Yes, that might be true, but when your death was upon you, I nursed you, I fed you, I provided a safe place for you, and then the thanks I get is deception." His brow wrinkled as the words left his mouth.

"I have never taken anything that wasn't intended to be mine. And I have no need to deceive a friend. But an enemy will feel me. No rules, no code, just wrath." Kayson wanted to send a warning.

Mr. Odoo huffed. "So the treachery your wife committed is her own?" He turned and looked at Kayson.

"My wife is a businesswoman who seized an opportunity. The treachery that has shown its ugly head came out of your house. The person you better direct the anger on is your son," Kayson spoke his words firmly.

Looking back at the chessboard he said, "Oh, don't worry about my house. I will handle that. But I need some punishment to surface in your house as well."

"Listen to my words very carefully. I never crossed you. I thank you for all that you have done for me. But I will tell you this. When it comes to my family, the words mercy, forgiveness, or friendship will not stop me from touching a muthafucka's whole generation," he angrily spat.

Mr. Odoo nodded. "Well, consider us enemies." He didn't even look up.

Kayson rose to his feet. "Well, all my enemies end up dead. Get your good suit ready," he said as he walked to the door.

Night got up. "Thanks for the hospitality," he calmly stated as he followed Kayson.

"You're not untouchable." Mr. Odoo looked toward the door.

Kayson paused and turned. "Neither is your daughter. You see her today?" He smiled before pivoting and walking out.

Mr. Odoo looked around the room, and then hurried to his desk to dial Yuri's phone that just rang continuously. He slammed the phone down on its receiver, replaying Kayson's words.

- 40 -
Coincidence

On their way back to secure the family and assets for the fall out that was about to happen, Kayson flew to St. Croix, and Night flew to Atlanta to make sure Goldie was straight. After an evening of going over protocol and procedure with her, he got up the next morning to catch a flight to New York.

"I'll be back in a few days. Pay attention and be on point. If shit don't look right, check into a hotel and call Chico immediately."

"Yes, I got it. Love you."

"Love you too." Night kissed Goldie on her forehead, rubbed her stomach, and left for the airport.

Goldie lay around for most of the morning, and then got up to prepare to meet the detective for what she was hoping was her last meeting. Ever since she had been serious with Night, she was holding out on giving him any pussy, and with her finding out she was pregnant, she certainly wasn't trying to fuck with him like that. She could sense his impatience, so she knew she needed to wrap things up.

Goldie pulled up with Detective Warren to the precinct on Centennial Olympic Park Drive.

"I need to run in here real quick. Come with me," he asked, feeling proud that he would get a chance to show her off.

Reluctantly she said, "Okay, I have to use the bathroom anyway." She shot him her pretty smile.

Reaching over, he kissed her on the lips, which made her almost throw up.

"Damn, you look so pretty today."

Forcing another smile, she mustered up some kind words. "That's because I'm here with you," she stated, and then grabbed the door handle in an effort to avoid any more physical contact.

Walking inside, he grabbed her hand and pulled her close.

Greg strutted to his desk like a proud peacock showing off all his feathers. All eyes were on him, and he was milking it all up.

"Where is the bathroom?" she asked, pulling away from his grip.

"Right down the hall." He pointed to the right.

"I'll be right back," she said, walking away.

Greg sat in his chair, quickly flipped through and signed some paperwork, and then checked his messages.

As he was about to walk to the copy machine, he ran into Damien.

"What's up?" They shook hands.

"Nothing much. Just stopped in to wrap up these reports. He displayed the files in his hand.

"I see you brought a little show and tell to work today," Damien said, referring to Goldie.

"Just a little sumthin-sumthin," Greg responded, placing the documents into the automatic feed.

"Where you meet her at?" he asked with a curious look.

"I met her at a club. Why? You know her?"

"Nah, just asking," he said as the wheels in his head began to turn.

"Ai'ight let me get outta here. I'll catch you tomorrow." Greg walked off.

"You ready?" Goldie asked, coming up behind him.

"Yeah, just let me put these files up."

"Okay." Goldie headed to the bench to sit down. She reached in her purse and pulled out her mirror and lip gloss and began to apply it. When she looked up, a sister coming out of an interrogation room caught her eye. The woman had on plain clothes but wore a golden badge at her waist. "Hold the fuck up!" she mumbled. Quickly, she walked over to the water fountain and dipped down, pretending to take a drink until the female passed her.

Goldie turned her head to take one last look at the woman headed to the door. "Ain't this a bitch?" she said to herself.

"I'm ready." Goldie put on a sad face as she turned to him.

"What's the matter?" he asked, seeing her face all tore up.

"I don't feel well. I think it was something we ate at lunch. I need to go lie down. Can you drop me off?"

"Yeah, I'll drop you off. You need anything on the way?"

"No, I have something at the house."

When they hit the door, Goldie's eyes were in all directions. She was looking for somebody, but unbeknownst to her, somebody was looking at her.

- 41 -

Running Out of Time

Tyquan sat at his desk running the numbers repeatedly. Anxiety overwhelmed him as the figures continued to disagree. Springing from his chair, he hit the lever to the safe and hurried over and punched in the code.

Grabbing a file from inside, he opened it, plopped back in his seat, and typed in the codes from the sheets of paper. "Shit!" he grumbled. He sat back and thought for a minute.

Instinctively, he picked up the phone and called the fifteenth floor.

"Hello, Conway and Gibbford."

"Hey Beth, did Conway ask you to run any figures this week?"

"No sir, Mr. Wells. I only run figures on Friday."

"Okay, thanks." He disconnected the call and ran the figures again. But the hundred million dollar difference continued to haunt the screen.

Tyquan went to the wet bar and poured himself a tall glass of bourbon and stood sipping from his glass, trying to figure out what happened. While taking a big gulp, it came to him. "That fucking bitch!" he said, slamming his glass down. He grabbed his jacket and headed to the door.

"Have my car brought to the front," he said to the temp as he headed to the elevator.

Tyquan walked swiftly out the doors, jumped in his car,

and sped off.

Forty minutes later, he was standing on the porch of Deborah's home in Nyack, New York. His pressure went straight up when he looked through the emty windows and saw all the furniture gone. He stood for a minute looking around, and then headed back to his car. When he got to the driver's side, he saw the neighbor coming out walking her dog. "Excuse me, I'm Mr. Wells." He walked over to the woman.

"Good afternoon, I'm Jackie." She extended her hand.

"The lady that used to live here. How long has she been gone? I'm her uncle. I was trying to surprise her."

"Oh, I'm not sure. All I do is work." The woman looked at Tyquan and became uneasy with his body language.

Sensing her hesitation, he ended the conversation. "Okay, you have a good day."

"You too. Come on, Santana," she said, snatching the dog by the leash and hurrying back into her house.

Tyquan jumped back in his car and pulled off. "Damn, I knew I should have killed that bitch when I had the chance," he said aloud, heading back to his office. He needed to make shit right and quick, because the men that, that money belonged to, were the type he was not prepared to war with. He knew they were relentless, and hiding was not an option.

"Where is my mother and son?" KoKo asked as she hurried to the bedroom of her island home and closed the door.

"Baby, he's safe." Kayson said into the phone.

"Kayson, please don't play with me. Why would you move him without telling me?"

"Baby, stop tripping. I moved everybody. We got to shut shit down and change all routines. And his life is one that I am not prepared to bargain with."

"Okay, where are you?"

"I'm standing in the other room listening to you act like a fucking fool."

KoKo turned and looked at the door. She hung up her phone and tossed it on the bed.

When she opened the door, Kayson stood there smiling.

KoKo punched him lightly in the chest. "You play too much."

"I'm sorry. I didn't have a chance to say anything. You came right in the house and started bugging the fuck out."

"Whatever. You know he is all I have. I can't play when it comes to him."

"I closed down both mansions and the pool hall. I also had your apartment on Park Avenue sold and all your shit shipped to the new location. The only thing still in business is The Lion's Den and Golden Paradise. I made sure all the paperwork and shit was straight. And I changed all the bank accounts and moved all assets."

KoKo stood listening to him. The reality of what was happening weighed heavy on her heart. They had spoken about moving out and doing shit different for years, but the hour had come, and she was relieved she had Kayson there to make everything happen.

"So, this is it?"

"Yes, we outta these streets, baby. We can't go on like this. We have to back up and let this shit blow over."

"What are we going to do about Baseem and the crew?"

"Bas is going to do the underground thing for a minute. But he already told them they have to be big boys and girls. Night is going to most likely try to come where ever we are."

"Damn, Kay. This shit don't seem real."

"I know, but that belly is real." He looked down at KoKo's now protruding stomach, and then reached out and rubbed it.

"Yes, and it is starting to slow me down. I was so sleepy the other day, I almost yawned while I was cussing a bitch out. How gangsta is that?"

"See, that's why I'm retiring your sexy ass." Kayson kissed her sweet lips.

"Only for a minute. I have to keep my pimp hand strong." She looked at her hand and turned it from side to side.

"Yeah, so you can pick up kids from school and check homework like normal mothers." He grabbed her in his arms and walked her over to the chair, where he sat down and perched her on his lap.

"Normal? What is that?" she said, laying her head back on his shoulder.

"I don't know, but we gonna look that shit up and try it for a little while and see what it's all about." He kissed her face.

"Well, as long as normal has you in it, I'll give it a try." She closed her eyes, enjoying being in his arms.

KoKo and Kayson sat like that for an hour talking and laughing as they stared out at the water. As the sun began to leave the sky, KoKo got up cooked, cleaned, and then gave the boss some of that hypnotic.

Wrapped in the euphoria of their little tryst, they both fell fast asleep.

- 42 -

Good Night

"Stop! You so crazy." Goldie pushed Night's head off her stomach.

"I'm trying to hear what my son has to say," he joked as he sat back in his seat.

"You don't even know if it's a boy," Goldie said as she smiled and giggled.

Today was their first ultra-sound. They had heard the heart beat, and Night was beaming.

"So, when are you going to be ready to make the move with me?" he asked.

"I am ready whenever you say it's time. But I have to keep my house in the 'A'. I love it down here. Plus, this is the first thing I ever owned. It means something to me," she said as her chest filled up with pride.

"I understand. We can keep your house, but I need you in mine every day. I need to be able to wake up and see your eyes and rub your big belly." He placed his hand on her stomach.

"Awww . . . baby." Goldie leaned over and kissed him on his lips.

"You know I got you. You ain't gotta worry about nothing."

"I know." She looked into his eyes. "I got something for you."

Goldie reached in her pocket book to grab a gift she had for him. A car pulled up next to theirs, and without warning, bullets blasted the windows.

Night dove on top of Goldie, covering her body with his.

Just like that, the car sped off.

Goldie struggled to lift Night's body from hers, looking around to see shattered glass everywhere. Gazing down, she saw a gaping hole in Night's head.

Hysterical, she picked up parts of his brain and began trying to put them back in place. "Oh God no! Please!" she cried as she rubbed her bloody hands on his face and hands.

Over and over, she screamed his name. Three men ran to the car, opened her car door, and pulled her from under Night's dead body.

"You alright?" one of the guys asked as he began to touch her to see if she was hit. She had a few scratches from the glass, but had not been hit with one bullet.

"Save him!" she yelled out as she watched the men pull him from the car and lay him on the sidewalk.

The guy at her side grabbed his cell and dialed 911, as the other two tried to apply CPR to Night. A task that would be fruitless because he was already gone.

Goldie sat on the hot concrete and cried hard. The man grabbed her in his arms and held her tight. Her blood curdling screams were like a punch to his gut.

When the two ambulances and police cars arrived, they quickly swept her in one and Night in the other.

Goldie watched as they cut Night's clothes from his body and pressed his chest. Goldie was in a daze. It seemed like everything was moving in slow motion. Questions were being hurled at her, but her eyes stayed fixated in one direction.

Nurses picked and probed at her, but she didn't feel a thing. She was numb from head to toe.

THE PUSSY TRAP 3: *Death by Temptation*
~ N E N E C A P R I ~

"What is your name, ma'am?" the nurse asked for the tenth time.

When Goldie still didn't answer, she reached in her pocketbook and pulled out her wallet.

"Geneva, can you hear me?" the nurse asked, repeating what she read off her license.

Goldie still didn't say a word. Slowly, she looked down at her purse, reached inside, and pulled out the ultra-sound picture and again became hysterical. "Nooooo!" she yelled at the top of her lungs. Her voice caused pain to the soul of everyone within earshot.

The nurse grabbed her and held her tight. She knew her pain. She had seen it too many times. That feeling that cannot be cured with words or time.

"Let it out. I understand." The nurse put her hand on Goldie's head and brought it to her shoulder.

"Whyyyyy!" Goldie yelled out, causing her voice to crack.

The stress in her cry brought tears to even the cop's eyes.

Chico walked through the doors asking questions and looking around. He was pointed in Goldie's direction.

Standing right by her, he placed his hand on her back. "Goldie, I'm here," he said as comforting as he could.

Goldie had cried so much that there were no more tears, only sound.

With glossy, puffy, red eyes, she tried to focus on Chico.

"They killed him," she said. The reality of her words caused her to shake and scream.

Chico began to breathe heavy as he felt tears threaten to flee his eyes. He brought his hands to his face and rubbed his eyes.

Goldie fell over on him and repeated, "Make them pay. Please make them pay."

"I got you. On my kids I got you." He held her head on his chest as a single tear rolled down his cheek.

After an hour, the doctors came out and handed Goldie everything in Night's pockets.

Chico and the crew came to attention as the doctor delivered the news that they had already known.

"We did everything we could."

Every one became uncomfortable as rage filled their hearts.

Goldie, now depleted of all tears, just looked up at him as she processed his words.

"Come on, ma. I called KoKo. She's going to meet us at the house," Chico said, trying to bring Goldie to her feet.

Goldie wanted to stand but couldn't. She was totally exhausted, mind, body, and soul.

"Yo, go get the car." He tossed the keys to Paco. He grabbed them in the air and moved out the doors.

"I got you. Just hold on to me." Chico picked Goldie up and cradled her in his arms like a child.

Goldie put her arms around his neck and whispered, "Make them pay."

"I promise," he said, walking out the exit to the car.

Everyone was sitting in Goldie's living room plotting and planning when they heard the bell ring. Then a series of knocks followed. They all grabbed their guns and moved through the house. Chico peeked out the window to see it was KoKo and a tall nigga with a hood over his head.

Chico moved to the door, opened it up, and KoKo walked in with the man trailing behind her.

"Hey, ma. You good?"

"Where is Goldie?" KoKo got right to the point.

"She's in the living room," he said, closing the door and then looking out the curtain.

KoKo walked into the living room scanning the room to see

who was all in attendance. Then her eyes settled on Goldie. She was sitting on the couch covered in blood and staring off into space.

KoKo went over to her and sat on the coffee table. "Goldie? I'm here," she said in the softest voice she could form.

"KoKo, they killed him."

"Who killed him? Did you see who did it?"

Goldie looked at her and then blanked out again.

Kayson pulled his hood back and sat next to KoKo. "Goldie, I need you to tell me everything you remember," he asked, trying to remain calm on the outside. However, on the inside was a burning fire, fueled with anger and hate.

"Goldie, we need you to try and remember. We gotta go get them niggas," KoKo said, her voice raising a few octaves.

The sound of KoKo's voice brought Goldie out of her trance. She looked back and forth at KoKo and Kayson and mumbled, "Diablo. That bitch looked right at me."

KoKo's heart skipped a beat as her mind tried to make sure her ears just heard what they heard.

Kayson stood up. "I'll be back."

KoKo followed Kayson to the door.

"Hold up, KoKo. Let me ride on this one," Chico said as he moved behind her.

"Nah, y'all stay here and keep her safe."

"Hold up. You gonna let *him* go ride on this nigga without us?" Brian, Goldie's brother said with a puzzled look on his face as he pointed his thumb at Kayson. "We don't even know him. We got this."

Kayson stopped in his tracks. Turning, he looked at ol' boy with those piercing hazel eyes and it was on. "Muthafucka, do you know who the fuck I am?" he barked, moving toward him.

Brian wanted to speak, but the power in Kayson's eyes paralyzed his thoughts.

"That nigga you consider a friend is my brother. This shit is way past business and personal. It's about family. My fucking family!" Kayson's voice reverberated throughout the room as he looked around, catching every man's eye. "Ain't nobody handling this shit but me!" he yelled, causing even the air to quiver. "Y'all niggas already dropped the fucking ball. My nigga laying on a cold fucking slab! Stay the fuck outta my way and do whatever she tell you." Kayson looked around the room, praying for some discord. He was ready to make something bleed. All he needed was an open invitation, and he was going to step in and act the fuck up.

Kayson turned to the door. "As a matter of fact, you stay here with them and make sure they do what they gotta do."

"I need to be with you. I gotta do it for Night," KoKo said, apparently disappointed.

"No. This shit gotta be by my hands." He pulled his hood over his head and walked out the door.

KoKo stood there with her hands on her hips.

"No disrespect, ma. But who the fuck is that nigga?" Brian asked.

"That's the boss," she said, turning to the men and taking a seat. She began assessing the situation and regrouping.

Once she had every one settled into their next move, she took Goldie upstairs, stripped her down, and put her in the shower.

Goldie just stood there allowing the water to rain on her aching body. When she looked down and saw Night's blood running off her skin she began to cry.

KoKo rubbed the cloth over her skin trying to wash away any trace of blood. She knew just how Goldie felt. With every tear and whimper, KoKo relived the horror of her own experience.

After her shower, KoKo dressed her and forced her to eat and drink a little something. Then she put Goldie in the bed.

"Don't worry, momma. You'll get through it." KoKo sat next to her and rubbed her back. Although KoKo wasn't really the friend type, today she knew that she had to be more than a boss.

Goldie softly sniffled as she tried to doze off.

KoKo's mind raced a mile a minute. For the first time she was going to actually listen and hold shit down. Plus, she was tired. Tired of killing and tired of death. Tears began to fall down her face as she thought about how Night had been there for her. He held her hand every step of the way, making the journey without Kayson a much less painful. Her throat became sore as she tried to choke back the tears. Easing off the bed, she moved into the bathroom and closed the door. KoKo turned on the shower, sat on the toilet seat, and cried. Her whole body ached with sorrow. As the steam clouded the bathroom, KoKo's mind fought back the vision of having to see Night lifeless. She hugged herself and rocked back and forth as she tried releasing some of her agony. In the past few years, she and Kayson had lost more than a few good men. They had lost their whole family. She had to admit it, she was ready to fall back and let Kayson do what he does best, lead.

- 43 -
Dance With the Devil

Kayson stalked the streets of Atlanta for hours tracking Diablo down. He had found out that she would be at a private passion party in Marietta on some kinky, orgy type shit she hosted every so often. Kayson caught a cab to Lenox Mall and grabbed a two-piece suit and some Ferragamo loafers.

He rented a room at the Renaissance Concourse Hotel near the airport to get dressed and clear his mind.

When he got out the shower, he hit the mini bar and hard, downing bottle after bottle until he couldn't feel the agony. Night had been there for him for over fifteen years. And the one day he really needed him, he was nowhere around. Those thoughts brought back the pain of the night his uncle got killed. He didn't know whether God was saving him or punishing him.

Once he got his thoughts together, he went into executioner mode. He cleared his mind of all happy thoughts. Kayson needed to detach himself from everything he loved and turned all his feelings cold and hateful. He wanted to do Diablo dirty and didn't want an ounce of compassion flowing through his blood.

Kayson left his room with a slight look of malice mixed with success. His suit lay on his frame like lotion, smooth than a muthafucka. He grabbed a cab and headed to the party.

When Kayson arrived outside the house, he watched as

niggas and females pulled up and piled in. He posted up by a Benz and waited for the right rat to bite.

"Damn, you fine as hell," this high yellow chick said in a thick southern accent as she looked him up and down.

Kayson looked in her direction. "You sexy as hell your damn self," he said, taking her by the hand. "Come here for a minute." He pulled her to him. "One of these niggas claiming you? Or can a nigga get close to all that ass?" he asked, looking behind her.

"Don't no nigga claim me. I claim niggas. You look like you want to be chosen," she spat back, trying to put her so-called game on Kayson.

"Is that right?" he asked.

"Yeah, that's right," Dar'chelle said, looking at him like she wanted to go to her knees right there.

"I was invited to this party by the DJ, but I really prefer private gatherings."

"Who, Mustafah?" she asked, frowning. "That nigga swear he the shit. Look, my boy Veno invited me. Come in with me and let's have a little fun. Then maybe later I can let you have some ice cream and cake." She turned and brushed her ass against his dick.

Kayson allowed the Enforcer to stand up as he pulled her in place to feel that rise.

"Yeah, I'll come with you. And later, you can come for me." She began to blush and smile.

"Sounds like a plan." She pressed against him a bit harder to get the full effect, before taking him by the hand and leading the way inside.

"What's your name?" She looked over her shoulder.

"Killah."

"Damn, is it like that?" she asked as they approached the

door.

"You can tell me later," he said as they passed the bouncer.

When they got inside, Kayson looked around the smoke-filled room trying to identify his target. His eyes feasted on the many small round couches full of pillows and people kissing, rubbing, smoking and drinking. There were groups of men on men and women on women, a whole mini Sodom and Gomorrah right in Georgia. There were tables full of toys and people gawking at them ready to try them out.

"Is this your first party?" Dar'chelle asked, feeling the tension in his hand.

"Like I said, I like to do my freaky shit in private." He looked at her with an intense gaze.

"Well, let's find somewhere real private."

"Lead the way," he said, following behind her.

Moving through the sea of people and sheer veils that hung from ceiling to floor, Kayson gazed in each corner of the room to find his victim.

Once he got to the second floor he was rewarded. Carefully, he glanced in each room as they passed by them. With the doors wide open, there were full fuck fests going on. Several people were standing and watching. At the end of the hall was a huge room with the door open with only women putting on a show. Sitting right in the middle of the action was Diablo.

Jackpot! Kayson thought as he positioned himself outside the door to spectate.

"Oh, so you wanna watch this, huh?" Dar'chelle asked as she began rubbing his dick.

"Yeah, I can watch pussy bump. I can't watch no fucking balls swinging."

"Typical," she said, trying to work him to full girth.

Seeing his target locked in his scope made his shit swell

right up.

"Damn," she mumbled as she took it firmly in her hand.

Kayson put his hand on the top of her head and guided her to her knees.

"I thought you wanted a private party," she moaned.

"I want something very private, publicly." He continued to push her to his waist.

Standing in the doorway of the room of pleasure, Dar'chelle took him in her mouth and began to work her show.

Kayson focused his eyes on Diablo, watching for her weakness, searching for his moment. He watched like a lion going in for the prey.

Pleasantly distracted by all the tantalizing eye-play going on around her, Diablo missed the deadly gaze carefully sizing her up. She whispered in one female's ear and pointed to a door on the left.

He knew this would be his window. "I'm good, ma," he said, pulling Dar'chelle to her feet.

"Damn, daddy. I wanted to make you come," she whispered and tried to kiss his neck.

Kayson moved back. "Oh, don't worry. I'm about to bust off." He put his dick back and zipped his pants. He took her by the arm. "Go have some fun. I'll be right back."

"You promise?"

Kayson didn't say a word. He carefully watched as Diablo followed the woman into the room. He allowed a few moments to pass, and then moved swiftly to the door. Carefully, he turned the knob and watched through the crack as Diablo got into position. When he saw she was good and distracted, he reached for his nine, silencer in place. Positioning himself in the room, he gently closed the door and aimed his gun. The shots hit the woman once in the head and then in the stomach, sending blood splashing all over the bed and Diablo's naked body.

Diablo came up from between the woman's legs, wiping blood from her face.

"What the fuck is wrong with you?" she yelled out.

"I thought all niggas like wet pussy?" he said, gun securely in place.

"Nigga, who's your problem with? Me or this bitch?" she stated, trying to sit up.

"Don't ask me no fucking question; just give me your soul." He moved toward her and jammed the gun in her face, and then shoved it in her mouth knocking out several teeth.

Diablo struggled for air as teeth and blood slid down her throat. "Nigga, you better kill me!"

"No problem," he said, releasing every round he had, blowing her head all over the room. "You touched the wrong muthafucka." Kayson hawked and spat right on what was left of her face.

Kayson stepped back and looked at Diablo. The deed was done, but he didn't feel any better. He had taken her life, but doing so could not replace what he lost.

Days after the brutal murder of Diablo, Atlanta was turnt all the way up. Baseem went down there wildin' out. He put heat on all of her top men and closed all her spots. A few of Chico's workers caught a hit, but the top dogs were safe and sound. The heavy police presence made it hard to do any real work, so they shut shit down and moved the operation to Dade County. With the shipment coming through there anyway, it was less risky moving it, so it worked out.

It took two weeks to get everything finalized for Night's funeral, and when they did, that shit was packed. Night's generosity over the years had reached many, and they showed up in force to pay their respect.

KoKo and Goldie sat in back of the limo watching all the people piling into the funeral parlor. Goldie had been crying all morning. Eyes puffy and red, she looked as if she hadn't slept since the night of the murder. She reached in her bag, pulled out her mirror, and looked herself over. Sniffling and wiping her tears, she tried to apply her lip gloss.

With shaky hands, she pushed her sunglasses on and tried to pull herself together.

"I don't think I can do this, KoKo," she said, lifting her shades to wipe her tears.

"You can do it. You're stronger than you think." KoKo tried to comfort her.

"This is fucked up." She rubbed her hands up and down her arms.

"Don't worry. We'll be here for you." KoKo put her hand on Goldie's leg.

"Thank you." Goldie gripped KoKo's hand

"It's all good. Now get yo' shit together. You know you the other woman. You can't be walking in here looking all fucked up." KoKo smiled at her, trying to lighten the mood.

"Oh shit, you ain't right."

"Sheeeit . . . I'm real. If I was Kayson's sidepiece and carrying his baby, I would walk up in that muthafucka, head held high, stomach out, with a neon sign on my back that says I rode that dick well. Fall back bitches."

They both burst out laughing.

Their mood was broken when a tap rang out on the window.

KoKo looked over to see Kayson and Baseem along with five of their goons.

The door came open and both ladies felt drained as they

stepped out the car. The walk to the door created a sinking feeling in both of their stomachs.

Goldie grabbed tight to Baseem's arm, and KoKo grabbed tight to Kayson.

When they stepped inside, Goldie looked down the long aisle at his gold coffin, and the tears flowed rapidly down her cheeks.

Kayson stopped at the doormen and ordered, "Lock all the doors and put all men in place inside and outside the doors. If muthafuckas wanted to be inside, they should have been on time." He continued to walk KoKo to her seat.

Goldie almost lost it, until KoKo's words came to her mind. *Hold your head high.* Instantly, she threw her head back and rocked her sexy ass down the aisle on Baseem's arm.

All eyes were on them as they passed the crowd.

Rain was already seated with the other wives and girlfriends on the front row on the left. KoKo and Goldie were escorted to the empty front row on the right.

Goldie looked up at the closed coffin with the picture of him perched next to it, and she became sick. She wanted to get up and run out, but she knew Night would want her right there by his side, and she was not going to let him down.

When the Imam began his speech, the tears and sniffles began.

KoKo looked around at all the faces and then turned back to face the front. *It always surprises me how there's always standing room only when you're gone, but when you're alive doing the wrong shit, the same niggas will encourage you to fuck up. Now they have kind words when Night can't even hear this shit.*

As the service came to a close, Kayson positioned himself in the back, and man after man came up to him, putting envelopes in his hand and confessing their condolences.

THE PUSSY TRAP 3: *Death by Temptation*
~ N E N E   C A P R I ~

KoKo watched as they walked up to him as if he were the king and paid their respects. With unfinished business to handle, she scanned the room for her girls. This was the perfect time to do so.

Calling Shameezah and Porcha over to the side, she began dropping the plan in their laps to put a big ass monkey wrench in the Atlanta PDs investigation. Just as KoKo was at the end of her plot with the girls, she heard a little ruckus to her left. When she looked up, she saw Rain and a few of the other wives going in on Goldie, necks and eyes rolling and all.

"Hold that thought," KoKo said as she headed in their direction.

Aware of KoKo approaching, one girl tapped another and shut up real quick. But Rain, being in her moment, missed the warning and kept on going.

"I don't even know why you're here. You're side pussy. You don't even deserve the right to stand next to the dirt that will cover his coffin."

KoKo walked up and snatched her by the arm, damn near yanking it out of the socket. "Bitch, you must have lost your gotdamn mind," she said through clenched teeth.

"Let me go!" Heartbroken, Rain snatched away from KoKo with tears flowing down her cheeks. "*You* let this happen to him. He was too loyal to you."

"Bitch, how the fuck you gonna be mad at me 'cause you lost your spot? I guess your pussy wasn't good enough. I understand your pain, no doubt. But I'ma tell you one thing. You are not going to act like no fucking fool while we trying to put him to rest."

"You don't get to control how I mourn for my man," she said with all the hate she could muster up. "You make me sick. All this blood is on your hands. He was always popping that *live by the code* bullshit. All he did was follow your ass to his death. Then you bring this bitch in my face and with a straight face ask me to repect her. Fuck her and fuck you too!" Rain said with tears streaming from her eyes.

KoKo looked to the side. Kayson caught her eyes and shook his head no. She understood his gesture loud and clear, but chose to go with the moment. With bald tight fists, KoKo two-pieced Rain dead in the mouth. Rain hit the floor hard and sloppy. Legs one way, body the other. Gasps filled the room as she pulled out her gun, and of course, a lesson had to be taught.

Putting one in the chamber, she yelled out, "Do you wanna go with him?"

Rain looked up in sudden panic, paralyzed with fear and unable to speak.

"Do. You. Want. To. Go. With. Him?" she repeated.

Rain sniffled and shook her head no.

"All right then. Act like you got some sense. You up here fighting over a dead dick neither one of y'all can get. He spent his last days with this woman. He died in her arms. Fuck you mean she don't have the right to be here? Now, I said I understand your pain, and by all means, mourn, bitch, in any way you please. But don't have disrespect for me or her in your mourning plans."

Rain tried to sit up slowly. "KoKo, please," she pleaded.

"Apologize!" KoKo yelled out.

"I'm sorry," she whined, covering her face.

"Get this bitch off the floor. Fuck is wrong with you? Coming all outta pocket. This bitch ain't yo friend." KoKo tucked her gun away as Lynn helped Rain to a seat. "Bitches be having the game twisted. You don't approach the other bitch unless she is your friend. If she don't know you, what the fuck is you mad at her for. Be mad at that nigga. He was lying to both of y'all. And in this case, he is gone. All we can do is move forward. Respect this man for who he was, and where he laid his dick does not sum up the kindhearted, loving person he was." KoKo got choked up as she thought of how he took care of her and Quran when Kayson was gone.

Kayson came over to her side. "Ai'ight, break this shit up. Rain, you know I got you. I know what you meant to Night. They are going to take you home so you can get some rest."

"Thank you, Kayson. He always spoke very highly of you."

Kayson nodded as she passed him. He put half of the money in her hand. "This is just to get you moved and situated. I'll send more shortly."

"Thank you." She clutched the money to her chest and walked out with her crew in tow.

"Why you always gotta go in?" Kayson asked KoKo.

"You know I have a very low tolerance for bullshit. Plus, Goldie didn't need them all in her face. They lucky she didn't pull out. She's very unstable right now."

"And so are you."

"Whatever!" She turned to Goldie. "Come on, ma. This shit is for the birds." She started to walk toward the door.

"KoKo," he called out. "Calm yo' ass down."

"Yes, sir boss." She saluted him and then kept on walking.

Kayson looked at Baseem.

"You wanted to know when I was going to get settled down. Never. And KoKo is reason number one through ten," Baseem said.

"Make sure they get to the hotel safely. I gotta check on some shit. I'll catch up with you in a little while."

"Got you." Baseem rounded up the crew to escort the ladies to the hotel.

Kayson stood reflecting on KoKo talking in the corner with

her hit squad and wondered what she had up her sleeve. Knowing her, she was plotting someone's demise. And the fact that she had not run it past him, made him think she had something to hide. But what?

Payback is a Bitch . . .

As soon as Kayson left for Vegas, KoKo was on the first thing smoking to Atlanta. KoKo arrived at 9 PM and drove to the address she was given for Detective Sandra Benjamin. Yes, the woman Goldie saw that day in the police station was indeed the same bitch Rock considered a friend. Positioning herself a block away, she deaded the engine and waited.

An hour later, Sandra was pulling into her driveway. KoKo waited until she got in the house, turned on the lights, and began to get settled.

KoKo tightened her vest, secured her guns, and then got out. With stealth she moved speedily up to the door and looked around. Pressing the doorbell, she anxiously waited.

Sandra looked out the curtain, wrinkled her brow, and then headed to the door.

"KoKo?" she asked, pulling her robe together and looking up and down the street.

"I was in your neighborhood. I thought I would drop in," KoKo said, locking eyes with her.

"Oh, okay," she responded, trying to smile.

"Can I come in for a minute?" KoKo walked in, not waiting for a response.

"Umm . . . sure. Please come in," she said, shutting the door.

"Damn, I like your little place," KoKo sarcastically stated, looking around at her all in one ranch style home, cheap furniture, and small television. It looked like everything was in the same room.

"Thanks, I try." Sandra moved to the kitchenette. "Would you like something to drink?"

"No thank you. I'm good."

"So what do I owe to this visit?"

"Nothing much. You know I'm down here often, so I figured I might want to get me some employment. Are they hiring at your job?" KoKo looked at Sandra's body language.

"At my job?" Sandra wore a bewildered look on her face. She turned to the refrigerator to grab a bottle of water.

"Yeah, your job. You know . . . At the police department."

Sandra froze in place. Panic set in when she realized her gun was in the other room.

KoKo pulled out both her guns and placed them at her side. "Move too fast and I will blow your fucking head off," she warned.

Sandra slowly closed the refrigerator door and turned to face KoKo. Standing in between a rock and a hard place, she tried to talk KoKo down. "Look, I don't know what you're talking about. You need to put those away, and let's have a rational conversation."

"Bitch, this ain't Dr. Phil. Fuck is wrong with you? Yo' ass is in total violation. I'm here to check that ass." KoKo slightly raised her voice.

"Okay, I will be honest. Yes, I am a cop, but I didn't come for you. You ended up in my world."

"What the fuck are you talking about?"

"We have been following Rock's paper trail for a year, and when he brought you into his house that night. That is when you got on our radar."

"At what part in that explanation did you think I was a fucking fool?" KoKo tilted her head.

Sandra swallowed hard as she tried to gather her thoughts.

"You don't want to have the blood of a cop on your hands."

"You see this bitch right here?" She held up her nine. "She don't give a fuck about your fucking career path!"

"KoKo please," she begged as tears formed in her eyes.

"Sit down and shut the fuck up," she ordered.

Sandra slowly moved to the counter and sat on the stool.

KoKo tucked one of her guns in her waist and pulled out her cell. She put the gun to Sandra's mouth. "Shhhhh . . ." she said as she dialed Rock.

"Yo, where you at?" she tried to sound upbeat.

"On my way home. Why?"

"I need you to meet me at Sandra's house. I ran into a something. I need your help."

"I'm on my way."

Meanwhile in Vegas . . .

Kayson walked down the long hallway with a duffle bag full of money headed to Mr. Lu Chi's hotel room. He posted himself in front of the door and contemplated how he was going to deal with his betrayal. Kayson placed all his thoughts in the right place and then knocked on the door. When it opened, he was greeted by Mr. Lu Chi himself. Kayson's eyes roamed the room for security, but there was none in sight.

"Kayson, how are you? Please come in," he asked, patting him on the back. "So I take it your flight went well," Mr. Lu Chi said, walking quickly to the seating area to join Kayson.

"It went well." Kayson was short and to the point.

"So what do you have for me?" he asked excitedly, ready to get his hands on the bag of money.

Kayson sat the bag between his feet. He looked down at it for a few brief seconds and then locked gazes with Mr. Lu Chi.

"What do you call a man that is more interested in greed

279

than money?"

Mr. Lu Chi thought for a few seconds. He replied, "A fool of course. Any real man knows that being greedy can in turn get you swallowed up."

"So, I guess it's safe to say that greed destroys men."

"At times. It can also motivate at other times." Mr. Lu Chi looked at Kayson with inquisitive eyes. "Where is this coming from, Kayson?"

"Just trying to figure out, how is it that a man can ask for loyalty and then look you in the eyes and try to fuck you in the ass." He sat back, rubbing his hands together.

"Again, I will ask you. Where is this coming from?" Lu Chi's anger began to form in his gut.

"You crossed the wrong man," he said as his nostrils flared and eyes lowered.

Mr. Lu Chi chuckled. "I never crossed you. I am a businessman. And the minute that you forgot that, you crossed yourself." He sat back, feeling he had regained footing.

"And I'm a coldhearted muthafucka. And the minute you forgot that, you crossed yourself." Kayson grabbed the bag and placed it on the table. "Today, our business is done. Here is the last of your money."

Again, Mr. Lu Chi chuckled. "Last? There is not a last to this. You are in this until the day you die. And right now I control that," he said with a smug attitude.

Kayson nodded. "Well, I guess you won."

"Of course. I hold all the cards, and when I'm done playing, I will cash them in and walk away with the prize." He paused. "When they came to me to help with their plan to get rid of you, I started to turn them down. They offered me money and powerful friendships, but I have all that. Then I realized, what I really am is a collector of rare things. You being the rarest thing I could collect, I figured I could add your head to my collection," he smoothly stated.

Kayson sat calmly looking at Mr. Lu Chi's arrogant disposition. "Thank you for being true to yourself."

"And thank you for being a good boy." He leaned forward and unzipped the bag. A smile came over his face when he saw all the neatly stacked bills. "Just make sure you have my money on time." He looked up at Kayson and then reached in the bag to collect a stack.

"Ahhh . . . shit!" he yelled as he drew back his hand. There were two holes with blood oozing from them. His eyes widened as a small spider crawled from the bag.

"You feel that? That is the sting of greed." Kayson looked at Mr. Lu Chi holding his chest and pulling at his tie, gasping for air. The venom coursed through his veins, triggering his already massive heart problems.

"The wandering spider is one of the most deadliest spiders in the world. Something I picked up from your friend, Mr. Odoo. The thing I like most about him is he will sit back and let you get dangerously close, and then he strikes." Kayson watched as his once friend and mentor struggled for life. "You once told me that loyalty is everything. Then you crossed me. Never cross the man that has nothing on his side but a bad bitch and a big ass gun." Kayson pulled out his silver 9-millimeter with a black diamond handle and put two in Mr. Lu Chi's chest, making sure to hit him in the heart. "Muthafucka!" He grabbed the bag of money, pulled his hood over his head, and headed to the door.

Rock pulled up to Sandra's house, parked, and then moved swiftly to the door. His mind was all over the place and anxiety high. He was hoping KoKo wasn't hurt or injured.

Knocking on the door, he impatiently waited for someone

to answer.

Sandra opened the door with paranoia in her eyes.

"What's wrong?" he asked as he pushed past her. When he saw KoKo standing behind her with a gun to her head, he froze in his spot.

"What the fuck is going on?"

"You sent this bitch after me?" she asked, one hand on Sandra's shoulder and the other one with the gun cocked and loaded at her head.

"Sent her after you?"

"Did you know this bitch was working for the po-po?" KoKo yelled, pushing her to the floor.

Rock looked at her for a few seconds, and then looked down at Sandra, who was on the floor shaking and afraid.

"What the fuck is she talking about?"

"Rock, please. You don't want to do this. She ain't worth it."

He looked at KoKo and then looked back at Sandra. Rock reached in his jacket, pulled out his .45, and shot her in the knee.

"Ahhhhh . . ." she shrieked as she grabbed her leg.

"The one thing I hate more than a liar, is fucking pig!" He shot her in the other knee.

"Rock, please!" she cried out.

"Please what!" Rock was in full murder role. "How much this bitch cost you?" he growled.

"She almost cost me my life," KoKo answered.

"There is nothing better than a snitch except a dead one." He aimed and shot her in her chest. Rock stood over Sandra with his gun at his side. Not even looking up, he asked, "Me and you good?"

"For now," KoKo said.

"Go 'head. I got this. It's my mess. I'll clean it up," he ordered.

"I hope your trust in this bitch don't cost me anything else," she warned as she walked away.

- 43 -

Happily Ever After?

Six months had passed, and Kayson and KoKo were enjoying the married life. With all that they had been through, they deserved all the happiness in the world. Kayson relocated Goldie and the immediate crew, sold all the property in St. Croix, and then moved to another island in Dubai. Before Baseem went underground, Kayson put him on Detective Greg and Damien. With the help of Porcha and Shameezah he did them real dirty, a perfect going away present for Mr. and Mrs. Wells. Once Kayson and KoKo were safe, Mocha released Yuri to Mr. Odoo with a stern warning, making him realize he was not untouchable. Forcing him to back the fuck up. Tyquan had gone on the run, leaving them one enemy unaccounted for, but Kayson vowed to continue his search. Keisha remained in their care while recovering, and yes, Mrs. KoKo was on house arrest again. Kayson had set their life on a new path and was working with KoKo on stopping the chase of the demons of the past.

"Oh shit!" Kayson moaned out as he slow stroked KoKo from the back. Shortly after, he was releasing long and hard. He looked down at the sweat glistening on her back and placed soft kisses up and down her spine. Then he whispered in her ear, "Doggie in the morning. The breakfast of champions." He chuckled as he pulled out and stood up.

"You are so spoiled," she stated as he pulled her to her feet.

"Sheeit . . . I'm not spoiled. I'm blessed." He kissed her lips.

"Whatever, Mr. Spoiled."

Kayson admired her sexy body as she walked to the bathroom. He had missed her being pregnant with Quran, and was enjoying watching her belly swell and was staying close to home so as not to miss anything.

"What are we doing today?" she asked as she adjusted the water.

"I can't think right now. I'm fucked up."

"Get it together, Boss. You owe me a date. I want to have my last hurrah before your daughter invades my life."

"I'm trying to pull it together, but my nigga Trae said it best. Pregnant pussy is to die for."

KoKo laughed. "You are so stupid. Well, I'ma tell you right now, you ain't gonna have a bitch bloated every year, so get that shit outta ya head. I ain't Tasha Macklin."

"Whatever. You gonna do what I tell you," he said, coming up behind her and reaching around to rub her stomach. KoKo leaned back and rested her head on his chest.

"Thank you, baby," he said.

"For what?"

"Loving me."

"I told you I will love you a day past forever, and if I go first, I'ma haunt yo' ass for the rest of your life."

Kayson burst out laughing, "That's fucked up. How you gonna rest in peace?"

"You get another woman, it ain't gonna be no peace. I'ma be up in your house rattling shit and knocking shit over."

"That's selfish. You gonna let all this good dick go to waste?" he joked.

"No, 'cause I'm taking that muthafucka with me."

They both burst out laughing. "You crazy as hell."

THE PUSSY TRAP 3: *Death by Temptation*
~ N E N E   C A P R I ~

"And don't forget it."

Within the hour, KoKo, Kayson, and Quran were so fresh and so clean, ready for a family day out.

Kayson smiled, watching as KoKo tried to keep up with Quran with her big belly.

Their family day was just about over, and Kayson had KoKo drive him to the airport. He needed to meet up with Baseem to handle some business. Then he was going to be stationary until the baby was born.

"I'll be right back," he said, kissing KoKo on the lips.

"Bye, daddy." Quran grabbed him around the neck.

"Why you always blocking?" he said, pulling him to the front seat.

"I'm not blocking." He giggled as Kayson tickled his neck.

He pulled him into his arms and hugged him tight. "See you in two days." Kayson put his fist out. "You're the man of the house. Hold it down for me."

"Okay." Quran hit his fist and then crawled to the back.

Kayson leaned over and kissed KoKo again.

"Hurry up back. I think your daughter wants outta here." She looked down at her belly.

"Trust me. I will not miss this one being born." He hopped out and shut the door.

KoKo watched until he was inside the private plane.

"Mommy, what's blocking?" Quran asked.

"It's what your father does to keep me from being in charge." She smiled.

"Why you wanna be in charge? Daddy's in charge."

"Fasten your seat belt." KoKo shook her head and pulled off.

Quran shrugged his shoulders, buckled up, and looked out the window.

An hour later, Quran and KoKo walked into the house. She fixed them a little snack and an ice cream sundae. Later that evening, she put Quran in the tub. Dressed in his pajamas, he joined KoKo in the living room for their movie night. The moment she saw his eyes closing in the middle of their Disney movie, she tucked him in her bed. KoKo picked up his toys and then cleaned the kitchen.

On her way to the shower, she checked the alarms, peeked in on him, and placed her gun under her fluffy pillow.

As KoKo lathered up, she felt a slight tightness in the bottom of her stomach.

"Don't you start, little girl. Your daddy is not here. I need two more days." She looked down at her stomach.

By the time she got out, she felt a few more pains, and they were sharper.

"Not now, momma." She walked to the closet and grabbed a sundress. She wanted to be dressed just in case.

KoKo lay down and dialed the phone on the plane.

"Hey, baby. You miss me already?" Kayson asked.

"Yes, of course. But I think I'm in labor."

Kayson got quiet. "What happened?"

"When I got in the shower the games began. You know this is your fault."

"How is it my fault?"

"You and your doggie style."

"You and your 'not until six weeks'. The Enforcer don't play that."

"Whatever!"

"I'm on my way back. Keep me posted."

"Okay, baby. Hurry!" KoKo felt another sharp pain.

She tried to remain calm and fall asleep, but the pain and pressure began to take over. She got up and attempted to walk to the kitchen to get some water. When she turned the corner, she felt a heavy object hit her head, and then she saw black.

"Wake up, KoKo," she heard the soft yet commnding voice say.

Struggling to open her eyes and lift her head, she sat half way up and got the shock of her life. Keisha stood over her with a gun in her hand.

"What the fuck!" KoKo mumbled. She tried to move her hand, but it was cuffed to the pipe under the kitchen sink.

KoKo yanked her shackled hands, trying to break free. "What are you doing?" she asked, trying to bring her head to her hands. And as she did so, she pulled back a handful of blood. KoKo tried to speak as calm as possible.

"See, I tried to be patient. I tried to wait and see if the animals would wipe themselves out, but you are fucking relentless. I put Mo on you. I put Boa on you. I *even* put the cops on you, and for some reason you just won't fade the fuck out!"

"What the fuck is wrong with you?" KoKo looked partly confused and shocked.

"*You're* what's wrong with me. *You're* the reason Malik did not love me. *You're* the reason why my daughter is gone!" she yelled.

"I am your daughter." KoKo tried to bring her back to reality.

Keisha laughed hard and loud while holding her stomach. "You are soooooo *stupid*. Didn't Tyquan tell you to open your eyes?" She leaned down toward her. "I am not your mother. Nine tried to tell you everything. I kept telling Mo, 'That bitch is smart. She is going to figure this whole thing out. But Mo said, No she won't.' It was the death of her, but I ain't going out like that." She leaned in and held the chain in her face and with gritted teeth she continued. "You took my Star. She was all I had in this world. You owe me, and just when I was about to cash in, that nosey husband of yours fucked with the accounts. Now, I need you to tell me where my money is."

"I don't know shit about your money," KoKo said as the crease in her forehead appeared.

"I figured you would say that. So I guess I will have to go to plan B." Keisha pulled a metal object from a bag and walked over to the stove. She turned the fire up high and placed the object on the flame.

"This is all about money?" KoKo asked as a sharp pain struck her stomach and back. Her head throbbed.

"It has always been about money." She leaned back down. "They owe me. I sacrificed everything, and I want what's coming to me. They didn't give it to me, but you will." She stood and walked back to the stove.

KoKo could hear her phone ringing incessantly. She knew Kayson was calling her back to back.

"So where did you say my money was?" Keisha asked, coming toward her with the hot object.

"Fuck you!" KoKo shouted.

Keisha stepped over her and placed the red, hot tip on her leg.

"Ahhh!" KoKo yelled out as the pain shot through her body.

"You still don't know?"

"I don't know shit!" KoKo spat in her face.

Keisha smiled, wiped the saliva away, and then burned KoKo again.

"Muthafucka!" KoKo screamed out this time. The pain was so severe, her water broke.

Keisha went back to the stove. "Let's see how much Kayson will love you with the skin burned off your pretty little face." Keisha placed the object back on the fire.

THE PUSSY TRAP 3: *Death by Temptation*
~ N E N E C A P R I ~

Tears came to KoKo's eyes, but she would not let them fall.

Keisha pulled up a chair and looked at her watch. "I gotta let it get good and hot." She crossed her legs.

"Bitch, you better kill me."

"Oh, don't worry. I am. But I want to do it real slow. While we wait, I want to tell you a few things. I don't know if you knew this, but Monique really did like your little orphan you're going to leave behind. We had so many arguments over if we should kill you or not. She was real conflicted. Thank god you got to her because she was really getting ready to fuck things up with her guilty conscience. Especially when her son came back into the picture. And Boa, you must have been fucking him real good because he was flip-flopping. Mo had to pay him big time, and if Boa's suicidal girlfriend wouldn't have pulled her stunt, I would have been living free by now."

She paused and looked at her watch again. "Oh well, water under the bridge." She rose to her feet, heading toward the stove.

Again, KoKo could hear her phone ringing off the hook.

"Bitch, you better hide good because Kayson will not rest until your grave is cold."

Keisha turned toward KoKo and then squatted beside her to look in her eyes. "I'm not afraid of your husband." She smirked. "To be truthful, you have no idea who he *really* is," she stated, lowering her eyes. "Let me ask you something." Keisha shifted her weight from one side to the other. "When he crawls between your thighs and gives you all that power inch by glorious inch, making you see what he wants you to see, hear what he wants you to hear, feel what he wants you to feel, rendering you incabale of thought and control." She paused. "Can you really say you *know* who he is? You climbed into a dangerous game with some very powerful players. Each one led by their desires. Money. Power. Greed. Sex." She chuckled. "I think they call it . . . temptation. And oh, it can be a beautiful thing in the hands of the right person, but in the hands of the wrong person, it can be deadly. And you, my dear, were dealt a very deadly hand."

KoKo stared in her eyes, unfazed by her little speech.

"Finally, your smart ass mouth is closed." Keisha slowly stood up and headed to the stove.

KoKo's pains were coming faster and faster. She needed to say something to distract her.

"The only thing worse than a greedy bitch is a thirsty one. Bitch, you ain't 'bout this life. You ain't worthy enough to suck a dog's dick."KoKo looked at her with low eyes and flared nostrils.

"I didn't climb into this game. I walked in the front door and sat right down at the muthafucking table. And I have been trumping you muthafuckas from day one." KoKo continued to taunt her.

Keisha turned the metal object over the blazing flame as she began to feel the sting of KoKo's words.

"While you trying to keep up with who and what I know, Tyquan played the shit outta your dumb ass," KoKo said with a devious smile.

"What the fuck are you talking about?" Keisha picked up the hot object.

"It's okay. He's that type of man. Fuck a bitch then trick a bitch."

"You don't know what the fuck you're talking about!"

"I can't tell. He's laid up with Deborah right now, while you're standing here broke. I guess your pussy wasn't as good as you thought it was," KoKo said, trying to throw her off her square.

THE PUSSY TRAP 3: *Death by Temptation*
~ N E N E C A P R I ~

Keisha thought for a minute.

"Yeah, look at you. You're weak. He don't want no weak, broke bitch."

Keisha's breathing quickened with every word. She threw the object across the room, barely missing KoKo's head.

She reached in her robe pocket and grabbed her gun. Breathing heavy, she pointed the gun at KoKo's head. "You don't know what you're talking about. Tyquan loves me. He has always loved me!" she yelled.

"Bitch, you're weak!" KoKo taunted.

"You and that fucking Sabrina took everything from me!" She stood, shaking and crying. "Now I'ma take everything from you." She pointed the gun at KoKo's stomach.

"You can take whatever you want. But the only thing I won't *give* you is my soul." KoKo closed her eyes.

When she heard the first shot, she braced herself for the pain but didn't feel anything. Slowly, she opened her eyes and saw Keisha fall to her knees coughing up blood. Then her head hit the kitchen floor.

When she looked past her, she saw Quran standing in his pajamas with her .22 tight in his grip.

"My daddy said I was in charge. He said 'protect your mommy'."

KoKo began to cry at the sight of her baby at the other end of a gun. A ton of emotions flooded her body at once. Pain, fear, regret, and lastly, pride.

"Keep it pointed down and walk slowly to Mommy," she instructed.

Quran walked slowly around Keisha's dead body. When he got to KoKo's side, he stood next to her with his eyes fixed on the woman he had affectionately called MiMi.

"It's okay, baby. You didn't do anything wrong." She tried

to soothe his little soul.

KoKo began pulling at the pipe in an effort to free herself. Then she heard keys in the front door.

Kayson opened the door and unarmed the beeping alarm. He frantically called her name. "KoKo! Baby, where you at?"

"I'm in here, Kay!" she yelled back.

Kayson ran to the kitchen and almost lost it at the sight of KoKo tied up, Keisha laid out bleeding with a gunshot to the back, and Quran standing with a gun in his hand. He rushed over and gently took the gun from Quran, put it on the safety, and laid it on the counter.

"Move over, son," he instructed as he began yanking at the pipes to free KoKo's hands.

"Baby, look in that bag," she said as she grimaced in pain.

He grabbed the bag, pulled everything out and turned it upside down. A key hit the floor. He unlocked the cuffs and then untied her feet.

"Ohhh . . . baby, be careful," KoKo moaned as he moved her leg.

Kayson ran and got a towel, rushing back to her side. Wrapping it around her, he picked her up and held her in his arms. Moving to the phone on the wall, he called 911 and waited for the fall out.

Quran grabbed onto his father's leg. "I kept her safe, Daddy. Right?"

"Yes, you did, son. Come on," he said as he walked to the front door to meet the ambulance.

"Baby, what the fuck happened?" he tried to ask. KoKo lifted her head off his shoulder and looked in his eyes.

"As hard as we prayed that he would be better than us. He now has blood on his hands."

THE PUSSY TRAP 3: *Death by Temptation*
~ N E N E   C A P R I ~

A week later, KoKo was sitting in her bed watching Kayson smile as he looked at his baby girl Malika Kah'Asia Wells. KoKo beamed as he held his daughter while little Quran sat next to his dad rubbing her tiny hand on his face. Even though they had everything to live for, the pain of the past would not allow her to give up the search. She was determined to be a woman of her word and make everybody pay their debt, and the sacrifice wasn't shit. She couldn't wait for the baby to get old enough, because she was going after whoever was left and their whole family. For every devilish temptation within their darkened hearts, all their jealousy, power, and greed, she would use against them to set a trap that would ultimately end in death.

"Hello," Tyquan answered as he ran on his treadmill.
"You know we can't let that muthafucka live in peace, right?" the cold, malicious voice boomed
through his speaker.
"Brenda, I got it." He stopped the treadmill and grabbed his towel.
"No, I got it. You have had enough time to fuck shit up. From here on I'll handle it," she abrumptly disconnected the call.

Book Discussion Questions

1. Was Baseem justified in killing Mugsy?

2. Should KoKo have told Baseem about Kayson to keep him from going off?

3. Did you see the twist with Keisha coming?

4. What will come of little Quran?

5. Did Goldie and Night cross the line? Was his death punishment for his disregard too orders?

6. Will KoKo stop or will she always be driven by her thirst for revenge?

7. Do you think there are any more weak links in the crew? If so who?

8. Was letting the Dutches live a smart move for KoKo or is she planning a bigger move?

9. What will become of Tyquan and will his treachery destroy everything Kayson and KoKo hold dear.

10. Who is Brenda Watson?????

THE PUSSY TRAP 3: *Death by Temptation*
~ N E N E C A P R I ~

WAHIDA CLARK
PRESENTS
BEST SELLING TITLES

Trust No Man

Trust No Man II

Thirsty

Cheetah

Karma With A Vengeance

The Ultimate Sacrifice

The Game of Deception

Karma 2: For The Love of Money

Thirsty **2**

Lickin' License

Feenin'

Bonded by Blood

Uncle Yah Yah: 21st Century Man of Wisdom

The Ultimate Sacrifice II

Under Pressure (YA)

The Boy Is Mines! (YA)

A Life For A Life

The Pussy Trap

99 Problems (YA)

Country Boys

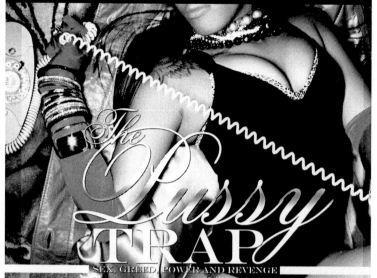